Replenish the Earth

Anna
JACOBS
Replenish
the Earth

CANELO

First published in the United Kingdom in 2001 by Severn House

This edition published in the United Kingdom in 2018 by

Canelo Digital Publishing Limited
Third Floor, 20 Mortimer Street
London W1T 3JW
United Kingdom

A CIP catalogue record for this book is available from the British Library.

Print ISBN 9781 78863 150 1
Ebook ISBN 9781 91142 097 2

Look for more great books at www.canelo.co

Printed and bound in Great Britain by Clays Ltd, Elcograf S.p.A.

Chapter 1

Late February, 1735

A fire of seacoal glowed dimly in the grate and a shaded candle flickered in one corner of the room. The sound of the sick woman gasping for breath woke her daughter, who was dozing fitfully in a chair by the bed, and Sarah leaned forward anxiously. When her mother sighed into sleep again, she leaned back, closing her eyes as worries chased one another round her mind.

How would she manage once her mother died? The small annuity would die with her, and then Sarah would not only be alone in the world, but penniless and without friends or relatives.

She glanced down at her capable hands, reddened from all the washing, and spread them before her. Strong hands in a tall, strong body. Could they earn her a living? She fingered one strand of the honey-coloured hair lying loose about her shoulders, smiling wryly. Her mother said her hair was beautiful, and perhaps it was when it was curled and fussed with. But Sarah had no time for such frivolities these days. She'd only had time to care for her ailing mother during the past few weeks.

'Sarah. We must… talk.'

She glanced up again to see her mother gazing at her anxiously. 'You need to rest, not talk, Mother.'

'I need to... tell you something.'

Sarah knew it would do more harm than good to try to prevent her mother speaking, so she smiled at the figure in the bed.

'You look pretty when you smile, dear. Life... hasn't been kind to you. You deserve better.'

'Let me get you a drink first, then you shall talk.' Sarah limped across to the tiny fire and swung the kettle over the flames, rubbing her bad hip, which always ached in the cold weather. 'Here, try the new cordial the apothecary mixed yesterday. He thought you might find it an improvement on the other.' And that's the strongest he can make it, she thought. Pray God it will ease the pain for as long as need be!

'When I'm gone...'

'Ah, Mother, don't!'

'I must! I worry for you. Afterwards, Sarah – you are to see the lawyer, tell him...'

'I saw Mr Peabody last month to collect our money. He knows about your illness.'

'Not him!' Her fingers tightened on Sarah's hand. 'You must go and see my father's lawyer – Mr Jamieson – at the Sign of the Quill in Newbury Square – and you *must* ask him for help.'

Sarah's mouth tightened to a narrow, bloodless line. 'I want nothing to do with any of your family! If they disowned you when you married Father, then they disowned me, too!'

'No! No! You must see him! You *must*!'

'I won't ask for their charity! And I doubt they'll offer any help.'

The thin fingers dug into her arm. 'You can't deny… — my last wish. My father must be dead by now, but my brother won't refuse to help his niece. And you – you must accept – that help.' Her face was deathly white and tears were running down her wasted cheeks. '*Promise me!*'

Sarah could hold out no longer. 'Very well. I promise.'

The grip on her arm relaxed and her mother let out a long sigh of relief. 'I can go in peace now. You'll keep your promise, I know.'

She watched her mother sigh into sleep. She would keep the promise. But she doubted it'd do any good, except to humiliate her. Well, she'd faced humiliations more than once since her father died. You didn't die of it.

–

In Dorset, Will Pursely took the lawyer's letter out to the copse and sat on the fallen log where he often sought refuge when things grew hard to bear, for he didn't wish to add to his mother's worries. The trees were leafless still, but the buds were getting fatter by the day and soon the tender green would burst forth. It was his favourite time of year. There was such promise in the surging growth of spring. Or there had been in other years.

For a moment or two he sat there, breathing in the cool, fresh air, enjoying the sound of the wind rustling the bare branches, letting the peace seep into his bones. Then, with a sigh, he unfolded the letter and studied it again. But no amount of reading would make the words say anything different.

My dear Mr Pursley,

I am in receipt of your letter of the second of this month, and I deeply regret that I can offer you no longer lease upon the home farm than a yearly tenancy. The will of Squire Bedham is still not resolved and in those circumstances no long-term plans can be made.

However, I sincerely hope that I shall be in a position to offer something more permanent by the time this new lease comes up for renewal.

In the meantime, I should be obliged if you would continue to act as our agent in Broadhurst, collecting the rents on the same terms as before.

Yours most sincerely
Samuel Jamieson

'But what the devil do I do about the farm?' Will asked the piece of paper, shaking it angrily. 'I need some more cows and I see a chance to get them.' But that would mean taking a risk. He'd already lost the main thing he cared about – his family's farm, where he had been brought up and had expected to bring up his own sons in due course. Unfortunately, after his father's death, it had been taken away from him by the new landowner, Matthew Sewell. He could feel anger stir in him at the mere thought of that so-called gentleman, who had quickly gained a reputation as a harsh master.

Will knew he was lucky to get the lease of this place at such short notice, but it didn't feel like *home* and it was small – heart-breakingly small after Hay Nook Farm. He slapped his palm against his thigh in frustration. What worth was a year's lease to a man who thought in terms of planting trees for the timber they would one day provide for his descendants, and breeding better stock over several generations of animals?

For a moment, bitterness scalded through him, then he tossed back the lock of dark hair that always fell across his brow and unfolded his long limbs. There was work to do done, always work to be done. No use sitting here feeling sorry for himself.

But if his mother had invited that silly Jen Tapper to tea again, he would walk out, he surely would, and go down to the village inn till she'd left. He hated young women mooning over him with foolish expressions on their faces. Didn't think much of Jen Tapper's face, anyway, come to that. She looked just like a cow he'd owned once, with her big eyes and heavy features. It had been a silly cow, but not nearly as silly as she was, however skilled she was in a dairy.

A man married more than a useful pair of hands. He needed someone he could live happily with, and bed happily, too.

It would be a long time before he'd consider marriage again. Once he'd lost the farm, Amy Barton hadn't wanted him any more. Her father had come to see him the very next day to break off the engagement. And she'd married someone else so quickly that Will felt furious every time he saw her flaunting her full belly.

One day, he'd have his own land again and she'd be sorry.

With a growl of anger at the whole world, Will went back to dig the garden, slamming the spade into the ground and turning the soil until his arms ached. Soon be time to plant some vegetables. You didn't need more than a year's lease to grow and harvest those, at least.

The following day, he drove his mother into the village to sell her cream cheese and butter at the small weekly market, though she had little to offer nowadays compared to her former produce.

While he was strolling round the village green, looking at what else was on offer, he found himself facing his enemy.

Sewell blocked his path deliberately, arms akimbo. 'Still here, Pursley? I thought I told you not to renew your lease on that hovel? I don't want trouble-makers in my village.'

Behind him, the bully boy who accompanied him everywhere snickered.

Will folded his arms across his chest. 'I'm not answerable to you, Sewell.'

'*Squire* Sewell to such as you.'

'Bedhams have always been squires in this village,' Will retorted.

'There are no Bedhams left.'

'There's an heir still to be found. And he'll be squire, not you.'

Sewell slashed suddenly out with his cane. 'Less of your impertinence, fellow.'

Will felt the sting on his cheek and snatched at the cane, taking Sewell by surprise. He sent it spinning across towards the duckpond and when the bully moved towards him, he smiled and made sure he was ready to defend himself. 'Come on, then, fellow! I could fancy a turn-to just now. 'Tis a pity your master's a bit old for fighting, but I'll make do with you.'

The man hesitated, looking to Sewell for orders.

Thad Honeyfield pushed through the crowd which had gathered to watch and came to range himself at Will's side, hefting his blacksmith's hammer suggestively. A couple of other men moved forward from the crowd and stood behind them.

The people who owed their livings and cottages to Sewell took care to move a step or two backwards, but lingered still to watch.

After a moment's pause, Sewell shook his head and gestured to his man to stand back. 'You have no place in this village now, Pursley. When will you recognise that?'

'I don't agree. I just had my lease on the home farm renewed, so it seems to me I do still have a place here.'

'No one would call that tiny patch of muck a farm!' Sewell scoffed. Turning on his heel, he strode off, pausing once to toss over his shoulder, 'You'll regret this.'

Will watched him go, then turned to his friend. 'Thanks, Thad. But don't put yourself in danger for me.'

The blacksmith shrugged. 'I'm already in his bad books because I refuse to sell him my land – he can't bear that I have two whole acres to call my own, that one. He must own every single thing in the village, it seems.'

Both men watched Sewell climb into his coach and be driven off.

'What was he doing here today?' Will wondered aloud. 'He doesn't usually honour our small market with his presence.'

'He came to see Mr Rogers.'

'If he's been bothering Parson—'

'He hasn't. Mrs Jenks wouldn't let him into the house.'

They both smiled. Parson's housekeeper would rout the very devil himself if he tried to disturb her beloved master, who was still recovering from a fever.

As his friend walked back to the forge, Will turned and glanced towards his mother, who signalled that she'd sold her produce and wanted to go home. She was looking anxious and he knew the encounter with Sewell would worry her.

Why could that man not let well alone? Hadn't he already turned the Pursleys out of their home? And done the same to one or two others. Did he want to grind the whole world under his heel?

–

Elizabeth Mortonby lingered for another week, drifting mostly in a merciful haze of laudanum, then slipped away quietly in the night, so that Sarah woke to a silent room and knew at once what had happened. Loneliness seemed to surround her like a high wall but she wouldn't let herself weep. What good would it do?

Widow Thomas, the landlady, flew into a rage when told of the death and was loud in her complaints that she had been deceived as to her lodger's health. A death on the premises was bad for business. Heartless wretches, they were, to damage a poor widow's livelihood! They wouldn't have got the room if she'd known how ill Mistress Mortonby was, that was sure!

'Would you kindly make the necessary arrangements as soon as possible, Miss Mortonby, because a corpse lying around will upset the other lodgers!'

'You can be sure that I shall do things in a proper manner.'

The vicar was sent for, but the curate came in his place, for it was a raw February day and the vicar was fond of his creature comforts. Mr Rawby, a studious young man recently ordained, peered at the corpse, but seemed disinclined to approach it too closely. He offered up a cursory prayer for the soul of… er, Elizabeth Mortonby', agreed to hold the funeral service the very next morning and volunteered to inform the sexton for 'Miss… er, Mortonby'.

He always had trouble remembering their names, Sarah thought bitterly, but he had no difficulty with the names of richer parishioners.

She had to brave the weather to make the practical arrangements for the coffin and its transportation to the church, and returned to a cheerless room, whose fire had gone out. Conscious of the still figure on the bed, she could eat nothing, but she did light the fire again and brew herself a dish of weak tea with some of the tea dust at the bottom of the caddy.

Later, two men came with the coffin, a poor affair of splintery wood and clumsy joints. The older one smiled sympathetically at Sarah. 'You sit down over there, miss, and we'll be as quick as we can.'

'Thank you.'

In between helping, the younger man gazed round the room, but said nothing.

'Your mother, is she?' the older man asked, squinting at her from under his lank hair.

'Yes.' Sarah dug her fingernails into her palms, determined not to give way to her grief in front of these strangers.

'Pretty she must have been once,' the man went on. 'Here, Bill, you take the feet. That's it! Gently does it.' He arranged the body, then stepped back to study it with the eye of a connoisseur. 'They don't always look this peaceful. Some of them has a terrible look on their face, like they've gone straight to hell.'

Sarah knew he meant well, but she wished he'd finish what he had to do and go.

'We'll set it on the floor or you'll have nowhere to sleep tonight.'

They had no trouble lifting the coffin. Her mother had weighed almost nothing at the end.

'Nail it down, shall I, miss?'

'Yes... no... I... just a moment!' She went to bend over the cheap, crudely-varnished box for a last look at her mother. Kneeling down, she kissed the wasted cheek one final time, noticed the locket round Elizabeth's neck and hesitated. It was gold and contained miniatures of her mother and father, not very good ones, but it was all she would have to remember them by. Steeling herself, she unfastened the locket and then, after further hesitation, slipped the gold wedding ring from her mother's finger.

Her mother would understand her desperate need, she was sure, but she still felt guilty, as if she were committing a theft. Poverty was a harsh master. Dropping the locket and ring on to the table, she watched bleakly as the coffin lid was secured.

The rest of the day dragged slowly past. She went out to buy a pie from a seller crying his wares, came back and tried to read. Unable to concentrate, she went to stand by the window and watch the people go past. Such a busy street, so many ragged people shivering their way along it.

–

In the morning, Sarah toasted and ate the last piece of stale bread, then put on her best dress, which she wore only to church on Sundays. The dark blue silk was faded and worn, and the dress offered little warmth on such a bleak day, but it was all she had to honour her mother's passing.

On a sudden impulse, she threaded the gold ring on the chain holding the locket and fastened it round her neck. They didn't show under her high-necked gown, but she could feel them and that comforted her.

When the men came for the coffin, she was sitting ready, her features set in a calm expression. She didn't intend to give way to her grief in front of these strangers, or in front of the curate, either.

After the funeral, at which she was the only mourner, she returned to Furness Road to find the door to her room, which she had locked carefully, standing ajar. That jerked her out of her lethargy. 'Dear heaven, no!' She pushed it open and sobbed aloud at what she saw.

The place had been ransacked and the thief seemed to have vented his annoyance at such poor pickings upon its meagre contents. Pieces of threadbare clothing were strewn around and her precious few books were tumbled on the floor, their spines broken, their pages spilling out. Worst of all, her mother's papers had been tossed into the hearth and had caught light. The grate was now full of ashes with only one or two singed corners remaining. Her mother's marriage lines, her father's letters, everything gone!

She choked on another sob and went to find Widow Thomas, who vowed she had seen and heard nothing, and grew angry when her lodger insisted on sending for the parish constable.

He came within the hour and examined the room, but could offer her little hope of catching the culprits. 'Times is very lawless and with no reward offered, well, who's to take an interest?'

When he'd gone, the landlady came up to rap on Sarah's door. 'I shall be obliged, miss, if you will leave my house immediately.'

'But we've paid until the end of the month!'

'I want you out now. Deaths and constables! What next, I ask!'

And suddenly it was all too much. Sarah took a step towards Widow Thomas, the pent-up anger exploding out of her in a rush of words. 'If you even *try* to turn me out before I'm ready, then I'll hire a bully-boy to come and smash your front door down – and I'll tell him to smash anything else he fancies while he's at it. See if I don't!'

Widow Thomas gasped and backed away, but Sarah was between her and the stairs, and she could only retreat to the end of the landing, stuttering in fright. 'Well, I... I... your mother just buried. A day or two – you shall have a day or two.'

'And the rent?'

'I shall refund what is not used.'

Sarah stood there for a minute longer, then laughed scornfully and moved away. 'I have to go and see my lawyer now. I trust you will keep an eye on my room while I'm gone? I should be very angry indeed if anything happened to what's left of our things. Who knows what I'd do then?'

She held the woman's eyes for a moment longer, then walked out.

Even though the sky was heavy with clouds and she would be lucky to escape another drenching, she regretfully refused the shrill offer of a passing sedan chair.

Her iron pattens were soon encrusted with mud and who knew what else. Since she didn't dare spend even a halfpenny on paying one of the urchins to sweep a crossing for her, she picked her own way among the refuse and slops, crossing streets when she could behind some wealthier citizen who could afford to have a path swept clear.

Impatiently, she waved away the pie seller who accosted her, as well as the hawkers of ballads and newssheets, clasping her purse firmly inside her worn rabbit-fur muff, instead of leaving it hanging by a tape beneath her skirt. Pickpockets were everywhere. It had nearly broken her mother's heart to be reduced to lodgings in Furness Road.

After a while, Sarah came to a more respectable area, where the streets were cleaner and people better-dressed. She asked directions from a motherly-looking woman standing in a shop doorway, and so found her way at last to Newbury Square. Wearily she limped round it in the drizzling rain, studying the signs swinging above the doorways.

When at last she found the Sign of the Quill she didn't let herself stop to think, but strode immediately up the steps and into the hallway, pushing open the door, anxious to have this humiliation over and done with. She was sure the lawyer would only tell her to go away, sure her uncle would refuse to do anything for her. But she had promised her mother to ask for his help – and she would keep her word.

Inside was warmth and order, with a cosy fire reflected in the gleaming oak panelling. She pushed her damp hood back and tried to think what to say. An elderly clerk was standing writing at a high, sloping desk by the window. The lad standing at the desk next to him didn't even raise his eyes from his work, but kept his quill scratching across the paper as if his life depended upon the speed of it. The older man set his quill down on the inkstand and looked questioningly at the newcomer.

'I would like to see Mr Jamieson, please,' she said firmly. 'This is his place of business, is it not?'

'Is he expecting you, madam?'

'No.'

'Then I'm afraid Mr Jamieson cannot see you today. He's a very busy man. Perhaps you could leave your name and come back next week?'

She could see his glance straying back to the papers on his desk, so let the anger that had never really subsided since her confrontation with the landlady rise again. 'My business is urgent. I *must* see Mr Jamieson today!'

'May I inquire as to the nature of your business, madam?'

'No, you may not!'

They stood arguing for a while, with the clerk becoming less civil by the minute and Sarah standing her ground. She *would* carry out her mother's last wish, and do so today.

Suddenly, a door on the other side of the room banged open, and a small stout gentleman came storming out. He had on a maroon waistcoat beneath his grey jacket, with grey knee-breeches, and an old-fashioned, full-bottomed wig crowning his rosy face.

'What is all this noise?' he demanded. 'Did I not expressly tell you, Pickersleigh, that I was not to be disturbed?'

Sarah stepped forward before the clerk could speak. 'Are you Mr Jamieson, sir?'

'I am, madam.'

'Sir, I beg you to grant me a few moments of your time. It's very important.'

He frowned at her, then pressed his lips together as if holding back a refusal.

'My name is Mortonby. I...' She stopped in bewilderment as the room grew instantly still, even the lad by the window stopping work to gape at her openly.

'Mortonby? Did you say *Mortonby*?' Mr Jamieson took a step towards her, his expression eager now.

'Yes.'

'Your mother's name? Her maiden name?'

'Elizabeth Bedham. But...'

'Aaah!' Mr Jamieson let out a long exhalation of satisfaction. 'You have seen our notice, no doubt, madam? The broadsheet?'

'No.' Sarah was bewildered, the anger ebbing suddenly and a great weariness taking its place.

'Then how did you know we were looking for you?'

'I didn't, sir. My mother died yesterday. She made me promise to come and see you.' Sarah's voice trembled for a moment and she had to fight for self-control.

His voice became gentler. 'I'm sorry to hear that, very sorry. But what am I thinking of, keeping you standing here like this? Pickersleigh, send out for a pot of chocolate and some pastries. The lady is wet and chilled, and could use some refreshment, no doubt. Leave your pattens by the door and come this way, my dear Miss Mortonby. I have a fine fire in my room. Dear me, have you hurt your foot?'

'No, sir. I've been lame since birth.' She was used to such questions, but he coloured and tried to hide his embarrassment by whisking out a handkerchief and blowing his nose loudly.

'Pray take a seat, ma'am! Pickering, the chocolate, the pastries. At once!'

Sarah sank into a huge, leather-covered armchair and held her hands out to the blaze, the muff dropping forgotten to the floor. Such an extravagant fire and sea coal four guineas the chaldron this winter! It was a long time since she'd enjoyed such wonderful warmth. 'Why were you seeking me, sir?'

'First, can you prove who you are? I'm not doubting your word, my dear, but 'twould all be much easier if you could *prove* your identity. Papers, your mother's marriage lines, for instance? Anything, really?'

Her heart sank. 'My room was ransacked while I was at the funeral. They burned all the papers.' Perhaps he wouldn't believe her now.

'Then is there someone who knows you? A clergyman, perhaps, someone who could vouch for your identity?'

'Not a clergyman. We have moved about so much, but,' her face cleared, 'would a lawyer do? My father's lawyer?

Mr Peabody has known me all my life. My mother had a small annuity, which he administered.'

Mr Jamieson beamed at her. 'Elias Peabody? Sign of the Red Seal, Hotham Gardens?'

'Yes. Do you know him?'

'I am not personally acquainted with the gentleman, but I know of him. His testimony would be quite acceptable. Ho there!' He sent the young man who answered his call off to find Mr Peabody, then turned to beam at Sarah. 'My dear lady, it is my pleasure, my very great pleasure, to tell you that if you are indeed Miss Mortonby, you have been left a legacy. Not a great fortune, you understand, but still… Miss Mortonby! Oh, my goodness! *Pickersleigh, come quickly!*'

For the first time in her life Sarah had fainted clear away.

She came round to a vile smell and feebly pushed away the burning feather, ruins of a quill, that the clerk was waving under her nose. 'I'm sorry.' She tried to sit up straight, but felt distant and dizzy still.

The outer door banged and the boy came in, staggering under the weight of an enormous tray containing a bulbous pewter chocolate-pot and a platter of sticky pastries.

Mr Jamieson brightened. 'There you are at last, Thomas! Put it down there, put it down! Now, my dear Miss Mortonby, I shall pour you some chocolate and you'll take a pastry, will you not? That'll make you feel better, I'm sure.'

This was such a rare treat that Sarah found herself eating and drinking almost as heartily as her host. She wouldn't now need to spend money on an evening meal… but

17

perhaps that didn't matter any more? The tide of questions could be stemmed no longer.

'A legacy, you said, Mr Jamieson?'

'Yes, indeed. Not a fortune, but enough to provide for you in modest comfort, once the house is sold.'

'House! I've been left a house?' she asked, dazed at the prospect. All her life she had lived in rented rooms. The thought of owning a whole house of her own was an astounding idea!

'On certain conditions.' He regretted the words as soon as he'd spoken them and added hastily, 'But those conditions need not concern us now.'

'What conditions? Why need they concern us no longer?' she asked quietly and a little grimly.

'My dear…'

'I insist you tell me.'

'Well, the bequest is from your grandfather and is upon condition you change your name to Bedham and—' He hesitated.

'And?' she prompted.

'And that your mother does not reside in the house with you or… or ever visit it.'

She said nothing, but he heard the quick intake of breath and leaned forward to say earnestly, 'He was not a forgiving man, I'm afraid, and he grew quite strange after his son's death. Sad to say, the only reason you have inherited the house is because there is simply no other family member left.'

She banished her anger resolutely. No use being angry at a dead man. And at least her mother could no longer be upset by the unkind conditions. 'He must have been very bitter.'

'Yes. With reason.'

'Whatever the reason for inheriting, it seems like a miracle to me. Tell me about my house, if you please. Where is it and why must it be sold?'

'Well, the house is Broadhurst Manor, of course, your mother's old home. And it must be sold because it's been let run to rack and ruin, and is now scarcely habitable. The roof leaks, the place reeks of damp, the gardens are overgrown... Oh, it must certainly be sold! And very fortunately, I have a buyer already waiting – indeed, he is pressing for a sale. There is some land, you see, as well as the house. We shall get you a fair price, don't worry!'

She leaned forward, her expression eager. 'But surely the house, or part of it, could be made habitable? Broadhurst has belonged to my mother's family ever since the Great Queen's day – Elizabeth, you know.' She beamed at him, joy flooding through her suddenly. 'My mother used to tell me all about her home, but I never thought it would belong to me one day, never expected to see it. I... I still can't quite take it in. Surely it can be restored, at least in part...?' She looked at him pleadingly.

'I doubt it, my dear. At least, not without great expense, and there is little money to spare until you sell. Mr Sewell is offering a fair price and might even be made to raise it a trifle.' He smiled at the thought, clearly looking forward to haggling about that.

'And what does this Mr Sewell intend to do with the Manor? Has he the money to restore it?'

Mr Jamieson sighed and avoided her eyes. 'I'm afraid he means to pull the house down. It's the land he wants, you see, to form a deer park. Even the cottages on the estate are to go – well, they're in poor condition, too, and the people surly. They say a bad landlord makes for bad tenants, do they not? Though it is not your grandfather's fault they've been sore plagued with cattle sickness in the district lately. No, that at least was not his fault. But as a result, some of the tenants have been unable to pay their rents in full for the last few quarters. You mustn't be thinking yourself a rich woman. There will be very little money until the place is sold, my dear.'

Sounds in the outer office announced an arrival. Mr Jamieson excused himself and left Sarah to ponder on the news. It was a few moments before he returned, accompanied not only by Mr Peabody, who smiled at her warmly, but also by the young gentleman who had gone to fetch him. Even the clerk, Pickersleigh, came into the room. She felt embarrassed to be the object of their stares.

'This is the lady in question,' said Mr Jamieson in a formal tone very unlike his former manner. 'I would be obliged, Mr Peabody, if you would tell us who she is and what you know of her.'

'Her name is Sarah Mortonby and I have known her ever since she was born. I know her mother, too, Elizabeth Mortonby, née Bedham. I administer a small annuity which her husband set up for her soon after they married.'

'Ah!' said Mr Jamieson in tones of satisfaction. 'Then I shall call upon you all to witness this due and proper identification.'

'By Jove, yes!' exclaimed Mr Lorrimer enthusiastically, for he was still young enough to see the romance of it all.

'Certainly, sir,' said Pickersleigh more formally. 'Shall I prepare the deposition?'

'Naturally. Three copies, I think. No need to make it very long. All quite straightforward. You'll stay and take some chocolate with us, Mr Peabody?'

'Delighted!' Mr Peabody eased his ageing bones down carefully into one of the armchairs and nodded to Sarah. 'How is your mother, my dear?'

'She's dead. I buried her today.'

His face fell. 'Why didn't you let me know? I would have wished to attend the funeral.'

Sarah flushed. 'I... It was a small affair – just myself. I couldn't afford more.'

'It will be necessary for you to come round to my rooms – when it is convenient, of course. There are certain formalities. And money is owing. One third of a quarter, to be precise.'

'I hadn't expected... I thought the annuity stopped at my mother's death.'

'And so it does – but not *before* her death! We are a full month into this quarter and the interest is accrued monthly, though it is only usually paid out quarterly.'

Sarah couldn't prevent herself from sighing in relief. 'I didn't know. I thought I was destitute.'

Her voice quavered on the last word and Mr Jamieson looked across at her anxiously. Was she going to faint again? Poor lady, she must have felt desperate! Imagine a Bedham reduced to such circumstances!

'I, too, have some money for you, my dear,' he said encouragingly. 'I have your rents, such as they are, from last year.'

'How much?' If it was unladylike to ask, Sarah didn't care.

'I have in hand thirty-two guineas, eleven shillings and sixpence. I'm sorry it isn't more, but there is some other money outstanding, to be paid as times improve.'

'It seems quite a fortune to me!'

'My dear,' said Mr Jamieson gently, 'when we sell, I have every confidence that we shall get more than a thousand guineas for your estate. With such a sum, you will be able to buy a small house somewhere more convenient – Tunbridge Wells, for instance, is a fine healthy town – and then you can invest the rest, hire a maid and live comfortably for the rest of your life. Either Mr Peabody or myself would be happy to advise you on how best to invest your money.'

Sarah wasn't really listening to him. 'My mother often spoke about Broadhurst,' she murmured in a bemused fashion, 'though I never thought to see it for myself.'

'But Miss Mortonby, I've just told you how it is! I cannot advise you even to visit the place. Let me arrange to sell it and—'

'Sell it!' She sat bolt upright and looked him full in the eyes. 'Sell Broadhurst! Oh, no, Mr Jamieson, I couldn't sell my mother's home, not without seeing it first, at least! And if it is at all possible, I should very much like to live there!'

'No, no, *no*! Believe me, *pray* believe me, it is not to be thought of! The place is a ruin!'

'It would seem very splendid to me, I'm sure, after Furness Road.'

He clicked his tongue. 'Furness Road! Dear me! I hadn't realised things were so bad. Tch! Tch! We must find you better lodgings immediately. Have you *any* money left?'

Sarah laughed, fumbled for the muff and untied the strings of her purse, emptying its contents into her lap. 'Oh, yes, sir. See… I have six shillings and five pence three farthings.'

She laughed again at the expressions of sheer horror on the two lawyers' faces.

Chapter 2

Three weeks later Sarah leaned her aching head against the hard back of the stage coach seat and wondered yet again whether she was doing the right thing. For she'd flown in the face of the two lawyers' considered and unanimous advice, and had insisted upon going to inspect her inheritance before she made a final decision about selling it, this in spite of all the warnings and dire prognostications of Mr Jamieson and Mr Peabody about the dangers that faced a lady travelling round the countryside on her own.

It had been a pleasant few weeks, for it was years since she'd eaten so well and that made her feel in much better health and spirits. She'd watched in the mirror as her face grew daily plumper, her cheeks rosier and her hair shinier.

Such a pleasure it had been to visit the shops with money in her purse! On one of her early outings she'd spent a delightful hour or two at a linen draper's, choosing the material for two new gowns. That hadn't really been an extravagance, because she had nothing decent to wear. She looked down at her skirt. Should she have chosen black, out of respect for her mother? No! The dresses would have to last for years and she didn't want to be in permanent mourning. Her mother would have been the first to agree about that.

Elizabeth Mortonby had always taken a great interest in clothes and one of her favourite pastimes had been to go out for a stroll in one of the great London parks and watch the fashionable world taking the air. After they got back to their room, her mother would discuss in minute detail what the ladies were wearing and what she would have liked to wear herself.

Sarah had finally chosen a dark blue calimanco, which she made up herself with a contrasting quilted petticoat in a blue and red figured chintz, which was not only fashionable, but warm. The other material was less sensible, but she assuaged her conscience by telling herself that it had been very reasonably priced and she would wear it only for best. It was a patterned lilac paduasoy, and she made it up into a simple closed gown, which showed off the beauty of the material. She was a good needlewoman and had contrived a modest imitation of the latest London fashions which would have delighted her mother.

She had also purchased fine lawn for her caps and kerchiefs, cambric for her under-petticoats and bodices and, rather guiltily, some lace, just a little, to trim her caps! And of course she'd visited a good staymaker.

In addition, she had ordered not one, but two new pairs of shoes from a shoemaker recommended by her new landlady. She wriggled her toes happily inside them at the thought. She'd never had such well-fitting shoes before. The cobbler had built up the sole of the left one very skilfully to reduce her need to limp.

When the tedious two-day coach journey from London to Poole was at last over, Sarah ate a hearty meal and stayed at the coaching inn overnight. She'd asked about a conveyance to take her to Broadhurst, but was told that the inn's small carriage wouldn't be available until later in the morning. It was frustrating, but there was nothing she could do about it.

But oh, she longed to see her family's home. She knew Mr Jamieson had written to Mr Pursley, the agent and tenant of the home farm, asking him to get things ready at the Manor, so was hoping to stay there.

By the time they arrived in Broadhurst, it was well into the afternoon and already dusk was threatening. Sarah felt happiness spread through her just to know that her mother and several generations of her mother's family had once lived in this village, and that gave her a sense of coming home she'd never experienced before.

The carriage stopped at the only inn, The Golden Fleece. It was an old-fashioned, half-timbered building, and stood beside a triangular village green. The inn looked tidy and well cared-for.

A burly landlord came out to greet her, took her inside and handed her over to his wife.

'My name is Mort... er, Bedham.' Sarah still had trouble remembering her new name.

The landlady nodded. 'Will Pursley told us you were coming.' She studied Sarah's face. 'Are you really Miss Elizabeth's daughter? You don't look at all like her.'

'She always said I looked like her grandfather.'

'You do, too. Eh, a fine old gentleman he was. And to think you've come home at last!'

Sarah found herself being ruthlessly hugged, something she wasn't used to, but enjoyed. After that she was swept upstairs to the comfort of a cosy bedroom with a blazing wood fire. Chilled and hungry after her journey, for the heated bricks at her feet had grown cool long before they reached their destination, she ate her fill of a tasty chicken pie, some small cakes and a rather wrinkled apple. She finished this off with a dish of tea, clasping the little china bowl in both hands as she sipped, enjoying its warmth.

When Mistress Poulter herself came to clear the things away, Sarah asked if there was a gig available to take her to the Manor in the morning.

'Oh dear, it's hired out till noon, I'm afraid. But Jem shall drive you then, I promise you.'

'I can walk, surely?'

'Best not, m'dear. 'Tis over a mile outside the village and the lane's in a terrible muddy state after the rain we've had lately.'

Sarah felt too drowsy to argue, but she didn't intend to sit around all morning when she was so close to her new home. She had never, she thought, as she snuggled down in the big, soft feather bed, felt quite so happy in all her life.

The only sadness was that her mother wasn't here to share her good fortune with her.

—

The following morning after Sarah had broken her fast, she went to stand by the window of her bedroom and stare out at the village, then took a turn around the green. She was surprised when she saw so few people, but supposed they were mostly busy at work by this hour.

Eager to see her house, she decided to walk there. 'Can you give me directions for getting to the Manor?' she asked the landlady. 'It doesn't seem likely to rain and I shall enjoy a stroll.'

'Oh, my dear, I don't think that's wise.'

'My mind is quite made up.'

Mistress Poulter opened her mouth to protest, caught her guest's eye and closed it again. After chewing her thumb for a moment as if uncertain what to do, she gave the necessary directions.

Donning her rather old-fashioned cloak and the stouter of her new pairs of shoes, Sarah set off. The morning was cold and the ground damp, but today the sun was shining. She had no trouble following the landlady's directions and finding the lane leading to her house. It didn't seem well used. High banks at each side were covered in tangles of dead vegetation and there were deep ruts in places, half-filled with mud, around which she had to pick her way with great care.

For the first time she began to wonder whether she should have waited for the trap. Or at least, sent for Mr Pursley to act as her guide.

Not used to being alone anywhere, and unaccustomed to the quiet of the countryside, she looked around her a little nervously as she walked. What a fool I am! she thought after a while. Anyone would think there were wolves and brigands in the woods. The place will be very pretty in spring when the leaves are out, I dare say. But today, she couldn't deny that there was a sad feel to the damp brown landscape and try as she would, she couldn't shake off a feeling of apprehension.

Suddenly, a dog came bounding down the slope on her right, a great shaggy creature, barking furiously. Sarah cried out in dismay as it leaped up at her, sending her sprawling on the ground. A man's voice shouted angrily from somewhere and the dog, which had been standing next to her, still barking but wagging its tail furiously, rushed off again.

As she struggled to her feet, she found a strong hand under her arm making the task easier. She looked up to thank her rescuer and found herself gazing at a man of about her own age, whose face might have been deemed handsome had it not been marred by a scowl. For a moment, she forgot everything as she stared at him. He looked so healthy and strong, not pale like the gentlemen she had seen in London, nor shrunken and furtive like the people who frequented Furness Road.

It was unusual to find a man so much taller than she was. It felt... strange. It must be that which was making her heart pound and her pulse race. Or perhaps it was his stare, for he had the kind of eyes which seemed to probe right into you. Such dark, compelling eyes.

She realised he'd said something and found herself blushing like a ninny and stuttering as she tried to understand his question. What was wrong with her today? She must be more tired than she'd realised. Then she noticed the streaks of mud on her cloak and skirt, and that jerked her out of her silliness. 'Was that your dog, sir?'

'I'm afraid so.'

'You should keep such a brute under better control!'

He took a step backwards and his apologetic expression was replaced by the scowl. 'Santo's not dangerous! And anyway, it's his job to warn us of strangers walking along the lane. You should have kept to the public highway, madam. This lane leads nowhere but to Broadhurst Manor.'

She gave him back scowl for scowl. 'As the new owner of Broadhurst, I have *every right* to come this way, so you had better keep that ill-trained brute under more control in future, because I have no desire to be attacked every time I walk to and from the village!' She began to limp on.

'Wait!' He hurried after her. 'You've hurt your foot. Please let me…'

'I'm not hurt.' She set off again, but slipped on a patch of muddy ground and if he hadn't caught hold of her, would have fallen again.

For a moment, she couldn't move, because she'd jarred her bad hip. She closed her eyes and clung to him as pain washed through her.

His voice was a growl of sound from just above her ear. 'You *are* hurt.'

'I just… twisted my leg,' she said, through gritted teeth. 'It will pass in a moment.'

His voice was gentler. 'Hold on to me.'

She had no choice but to do so until the waves of pain had subsided. Most of the time she had no trouble walking, but just once in a while she jarred whatever it was that was wrong inside her. When she thought she could move without stumbling, she tried to pull away from him, but he kept hold of her arm, his eyes anxious.

'Are you sure you're all right now?'

'Yes.'

'You must have hurt yourself badly.'

'I was born lame, sir. Today's fall has merely jarred my bad hip. The pain will soon pass.' She could hear how sharp her voice was, but couldn't help that. She hated to display her weakness to anyone. 'Thank you for your help.'

'I'm sorry about Santo.' He turned to the animal and said, 'Friend,' loudly, several times, patting her arm. It wagged its tail even more furiously at Sarah and panted vigorously, its pink tongue hanging out of one side of its mouth as if it was grinning.

She couldn't help smiling at it, then stole a quick glance sideways. The man was standing so close to her she could feel the warmth where his body was shielding hers from the chill breeze. His dark hair was tied back in a plain bow – his own hair, not a wig – and his skin had that fresh colour to it that came from working out of doors. His eyes were so dark as to seem almost black, and he had a straight, well-formed nose and wide, generous mouth, though this was set in a grim line at the moment to match the frown lines on his forehead. And although he was dressed in working clothes, they were not poor men's clothes, but good, hardwearing stuff, a neat leather jerkin over a woollen overshirt to keep out the cold, knee breeches of broadcloth over knitted woollen stockings, and sturdy leather shoes with the low heels of a working man.

'Are you really the new owner of Broadhurst?' he asked abruptly.

She was glad of an excuse to feel annoyed with him. Anger was something she knew, something that kept you going, not like this... this other feeling he inspired, a feeling she definitely didn't trust. 'Why should you doubt what I tell you?' She drew away from him, relieved to find that her leg would hold her now.

'I'd not expected the new owner to walk up a muddy lane and arrive unannounced.'

'Well, I haven't got a carriage, and if the state of my house is as they tell me, I don't suppose I ever will have. *If* that's any of your business.'

He laughed, a short, mirthless bark. 'Oh, but you do have a carriage! Two, in fact. They're mouldering away in the coach house at the Manor. But you won't be able to use them, because there aren't any horses left to pull them.'

'Well, they can just stay there and moulder, then. I've no money for horses, or for a coachmen to drive them.'

The scowl returned. 'Then I take it that you'll be selling the Manor to Sewell?'

'That's my business, I think.'

She saw him open his mouth as if he was going to speak, then breathe deeply and clamp his lips shut. What a surly fellow he was! Still, if he was a tenant, he had a right to worry about his future, and she had lived with uncertainty about her own future for the past year and wouldn't willingly inflict it on anyone else. 'I'm not selling.' Honesty compelled her to add, 'At least, I hope not.'

He looked at her in both surprise and distrust, as if he didn't quite believe her. 'You're not? But... how shall you manage?'

'As best I can. And I take leave to tell you that you are impertinent, sir!'

He stiffened. 'I cry pardon! I meant no impertinence, Mistress Bedham. I was just... I should have introduced myself before now. I'm Will Pursley, you see. I lease the home farm from you and in addition, your lawyer has appointed me to act as your agent, collecting rents and so on. He said you'd be arriving, but not exactly when.' And the lawyer hadn't said she was so young. Will had expected an older woman, not one with pretty hair and clear grey eyes.

'Ah, yes.' Sarah inclined her head. 'Mr Jamieson has spoken of you.' Then she looked up at the sky which looked grey and full of rain. 'Perhaps you could call on me at the inn tomorrow to discuss how things stand? For the present, I'm eager to see my house and must be on my way.'

'You'll be quicker if you cut through the woods. I'll show you the path.'

She wasn't sure she wanted to spend any more time with him, but her hip was still aching and he seemed to take her acceptance for granted. Only burning curiosity made her continue. And hunger – such a great hunger for a home of her own that it was nearly devouring her. 'Very well. Thank you.'

Simple courtesy made him offer her his arm, but she hesitated before taking it. Touching him made her feel… strange. But in the end she laid her hand on his arm and they set off, with him letting her set the pace, thank goodness, which was very thoughtful.

He led her along the side of the lane, avoiding the worst of the mud. Since he made no attempt at small talk and she had never learned the art, they moved in silence, their breath clouding the air around them and the only sounds, the soft muddy beat of their footsteps on the ground. The sounds they made were accompanied by the panting of the dog, now loud, now faint as it quested to and fro.

At one point, a sheet of muddy water stretched across the whole lane and without asking, Mr Pursley set his hands on her waist and lifted her over it as if she weighed nothing. Sarah could feel her face grow warm with embarrassment. She wasn't used to the feel of a man's hands on her body.

He stared at her as he set her down and seemed about to say something, then clamped his lips shut again.

They came to a long, high wall, made of some local stone, and in it a gateway, with the wooden gate hanging useless from one hinge.

'This leads through the woods to the house.' He pushed the gate to one side.

Only when she thought things over that night, did she realise how instinctively she had trusted him. And yet she'd learned, in places like Furness Road, to trust no one, especially a man. But for all his surliness, Will Pursley had a wholesome air to him. One look at his face showed you an honest man.

Another thought followed that one in the safety of her bedchamber: he was a handsome man, as well.

The path through the woods was better drained, but still he kept an eye on the going, ready to point out a smoother route or guide her away from boggy ground.

'You seem to know these woods well,' she commented when the silence became too heavy.

'Aye. I've made it my business to know them since I took over as agent. And to keep a watch for people who shouldn't be here, but who try to make free of the game – and of other things, too, perhaps.'

'I thank you for your care.' What other things, she wondered, might people be seeking here?

Quite soon the trees began to thin out and the house came into view in the distance, surrounded by grassy meadows and occasional clumps of trees. She stopped, letting go of his arm to clasp her hands at her breast, unable to hold back a cry of sheer joy.

Broadhurst Manor lay nestled in the hollow below them as if it had always been there and had put down great roots to anchor itself securely to the land. It was four stories high at the front, if you counted the attics, and a storey less at the wings, which stretched backwards from where they stood. It was built of mellow red brick, with a neat portico over the front door and two broad, shallow steps leading up to it.

Sarah fell instantly in love with it, as if something within her recognised it. 'It's beautiful!' she breathed, totally forgetting her companion as tears welled unheeded in her eyes. And it was hers! She who had owned so little before, who had never had even a small house to live in, now possessed a handsome manor house. From where they stood it looked sound enough, and she couldn't understand why Mr Jamieson considered it uninhabitable.

'It could be beautiful,' Mr Pursley allowed, 'If someone cared enough to look after it.' Then he shook his head and the frown returned, not aimed at her, but as if it was his habitual expression.

They moved slowly forward towards the curving driveway and as she began to see more details, Sarah's heart sank. The windows were dull, one or two broken and gaping open to the weather. Grass was growing in the gutters, and there were dead branches and other debris scattered over what had once been a gravelled forecourt, but which now sprouted patches of dead weeds from the previous summer.

This couldn't all have happened in the year since her grandfather's death. He must have allowed the place to degenerate while he was still alive. How could he have done that? She would have boarded up the windows herself rather than leave them open to the weather's assault. There were broken roof tiles lying here and there on the ground, recent falls, by the looks of them. There must have been bad winter storms to do this. How much did it cost to get in a tiler? And a glazier? How bad were things inside the house?

Too bad for her to live there? Oh, please, no!

She stopped and pressed a hand to the hip that was aching furiously now. When she saw that Mr Pursely had noticed, she snatched her hand away, but the damage was done.

'How did the house get like this?' she wondered aloud to distract his attention from herself.

He ignored her question. 'Never mind the house, you need to rest that hip, Mistress Bedham.'

She nodded and let out a shaky breath. Useless to deny it. The house still lay some two or three hundred yards away. She might get there, but would find it difficult to return to the village on foot afterwards. 'I think perhaps I'd better return to the inn. I need not trouble you further. I can manage on my own, now that I know the way.' And would be able to go slowly, with rests to ease the hip.

'Nonsense! You aren't fit to walk far, so if you'll sit here in this arbour, I'll go and fetch my trap.' He brushed the dead leaves off a rotting wooden bench and guided her to it, making sure she had sat down before he stepped back. ''Tis only a short walk to the home farm through the woods.'

She could only nod and admit, 'I'd be grateful for your help, sir.'

She looked so white, Will ran all the way home, wondering how to warn her about Sewell and how best to help her settle in. For upon this woman depended his own future, his only hope of staying in the district. And he was determined to stay there, just as he was determined one day to make Sewell pay for what he had done.

'She looks like she needs cosseting,' he told the horse as he harnessed it. 'But she's a Bedham all right. She's not only got their height and colouring, but that stubborn chin, just like the old Squire's.'

As the horse clopped along the track to the big house, he could see her sitting in the old arbour, heedless of the dirt and spiders, her head leaning back and weariness in every line of her body. Something tugged at his heart, as it had when she'd leaned against him, fighting to hide the pain. It was strange, this urge he had to protect a stranger, a woman he had only just met.

He jumped down and helped her up into the trap, driving it gently back to the village via the farm lane, which was the longer way round, but in much better condition than the one she had arrived by.

At The Golden Fleece, he helped her down and wasn't surprised when she clung to his arm again to cross the muddy ground to the door, limping badly now.

Prue Poulter met them at the door, her face anxious. 'What's happened?'

Will answered. 'Mistress Bedham has had a fall and needs to rest.'

Sarah tried to pull herself together. She didn't need anyone to speak for her, even though he meant it kindly. 'I shall be all right now. I must thank you again for your help, Mr Pursley. I hadn't realised how long a country mile can seem.'

She saw him give Prue what could only be a quick warning glance. Warning of what? But the grinding ache in her hip was only too real and she knew that she must rest it for a while.

He stepped back. 'I'll come and take you to see the house myself tomorrow afternoon, Mistress Bedham. I can't come in the morning, as I have someone to see, but I know my way around that house as well as anyone, and shall be happy to be your guide.' He should know the house – he'd had to make quite a few emergency repairs lately to stop the old place going from bad to worse.

He was striding back to his cart before Sarah could say anything.

'Well!' She turned to the landlady. 'Does he always take charge like that and tell folk what to do?'

Prue shrugged. 'If there's something to be done, you can always rely on Will Pursley to get it done. And I'll feel better if you have him with you tomorrow, my dear.' For she, too, was afraid that Sewell's men might waylay the newcomer and she was uncertain whether to warn her guest about him and his bullies, or hope Sewell would not dare act against one of his own class.

Upstairs, Sarah lay down on the bed, sighing in relief as the pain eased a little once the weight was off her hip. She couldn't stop thinking about what she'd seen. How forlorn Broadhurst Manor had looked – and yet, how lovely it could be, for there was a harmony to the lines of the house that pleased her greatly.

'If it's at all possible,' she said softly as she got ready for bed that night, pinching out the last candle and pulling the covers cosily around her, 'I would like to live there.'

'There must be some way,' she muttered a few minutes later, as she slid towards sleep. 'There must.'

And why she should dream of Mr Pursley that night, she couldn't think. In the morning, she had to wonder at how unsettling her dreams of him had been – the feel of his hand on hers, the strength of his shoulders, the firm line of his lips. She'd never had such dreams in all her life before. But then, she'd never met a man like him. So strong. Not a mincing town gentleman, well not a gentleman at all, but a man of character, open-faced and quietly confident of himself.

And handsome enough to turn any woman's head.

Oh, she was being foolish! She drifted off to sleep on the less disturbing thought that tomorrow she would see her new home properly, go inside, take possession.

It would be hers for a time, even if she was forced to sell it. But she'd only do that as a final resort.

Whatever anyone said.

Chapter 3

The following morning Sarah woke early. Excitement hummed through her as she got ready, and images of the old house's exterior kept floating through her mind. Today she wouldn't be staring at it from a distance, but actually going inside. And if it weren't for her stupid hip, she'd have done that yesterday.

'Is your boy free to drive me to the Manor this morning?' she asked Prue Poulter, who carried up her breakfast tray in person.

'I thought Will Pursley was to take you there this afternoon?'

'I'm not going to sit around half the day waiting for him!'

'I... I...'

'This morning, if you please!'

Prue went away, shaking her head and muttering to herself.

'Mistress says I'm to drive you round by the farm lane,' the stable boy offered as they left the village. ''Tis a bit longer, but less muddy, easier on the pony.'

'Very well.'

Sarah watched eagerly for the first sight of her house, her face softening into a smile as they drove round a bend and on to the overgrown drive. When they drew up before the front door, she let out a long sigh of happy anticipation, allowed the lad to help her down, then told him to return for her in three hours time.

'Mistress Poulter said I were to stay here, case I'm needed,' he objected, edging from one foot to the other.

She set her hands on her hips and gave him a stern glance, the sort that had quelled impertinent folk in Furness Road. 'Well, you're not needed. And that poor animal is going to get chilled through if it has to wait here all morning.'

Truth to tell, she preferred to be on her own today, with neither the lad from the inn nor Mr Pursley, whose shrewd eyes had missed nothing the previous day, to witness her feelings. Indeed, she felt remarkably like weeping for joy already as she slowly mounted the shallow stone steps, studying the entrance.

Varnish had faded unevenly from the wood of the door and the hinges were rusty. It looked as if it hadn't been opened for years. A hole in the wall suggested that the bell pull was broken and hadn't been repaired, which seemed a strange thing to happen.

'Poor house!' she murmured, stroking the brickwork as if it were a living creature. She knocked on the door and waited for a minute or two, then hammered on it again, but there was no sound of life from inside. And yet, Mr Jamieson said there was a caretaker of sorts.

The door was firmly locked, so she set off to look for another entrance. A path which was only slightly less overgrown than the drive led round the side of the house. In summer it would be almost hidden by foliage, but now most of the plants showed only bare twigs, with some of them in bud. Here and there stood an evergreen shrub to cheer the eye, but they were growing untidily and clearly hadn't been trimmed for years.

As she followed the path, she began to get an uneasy feeling, as if someone was watching her. She stopped and looked round, but could hear nothing. 'Is anyone there?' she called. There was no answer. She was just being silly, she decided.

However, as she was about to start moving again, there was a rustling sound behind her. She spun round. There *was* someone following! Her heart began to pound and she moved to stand with her back against a tree. 'I know you're there!' she called, more loudly this time. 'Come out at once!'

Heavy breathing was the only answer. It sounded like an animal in distress, not someone out to attack her, but she bent and picked up a stick to defend herself with, just in case.

When no one appeared, she decided surprise was the best strategy. Rushing forward into the shrubbery, she pushed her way past the tangles of branches and there, behind one of the evergreen shrubs, she found a man in ragged clothes crouching. She stopped, holding the stick at the ready, but he remained where he was, hands clasped protectively over his head, as if he expected her to hit him. He looked up, whimpered, but made no attempt to speak to her.

'Who are you?' she demanded.

As she took another step towards him, he gibbered with fright, then lurched to his feet and ran away round the house, crashing through the shrubbery. When she called out to him to stop, he only sobbed and ran faster.

He was more afraid of her than she was of him, she decided then, feeling a little better. She was astounded at her own rashness in confronting him, but it *was* her house, after all, and she had every right to be there.

As she followed the path towards the rear of the house, she noticed that the brickwork here didn't match that at the front and paused to study it. From its dilapidation, she guessed this part must have been built at an earlier date than the rest, for the walls were sagging visibly, the mortar crumbling from between the bricks.

Rounding another corner, she found a paved courtyard enclosed by the wings of the house, with tumbledown stables and outhouses filling in most of the fourth side.

Limping on, still feeling apprehensive, Sarah finally came to what looked like the kitchen door. Inside she could hear a woman's voice scolding, such an ordinary sound that she closed her eyes for a moment in thankfulness before calling, 'Is anyone there?'

As she knocked on the door, the voice stopped abruptly and footsteps come shuffling towards her. The door opened a crack and an old woman, dressed in clothes as ragged as the man's, peered through it, brandishing a carving knife. She sighed in audible relief as she saw Sarah and let the knife hand drop.

'You'm missed your way, mistress. Village is down t'other end of the lane. There be no gentry livin' here now.'

She made as if to shut the door and Sarah put out a hand to stop her. 'I haven't missed my way. I'm Sarah Bedham.'

'Ah.' She stared hard at Sarah. 'Will Pursley said you were coming today, but he said this afternoon, not this morning. Said *he* were bringing you.' The woman peered around, as if expecting to see him nearby.

Sarah tried to be patient, though she was longing to go inside and the doorway was still blocked. 'Well, I've come on my own. I didn't want to wait.'

As the woman studied her face again, the fear and hostility faded from her eyes, and she let the hand holding the knife fall by her side. 'Be you truly Miss Elizabeth's daughter?'

What were she and her son so afraid of, Sarah wondered? 'Yes. And you are, I think, Mary Hames. Mr Jamieson told me you were living here.'

Mary nodded and glanced at Sarah again. 'You don't look like Miss Elizabeth.' Then she saw the locket and reached for it. 'But thass hers, right enough. I seen it many a time. Her godfather give it to her when she turned eighteen, Lord Tarnly.'

She studied Sarah again, then clapped her hands together triumphantly. 'You d'look like Old Master, thass who! Your great-granfer, not your granfer. He were a big man, Sir James, wi' grey eyes like yourn. I remember him well. There's a painting of him in the long gallery upstairs.' Tears tracking down the wrinkles on her cheeks, she reached out to tug at Sarah's arm. 'Come in out of the cold! And welcome home, mistress! Welcome home!'

So at last Sarah entered her house, and she cared not that it was by the back door. Her heart was too full for speech as she moved slowly inside, and once there, she could only stand and look around, swallowing hard and willing herself not to weep for sheer joy.

It was a large, square room with a bright fire of logs burning in an enormous grate over whose iron cooking rails hung an assortment of hooks and a kettle crane holding a big, blackened kettle trickling steam. There was a window on the yard side of the room, though the panes were dusty and some cracked. The floor was paved with great square stone slabs and those nearest the door had hollows worn in them, as if countless feet had left a lasting impression of their passing.

Sarah moved across to warm her hands at the fire. At one side stood an old-fashioned wooden settle with a high back and cowering behind it was the man who had run away from her in the shrubbery. He whimpered and hid his face in his hands as he saw her looking at him.

Mary came to stand at Sarah's side, 'Don't ee be feared of the lady, boy. She's our new mistress.' She turned to Sarah. 'My Petey's nervous of strangers, mistress. I know he ent got all his wits, but he wouldn't harm anything, that boy wouldn't. An' he's a good worker if you do but take the time to tell him slow what to do, an' maybe watch him do it once or twice.

'Will Pursley hires him sometimes for a day's diggin' or to help wi' the harvest an' *he* wouldn't pay out good money unless he got value for it! Yes, he's a good lad in his own way, is my Petey, but they boys in the village do torment him so! Then he hits out at them. S'only natural, that is, to defend yourself!'

'Yes, of course,' agreed Sarah. She had seen people bait idiots before and it had always sickened her. 'I'm sure he is a good... er... boy.' Petey looked to be at least thirty and his hair was starting to go thin on top. 'Mr Jamieson told me you two had been looking after the house.'

Before Mary could answer, the back door crashed open and a burly man with dark hair and a high-coloured complexion strode inside.

Petey shrieked and dived back behind the settle. Mary whimpered and edged closer to Sarah.

'Who's this, then?' the newcomer demanded, striking out with his riding crop and sweeping some things from the kitchen table.

Sarah was so stunned by this that she could only gape at him for a minute.

'Got us another idiot here, looks like,' he called to someone outside and another man stuck his head inside the door. He was thinner than his friend, with sparse, straggly hair and a front tooth missing, but he had the same cruel, gloating expression on his face.

Sarah recovered her voice. 'How dare you burst in here like that!'

'Oh, she has got a tongue, then!' the man mocked, using his riding crop to send another wooden platter crashing to the floor.

Before she had thought what she was doing, anger drove Sarah to forward to grab his riding crop. She took him by surprise and wrenched it away from him before he realised what she was doing. 'Get out of my house at once, you!'

He had stretched out his hand as if to grab his crop back, or maybe to seize hold of her, but as her words sank in, he stopped and stared. 'Your house? And just who are you to claim ownership?'

'The granddaughter of Squire Bedham, that's who. And I demand that you leave my house immediately.'

He let out a slow whistle of surprise. However, within a minute he was scowling at her. 'You're lying. There aren't any Bedhams left.'

'Who are you to know that?' She could feel Mary trembling beside her and Petey was still curled up in a moaning heap of rags.

'I'm the man who's going to stop cheats like you trying to lay false claim to this place.' He held up one hand to protect his face and came a step closer. When she lashed out at him with the crop, he fended off the blow with his arm and wrenched the crop back from her, laughing scornfully. 'Looks to me like you need a lesson about lying, mistress, and I think we'll send you on your way with a warning not to come back.'

Until now, anger had sustained her, but suddenly she began to feel afraid. Tall as she was, she would be no match for two of them, and neither Mary nor Petey was making any attempt to help her. This man was very muscular, for all his bulk. Although she fought back instinctively, shoving at him with all her might, she could not push him away or stop him fondling her body.

'Come and help me, Izzy' he called, laughing. 'She's a comfy armful, if a mite scrawny. Ouch! You'll pay for that, wench!'

There was a cry from outside and then a voice roared from the doorway, 'Let the lady go at once!'

With a curse, the man shoved Sarah aside and turned to face Will Pursley, who was standing with clenched fists half-raised as if ready for a fight. Beyond him, the other intruder lay sprawled in the mud of the yard.

Sarah seized the moment to give the man next to her a shove that sent him flying towards the door. By the time he turned round with a snarl and an upraised hand, she had grabbed a stool and was holding it between herself and him. She jabbed its legs at him and he retreated a step. Her mother didn't know half the tricks she'd had to learn to defend herself in Furness Road. The main thing was to show no fear and to take the initiative. And at the moment anger was burning so hotly through her veins that she wanted to hurt him in return for what he'd done to her.

As she glanced towards the doorway, she saw the man in the yard scramble to his feet and dive towards Will Pursley, so called out a warning. There was a short scuffle, then Will knocked the man down again and he lay there groaning. When the fellow near her would have gone to his companion's aid, she jabbed the stool at him again to distract him.

As soon as he had disposed of his opponent, Will Pursley came running back into the kitchen and grabbed the burly man from behind.

When another fight began between the two of them, Sarah didn't wait to see who would win, but snatched up a wooden platter, waited till the intruder's back was towards her and hit him hard on the head. He roared in pain, staggered and stopped fighting to clutch his head.

For a minute it was touch and go whether he'd attack Will again, then he glared at them both and began edging sideways towards the door. 'I won't forget this, Pursley.'

'Neither will I, Tensby. You're trespassing and if I find you here again, disturbing Mistress Bedham, I'll have you up before the magistrate.'

'I'm here at Mr Sewell's behest and *he* won't forget your behaviour, either!'

'He has no rights here.'

'He's buying the rights – not trying to steal them like she is.'

Breath hissed into Will Pursley's mouth and his fists clenched again, but he held back. 'She's the rightful owner,' he said.

'We'll see about that.'

The man outside got to his feet, clasping his jaw. For a moment, the two bullies stood shoulder to shoulder, and the malevolence on their faces made Sarah shiver. Then they turned and strode off. A minute later there was the sound of horses trotting away.

Will rounded on Sarah and asked angrily, 'Why did you not wait for me at the inn today?'

She blinked in surprise at his sharp tone. 'I had no intention of wasting the whole morning – and how did you know I was here, anyway?'

'I saw you drive past the farm, so finished what I was doing and saddled Dolly.' He ran a hand through his hair in a vain attempt to smooth it back and brushed some of the dust off his jerkin.

She felt obliged to say, 'I'm grateful for your intervention.'

For a moment a grin creased his face. 'I should thank you as well. Not many ladies would have been so... er, resourceful.'

She smiled back, then felt the smile fade as the worries returned. 'Who are those men and why do they feel they can just... walk in here and attack people?'

By now, Mary's son had crawled out from behind the settle. 'Hit him on the head, the lady did,' he announced, beaming at Sarah and miming her action. 'Hit him hard. Bang!'

Will turned to Petey, his voice gentler now. 'You go and give Dolly a drink, lad. Give Dolly a drink. Clean water, mind.'

Petey nodded and went outside to pick up the horse's reins and lead it across the yard, talking to it, repeating his tale of, 'Hit him on the head, she did,' several times, as if the animal could understand.

'Let me show you into the front parlour, Mistress Bedham. We'll be more comfortable talking there – and more private, too. Mary, shout for me if they return.' Will looked at Sarah as she moved towards the door. 'I should have told you yesterday about... about the danger you're facing.'

'You should indeed.'

He led her along a dark passage, whose only window was smashed and the gap boarded up.

'Why are so many of the windows broken?' she wondered aloud.

'Sewell's men do it.' He opened a door and led the way out into a broad hall, which led in turn to the front door she had knocked on in vain. Striding across to the left, he pushed a panelled wooden door open and ushered her into the room behind it. 'This is the great parlour. Your grandfather always sat here in the evening, so it's in better condition than some of the other rooms.' He frowned round. 'But it still needs attention.'

The place was filled with huge pieces of furniture, many shrouded in coarse sacking and yellowed cloth. It must have been very grand once, Sarah decided. The ceiling was patterned plaster, its white panels outlined in gold, but it was badly stained in one corner where rain had leaked in. As in the rest of the house, the windows were grimy with dirt and festooned with cobwebs. One pane was broken, another cracked. The hangings were deep red in colour, but were stiff with dust, and cobwebs stretched from their top corners to the wall. Over the fireplace hung a portrait of a lady with a sweet smile. Sarah moved over to study it more closely.

'Your grandmother,' Will murmured in a hushed, respectful voice. 'A rare kind lady. She used to give me sugar plums when I was little. Squire adored her and was never the same after she died.'

Sarah felt resentful that this stranger knew so much more about her family than she did. She moved across to another door that led out at the rear of the room, opened it and peered inside.

'The dining-parlour,' Will said in his abrupt way, not moving from his place near the window. 'Though it was never used again after your uncle's death. Your grandfather lived and ate in here. He would see no one once he'd found out about the debts, you see.'

'Debts?'

'Your uncle had many debts. No one knew about them until after his death.'

'To whom was he indebted?'

'To Sewell mainly, though to a few others as well. Squire was furious. He claimed Sewell must have encouraged his son to gamble. He felt shamed by this and that's why he wouldn't receive anyone afterwards, not even Lord Tarnly when he came over from Sawbury.'

He cleared his throat. 'Look... I need to explain. Even Mr Jamieson doesn't know all that's been going on here, because he wouldn't believe me about Sewell, who puts his best face on when dealing with the gentry.' He pulled the cover off a chair and gestured to her to sit down.

Reluctantly she abandoned her explorations. 'Who exactly were those men? And why did they behave so violently?'

'They're Sewell's bullies. Since he's offered to buy Broadlands and is not used to being denied, he already considers the estate his own and sends those two to keep people away. He also feels, I dare say, that the less attractive the house is, the lower the price he'll have to pay, so from time to time Hugh and Izzy come over and break windows, or do any other damage that amuses them.'

She sucked in her breath. Mr Jamieson has spoken of the man who wanted to buy her house. 'This Sewell is... an unscrupulous man, then?'

'By my lights, yes.' Will took in a deep breath. 'But you should perhaps ask someone else about his character. I must confess I have a personal grievance against the man.'

'Oh? May I ask what?'

'He bought most of the land your grandfather was selling and built himself a fine new house on it. That included,' his voice was thin and tight for a moment, 'buying the farm my family had leased from yours for over a hundred years. Sewell ordered us to quit our farm because he wanted to set out his pleasure gardens where our house stood – but we had a lease on the place still, for as long as my father lived. It was a three lifetimes lease, you see. So we stayed.'

His mouth thinned into a grimace of pain and he lowered his head for a moment, then raised it to continue in a dull voice, 'One day we found my father hanging dead in the barn. It seemed as if he had taken his own life. Only he would never have done that. Never! Sewell then claimed that debts owed to him were the reason and even produced papers with what looked like my father's signature on them to prove it. He not only turned us out of our house, but took half our possessions in payment for those so-called debts.'

And Sewell had laughed as he did so, while a group of strangers, hired for the occasion and led by Hugh Tenby, had taken the opportunity to beat the son who had tried to defend his mother from their cruel jokes.

Will closed his eyes as the now familiar pain racked him, but forced himself to finish the tale because Mistress Bedham needed to know what had happened. 'They... um, beat me senseless. While I was still recovering, Lord Tarnly himself came to Broadhurst to inquire into the matter – Parson had given us shelter, you see, so Sewell couldn't touch us further.

'Mr Jamieson found us a place to live – on your home farm – what was left of it. The tenant had died recently and his son wished to move to Bristol. But soon after that, your grandfather also died, this time of natural causes.' He hesitated, then said bluntly, 'If you can call an excess of port wine a natural cause.'

He didn't need to say that his new home was now also at risk, and depended on her good will. He could see in her face that she understood the ramifications. Admiring the intelligence that shone from her fine grey eyes, he stopped talking, watching her,. Sometimes he wondered if he wouldn't have done better to leave the district entirely – except that he hadn't given up hope of one day finding proof that his father had indeed been murdered and that the debts were forgeries. He was quite sure of that in his own mind. And anyway, it went against the grain to be chased away like a stray cur.

Sarah stared at the stiff figure, outlined against the window. She couldn't see his face, but every line of his body spoke of grief as well as anger. She, who had lost a beloved mother so recently, could sympathise with that. And having encountered Sewell's two bullies, she believed what Will Pursley had told her. She'd have believed it anyway. He was blunt but not devious.

'Well, Sewell won't drive me away,' she declared at last.

'How can you possibly stay?' he burst out, gesturing around him, for seeing the bullies attacking her so openly had made him realise the futility of his hopes. 'Look at the state things are in. Can *you* repair all this? Of course you can't. You're a woman alone, and you won't even be able to keep those louts from attacking you, unless you can afford to hire your own guards.'

It took a great deal of vigilance on Will's part to protect his own mother and their farm. He didn't always succeed where the property was concerned, but he'd kept his mother safe.

'I'll find a way. Perhaps Lord Tarnly can help me? I believe he's the chief magistrate hereabouts?'

'He is. And an honest gentleman, too. But he lives over in Sawbury. Too far away to ask for help if you're attacked like you were today, and I can't always be on hand to drive them away.' He shook his head, bitterness roiling within him in a greasy, acid tide. 'You'll not manage it, Mistress Bedham. If you had a husband and servants about the place, then maybe you could do something. There *is* some land on the estate which could be farmed to increase your revenue, and you do still own a few small properties. Most of the house is habitable, or could be made so.'

After a pause, he added quietly, 'But you haven't got a husband. And you told me yesterday that you haven't got much money, either.'

She knew he was only speaking the truth as he saw it, not trying to anger her. But she was angry at the thought that someone wanted to drive her away from her inheritance. Well, she wouldn't give in so easily, not when her mother's home had already touched her heart, not when she was longing to live here. She opened her mouth to speak, but he got in first.

'Face the truth, Mistress Bedham. For you, the most sensible thing would be to sell to Sewell – or,' and this was the best Will could hope for personally, 'to someone else.' *If* she could find anyone willing to buy. *If* Sewell's bullies didn't burn the place around her ears while she was trying to sell it.

Sarah took a deep breath. That was exactly what both lawyers had said to her in London. And she'd defied them to come here. Selling might be the easy way out of her troubles, but her heart told her to stay. It told her also that she was a Bedham and had a right to live here. She drew herself up and looked him straight in the eyes. 'Mr Pursley, I've never had a home of my own before and now that I've been given one, I'm not going to let anyone take it away from me.'

His voice was weary. 'It's a valiant thought.' If Sewell could kill his father, the man wouldn't balk at killing this lady. That thought sent chills shivering in his belly which surprised him. Something about her continued to touch him. Her courage, perhaps, or her clear, direct gaze. And he could understand her longing for a home. Oh yes, he could understand that completely. Feeling as if someone was pulling him to pieces, too, he'd stood in a nearby copse and watched as the farmhouse he'd been born in was torn down, stone by stone.

He glanced sideways at Mistress Bedham. She was thoughtful now, frowning into space. He remembered how she'd limped along the lane beside him, making no complaint, though her hip had obviously been paining her greatly. Even in the dimness of this gloomy chamber, he couldn't help thinking how pretty her hair was, just the colour of his mother's best honey.

'You could try to find another buyer?' he suggested as she continued to stand there with that stubborn look on her face.

'I'm not selling. I'm staying.'

'Have you been listening to a word I've said?' he shouted suddenly, unable to bear the thought of Sewell hurting her – or worse.

She drew herself up. 'Yes. I've heard everything you've said – but it hasn't changed my mind.'

Silence hung between them for a few more minutes, then he threw out his hands in a gesture of despair. 'For your own sake, I can only hope that after you've thought it through more carefully, you'll change your mind. In the meantime, I'll do my best to help you.' He cast a glance through the window. The day was passing and he had work to do. 'When shall I come to take you back to the village?'

'Are you sure you can spare the time?'

'I'll make the time.'

'In two hours, then, if that's all right.'

'Don't try to go back on your own.'

'No. I won't do that.'

He rode off across the meadows and through the woods, feeling angry and worried. All over a woman he'd only met for the first time the day before.

But he didn't forget to keep an eye open, and he decided to enlist the help of the other villagers in keeping a watch on the comings and goings of Sewell and his two bullies. Surely between them they would be able to keep her safe?

Chapter 4

When William Pursley had left, Sarah moved across to the windows and sure enough, a few minutes later she saw him striding away towards his farm. So much strength and energy! She envied him that free stride, something she had never experienced in her whole life.

Was she being foolish about this house? She didn't know. But a quiet life in Tunbridge Wells, a town Mr Jamieson had suggested as suitable for an unmarried lady of means, didn't appeal to her at all, while the thought of living here, of bringing the house back to its old self – ah, that appealed to her greatly. But if her grandfather hadn't been able to manage on his income, how could she? It would all need a great deal of thinking about.

A tap on the parlour door brought her out of her reverie. Mary peered in. 'Will says I'm to show you round.'

'Thank you.'

Mary pushed open a door at the back of the dining room. 'This was the still room, and beyond it are the store-rooms and you can get to them from the kitchen too.'

Sarah went to glance inside them, but they were all empty.

'Made some lovely perfumes, she did, your grand-mother,' Mary went on. 'And medicines, too. Had a cure for everything, she did. Her book of receipts is in the library. She wrote 'em all down.'

She led the way back into the hallway and across to the front room at the other side. This was a much smaller room, but still larger than any Sarah had ever lived in. 'This were your grandmother's own parlour. Used to be nice, it did. She allus put flowers round the place, an' branches of berries an' such in winter. But it ent been used since she died. Master wouldn't even come in here.'

Allowing little time to linger, she led the way briskly through yet another door into the room to the rear of it. All the main rooms seemed to lead off the hall or off one another in the old-fashioned way, Sarah thought as she followed.

'An' this were called the winter parlour. Family sat in here an' ate their meals in here too, when there weren't any visitors. Warm, it is. That grate throws out a good heat. Best fire in the house, that is.'

Sarah continued to follow quietly. Afterwards she would walk round again on her own. For now, she was content to get a general idea of what the house, *her house*, was like and to listen to Mary's rambling reminiscences.

Opening from the far side of the winter parlour was the library, a long narrow room, forming the west wing that jutted out to the rear, as the stillroom and storage rooms had formed the east wing. Her mother had described her old home often, but that was not the same as seeing it, especially when everything was so much bigger than Sarah had expected. According to her mother, the Manor had been built in bits and pieces, with each generation adding something new.

There were several rows of old-fashioned books along shelves at one side of the library, but they were as dusty as the rest of the house. There were yards of empty shelves too, as if the library had never been finished. Well, she couldn't afford to buy books, so they must stay empty.

'There!' Mary pounced on something. 'This is your grandmother's book.' She opened it and ran a finger over the faded black handwriting. 'Wish I could read it. She knew some clever things, Squire's lady did.'

Sarah looked at the book, promising herself to read it from cover to cover one day, then laid it down carefully, for Mary was waiting for her at the far end of the room, to show two more small rooms leading off it, one Squire's private cabinet and the other the estate office which had a door leading straight outside, so that tenants didn't need to pass through the house.

'Ent been any business done in there for years, though, mistress,' cackled Mary. 'Squire said there weren't enough of the estate left to need a bailiff, let alone an estate office an' he told us to shut that room up. Said it could rot, for all he cared. That Frenchie took care of most things after that – an' Will Pursley helped some. He might be young, but he d'know more about runnin' a farm than a dozen Frenchies what can't even talk proper!'

'Who was the… er… Frenchie?'

'Squire's manservant. Looked after his clothes an' such. Even at the end, your grandfather were fussy about his clothes an' you never saw him outside his bedroom without his wig.'

Up the wide, shallow stairs there were ten rooms, a number which took Sarah's breath away, most of them opening into the long gallery which ran the length of that floor. The great chamber was really a suite of rooms over the west wing.

'Just for dressin' in, these little rooms at each side were,' Mary said proudly, flinging doors open and sending them crashing back into walls.

Most of the other bedrooms were a jumble of furniture, some of it shrouded, some of it uncovered and dusty. Some had broken windows, partly boarded up.

'Will comes sometimes an' stops the worst of the weather from gettin' in,' Mary said. 'But it were me an' Petey what brung the old furniture down out o' the attics when the roof got bad. It d'get worse every year! Squire wouldn't hev the carpenter in, neither. Said the house'd last his time an' after that, he didn't care none.'

'Did he... ever mention my mother?'

'Wouldn't hev her name spoke, mistress, beggin' your pardon. Nor your uncle's, neither, after he died – not once Squire found out how much money Mr Ralph owed. Terrible lot, it must ha' been, an' the master left to pay it! Don't seem right, that don't, do it? Mr Sewell's got a good deal to answer for. My Harry was alive then an' we was livin' over the stables an'—'

'What did my grandfather do next?' Sarah interrupted, impatient of digression and desperate to understand how her family had sunk so low.

Mary screwed up her forehead in thought. 'Well, mistress, after a day or two Squire called all us servants into the hall, indoor an' outdoor, all of us together, an' he told us he'd hev to turn us off. Terrible shock, that were! Some of us had been here all our lives. He told us we could stay on till we found new places, but to be quick about it.'

'Why didn't *you* leave, then?'

'Because,' she shifted her feet uneasily, hesitating, then said in a rush, 'Well, truth to tell, it were on account of Petey. My Harry could've got a job easy, but folk was afraid of Petey. They wouldn't let us take him with us, an' me, I wouldn't have him put in the poorhouse. It'd kill my boy to be shut up in that place.'

She added, almost to herself, 'I don't know now if I did right. Fair broke my Harry's heart, it did, to go for a day labourer, him as had been under-coachman. When we couldn't find nowhere to go, Squire said we could stay on here if I did some cleanin' for him an' such. He couldn't pay us no wages, but we had a roof over our heads an' the leftovers, so we managed.

'Then my Harry keeled over in the lane and died one day. Sudden, it were. No time to say goodbye. After Squire died, I stayed on here. Don't allus eat so good, but we manage, me an' Petey do. He gets bits of work sometimes an' I do washin' an' such for Mrs Pursley. An' there's stuff growin' in the garden still.'

After a moment or two they continued the tour, but Mary kept harking back to the subject of the Squire's losses. 'Sold off Hay Nook Farm, your granfer did, and Downleigh Meadows and Uppercombe Edge. Sold some of his cottages in the village too.'

And his London house and business interests, mentally added Sarah, who had had the whole list from Mr Jamieson.

'That Mr Sewell bought 'em,' Mary went on. 'Bought everythin' he could lay his hands on. Foreigner, he is. Comes from up Bristol way. Made hisself a fortune from sellin' tea an' such-like, they d'say. He were wild to buy the Manor, but the Squire wouldn't part with that, choose how. Said he intended to die in his own home an' they could fight over it afterwards. He did it, too.'

'Did what?'

'Died here. Just like he said he would. Died in the great parlour. That Frenchie found him one evening, sat there in his chair, stiff as a board. An' now Mr Sewell tries to call hisself Squire. Built a big house down on Marsh Bottom, he has, an' calls it The Hall. I d'call it Marsh Bottom still! That'un's no Squire! Don't know nothin' about the land, he don't. Proper townie, he be.'

She scowled. 'Them as work there has to call him Squire, though, else they'll lose their places. Throw you out of your job an' cottage soon as look at you, he would. So folks don't dare say nothin' 'cept what he wants to hear – specially if those two men of his be near. Tell their master all they hear, they do. Then bad things happen to folk.' She looked sideways at Sarah and added, 'Be you goin' to sell to him, mistress, or be you goin' to live here?'

'I'm staying, though I don't know how we're going to manage,' she admitted. 'There isn't much money.'

'Old Master did allus live very fine,' volunteered Mary, 'right to the end. You could feed ten families for a year on what Old Master spent on clothes, let alone the wages he paid that Frenchie.'

Sarah stared at her. 'How much does it cost to buy food in the country? Can you tell me some prices?'

Mary blinked and struggled to gather her slow thoughts. 'I couldn't rightly say, mistress. Folks don't buy much food, if they can help it. They d'grow things themselves.'

'Grow what sort of things?' Oh, it was galling to be so ignorant of country life!

'Well, they d'keep pigs an' chickens an' such. White bread d'cost a lot, full sixpence a loaf over in Sawbury, but rye bread be cheaper. If you d'buy a rabbit, he'll cost you twopence, but my Petey d'catch 'em in the woods sometimes an' that costs nothin'.' She clapped her hands to her mouth in dismay at what she had revealed. 'Oh, mistress, don't have him taken up for poaching! They'll hang him for sure. What hev I said?'

'It's not poaching. They're my woods, and I give Petey permission to catch rabbits there any time he wishes. Go on! Tell me some more!'

Mary relaxed again, took a breath and rattled off a list of foodstuffs. 'Mistress Pursley d'make fine cheeses, but they be tenpence the pound. She sells the best ones in Sawbury, not here. Stewin' meat be twopence a pound when someone kills a beast. Roastin' meat costs more. We got plenty o' fruit, though, and that don't cost nothin'. There be some nice apple an' pear trees in the orchard. Me an' Daniel Macey d'make cider still, just for ourselves, like. Well, them apples'd go to waste otherwise, wouldn't they? Mr Jamieson said me an' Petey could eat the fruit, so I stored 'em up careful an' there be plenty left still. Bit wrinkled, but they d'make a nice pie. An'… Mistress! Mistress! What be you a–doin'?'

For Sarah had grabbed her by the waist and swung her round in a clumsy, lop-sided dance, which only came to a halt when they stumbled against the bed and sat down abruptly on it.

'Oh, Mary, Mary! That's it, don't you see? When Mr Jamieson told me I wouldn't be able to manage, I couldn't understand it. We managed on far less in London, with rent to pay and seacoal to buy. But he seemed so certain it was impossible – and my grandfather hadn't managed well, had he? But it was my uncle's debts which caused the trouble. I see that now.'

She paused a minute to frown and wonder why everyone seemed to have got into debt to Mr Sewell, then pushed that thought aside and continued eagerly, 'I'm sure I could manage here! I'm strong and healthy, in spite of my lameness.'

Then she became aware of the anxiety in the other woman's eyes and guessed what must be the cause of it. 'Will you stay and help me, Mary? You *and* your son? I can't afford to pay you wages, not at first, but one day, if things go well, I'll make that up to you. And I will feed you properly and clothe you better.'

The wrinkles on Mary's weather-beaten face multiplied a hundredfold as she smiled and reached out to grasp her mistress' hand. 'Aye, Mistress Sarah, we'll stay. This be our home too. An' don't you worry 'bout wages. Petey don't understand money anyway. It be kindness as he needs. Kindness an' shelter an' food. He's a strong lad an' he'll earn his keep, never you fear! An' I'm not too old to work hard, neither.'

Sarah persuaded her beaming maidservant to return to the kitchen and spent the rest of the time till Will Pursley came back for her going over her house on her own, peering into every chest and cupboard, gloating at the sight of so many things which she could use. Linen, clothes, tableware.

She decided to move in the next day and sleep in the great chamber. However, the room needed a thorough airing, because you could feel the dampness. She found Petey and directed him to carry the feather mattress down and put it to air before the kitchen fire. Mary was set to scrubbing the bedroom floor and washing the windows, while Petey took the carpet outside into the frosty air and hung it over a line, beating it with great gusto, clumsy thwacks that made him laugh aloud and also caused him much sneezing.

So when Will came back, it was to find a woman glowing with hope and bubbling over with ideas, a woman who wouldn't even listen to the fresh arguments he'd marshalled for her not living here.

Did she not realise that Sewell's bullies would be back? Or that Sewell would try other nasty tricks on her? She couldn't possibly manage on her own, however hard she was prepared to work.

When he left her at the inn, he went away to worry about it all, but for some reason, he couldn't get the memory of her glowing face out of his mind. She'd been so happy. He wished desperately that he could keep things that way for her.

There was too much unhappiness in this world, that was sure. And men like Sewell caused more than their share of it.

-

The following morning, Sarah again hired the gig from the inn, and got the lad to drive her and her luggage to the Manor, plus a basket of food packed by Prue Poulter. She'd borrowed a walking stick from Prue, one with a nobbly end to it, and she set it close at hand, keeping a careful eye out for attackers as they drove. But nothing disturbed the peace and beauty of the day.

Left alone with her new retainers, Sarah wondered that she felt no fear, only great joy at being here. But she couldn't spare the time to savour the moment, for two faces were staring at her expectantly, waiting for orders.

She unpacked the basket, whose contents brought tears to her eyes, for it was a gift from the landlady of the Golden Fleece and Prue had done her proud. There was a pie, a crusty four-pound loaf, a jar of fruit preserve, a pat of golden butter, stamped with a rose, two wax candles and a jug of milk, its top stoppered by a wrinkled apple.

She set to work to finish her bedroom, removing her grandfather's things from the chest and laying her own meagre belongings inside it instead. Not nearly enough to fill it – just as she would feel lost on her own in the huge bed with its high pedestal.

At noon she shared the food with her new retainers, watching them eat with the hunger that only long deprivation can give. She had lived among such hunger for too long to mistake it. If she was able, she vowed to herself, she would ensure that Mary and her son never went hungry again.

'I think I'll have to send to the village to buy more supplies,' she said while Mary was clearing the table.

'Yes, mistress. Janey Bell keeps a little shop there. She sells all sorts of things.'

'Would Petey go with me to carry the baskets, do you think?'

Mary's hand went up to her mouth in a gesture of dismay. 'Oh, mistress. Oh dearie me. I'm sorry to tell you no, but he daresn't.'

'Why ever not?'

'It's them men of Sewell's, mistress. They d'torment my poor lad something cruel. He ent been into the village for over a year, now. But if you ask her, Janey Bell will lend you one of her children for a ha'penny to carry a basket back for you. Or she has a handcart. Maybe you could use that – if you're buying a lot of things. If you got some wheat flour – she buys the good stuff from the miller in Sawbury – we could make proper bread.' She licked her lips at the thought.

'I'll go to see her myself tomorrow, then.' Sarah wasn't looking forward to the long walk, though – especially if those dark skies meant rain.

To her relief, Will Pursley turned up that afternoon to ask her if she'd like him to take her into the village to buy anything.

'That's very kind of you.'

'It was my mother who thought of it.' It wasn't, but he wasn't going to tell Mistress Bedham he'd been worrying about her.

They hardly spoke to one another on the way there. Perhaps one day she'd be able to afford a pony and a small conveyance of some kind. You needed them in the country, it seemed. She'd have to learn how to drive one first, but it didn't look hard, not on these quiet country lanes.

'You should call on Parson,' Will said after a few minutes' driving in silence. 'It'd be proper for you to make his acquaintance.'

'Oh, yes. I'd be happy to do that. Is he married?'

'No. And he's quite old now.' He pointed. 'Mrs Bell's shop is the third house after the inn, the one with the bow window. It's one of your properties still, actually, and she's a good tenant, Janey Bell is. I'll come across and tell you if Mr Rogers is well enough to see you. He's been ill. And 'I'll drive you back afterwards, if you like. I have some… er, things to attend to in the village.'

'Thank you.' She guessed he was waiting for her on purpose, but she couldn't afford to be proud. And in any case, she didn't think she could face the journey back to the Manor on foot, especially with a load of provisions.

Sarah went into the inn first to return Prue's basket and found herself being catechised about how she had found things at the Manor, all in a very respectful but nonetheless determined way. Prue had clearly decided to take Miss Elizabeth's daughter under her capacious wing.

Will peered through the open door to say, 'Parson's happy to see you, Mistress Bedham,' then vanished before Sarah could say anything.

Prue watched him walk away and sighed. 'Had a hard time, Will has. Fine young man, though. 'Tis a pity there aren't more like him.'

Sarah made her way across the village green towards the cottage that Prue had pointed out to her as Mistress Bell's shop. The door was open, but when she went inside, there was no one waiting to serve her. She could hear voices coming from the back room, so after a moment or two, she called out, 'Hello! Is anyone there?'

The sounds ceased abruptly and a thin-faced woman of about Sarah's own age peered through the low doorway at the back of the shop. 'Dear, oh Lord!' she exclaimed. 'I never heard that door go. Just a minute, please.' She vanished again, to be heard yelling, 'Susan! You see that our Bessie eats her bread, then you can scrub that table.'

When she reappeared, she was smiling brightly, ready to give her full attention to her customer. 'I'm that sorry, mistress. I usually hear the door opening when folks come in.'

'The door was already open.'

'Drat the boy! I told him to shut it behind him!' She looked at Sarah with frank curiosity. 'What can I get for you, Mistress Bedham?'

'I have a whole list of things that I need.' Sarah made as though to hand over the piece of paper and Mistress Bell went red.

'I *can* read a bit,' she said stiffly, 'but it'd be a sight quicker if you read your list out to me. I'm not very fast.' She went even redder and added, 'And I'll hev to ask you to pay for the things now, if you please. I can't afford to give credit, not even to the gentry. Hoping I don't give no offence, mistress, but me bein' on my own, I hev to be careful.'

Sarah smiled reassuringly. 'That's all right. I prefer to pay as I buy, then I know where I stand, too.'

Mistress Bell's sigh of relief was audible. 'What be you wantin', then, Mistress Bedham?'

'Just about everything, I'm afraid. Mary helped me to make a list, but if you think of anything else I might need, please tell me, for there are few stores of anything left at the Manor and I'm not used to country ways.'

'I'll be very happy to oblige.' Mistress Bell beamed at her, then yelled, 'Susan! Fetch my stool for Mistress Bedham this minute!'

The stool was brought within seconds by a little girl who gaped at the newcomer till her mother hissed at her not to stare like a scarecrow in a field! Then Mistress Bell settled down to fill a satisfying large order.

As Sarah left the shop, two men turned round to eye her speculatively and with a sinking heart she recognised Sewell's bullies. They were standing on their own in front of the blacksmith's forge and everyone was giving them a wide berth. However, they made no move towards her. More conscious than usual of her limp, she made her way across the green.

The front door of the parsonage was opened by a dignified older woman, who dropped a small curtsey and begged Mistress Bedham to step inside. 'Parson's waiting for you in his study. We've had to take the sofa in there for him, for he *would* be near his books!'

She bustled across the hallway and raised her hand to tap on a door. From inside the room came a scuffling sound. 'There!' she exclaimed, dignity forgotten. 'If he hasn't been an' got up off his sofa again!' She flung the door open. 'I heard you, Parson! You've been walking around again! What did the doctor say about resting? How will you get better if you don't do as you're told and rest! Now, here's Mistress Bedham come to see you,' She straightened the blanket over his legs. 'I'll go and fetch your tea-tray.'

Sarah looked across at Mr Rogers, longing to laugh, and he smiled at her conspiratorially. 'I can't call my soul my own,' he murmured, 'but she's an excellent house-keeper and makes the most splendid scones and cakes.'

'You're fortunate in having such a loyal servant, sir.'

'I am. The Lord has been truly kind to me. Mistress Jenks undoubtedly saved my life by her devoted nursing this winter. I'm well enough now to chafe at my bonds, but not well enough to be independent of her good offices. However, we mustn't waste your time today in talking about me. First, let me welcome you to Broadhurst and tell you how happy I am to meet you, my dear. I'm only sorry that I wasn't able to welcome you in person when you arrived.'

Sarah fumbled in her muff. 'I have here the deposition made to identify me, which you will wish to see.'

'No, no, my dear! I really don't...'

'I would prefer to show it to you, sir, in case anyone queries my right to Broadhurst. You are the proper person, I believe.'

'Well, if you insist.' He skimmed through the parchment rapidly, then returned it to her. 'All in order, as I expected, my dear. Now, is there some way I can help you?'

Sarah found herself telling him her whole story and asking for his advice.

'Well, if your mind is set on staying, I see no reason why you should not do so, my dear. The Manor has been sadly neglected, both house and land – what land is left, that is – and I would be glad to see it kept from Sewell, even if you cannot maintain it all in good repair. He's a harsh master, that man is, though I don't like to speak ill of others. As for Will, he's a good farmer and an honest man, and any advice he gives you about the Manor would be well worth following. I have to own to being a little prejudiced in his favour, though, for he is by way of being a protégé of mine.'

The door banged open and Mistress Jenks marched in, carrying a large tray set with a snowy cloth. On it stood a silver chocolate pot and a plate of fluffy scones. 'Now, you be sure to eat something, Parson,' she scolded. 'You won't get any better if you make such poor meals as you have lately!'

'Mistress Jenks... could we find a few of your delicious cakes or scones for Mistress Bedham to take with her, do you think? They'll not have had the chance to do any baking yet at Broadhurst.'

'Certainly, sir. That Mary Hames is no cook, though an honest body and a hard worker, and I respect her for keeping that son of hers off the parish. Yes, Parson, I'll see to it at once.'

As she left, Mr Rogers sighed and looked at the food. 'I would be glad of a dish of chocolate, my dear, but I must confess that I don't feel like eating.'

So Sarah found herself joining the ranks of those who loved and bullied their impractical and absent-minded parson. 'Just one scone. See, I'll spread a little of this delicious-looking preserve on it for you and you can eat it quickly while I pour the chocolate. Then it's over and done with, and I shan't press you to eat any more.'

Not for nothing had she nursed her mother over the last few months and learned how to coax a failing appetite.

After a while she saw him looking tired, so took her leave.

He clasped her hand in his for a moment. 'It's been a pleasure to meet you. You must come and visit me whenever you're in the village and I shall come and call on you when I'm recovered. And... I wish you well, my dear. May the good Lord keep you safe.'

In the hallway, Mistress Jenks picked up a loaded basket, covered with a white cloth, and handed it to Sarah. She waved aside any thanks and ushered the visitor politely but

73

inexorably out of the door, saying, 'For he'll not settle till the house is quiet again, mistress.'

Will Pursley was waiting across the village green, with Sarah's other purchases already loaded on his cart. After she'd paid Mistress Bell, he helped her up in silence and clicked to the horse to set off. Already the daylight was beginning to fade.

As they turned up the lane to Broadhurst, Molly slowed down to a walking pace to negotiate the ruts, seeming not to need her master's guidance. He let the reins lie slack in his hands and looked sideways at Sarah. 'Still determined to live here?'

'Yes.'

'Then if I'm to stay on at the home farm, I'll buy some cattle I've been offered. I didn't dare do that till I knew how things stood.'

'Mr Rogers speaks very highly of your ability as a farmer, sir. You must come and tell me how the rest of the estate stands and give me your advice.'

As they drew up outside the kitchen, she frowned, thinking aloud. 'I believe I'll need to hire another maid-servant, one who can help me round the house and go shopping into the village on wet days. I'm afraid I'm a little slow at walking and cannot always be troubling you for a ride. Do you know of anyone suitable?'

Will, who was now unloading her purchases, swung round at her words. 'A maidservant, did you say?'

'Yes. But not a lady's maid, just a woman or girl who is not afraid of hard work and who will turn her hand to anything. Why do you ask? Do you know of someone looking for a place?'

He nodded. 'Yes. She's called Hannah Blair, and she's the sister of one of my former cowmen. She's a widow and hasn't been in service before, but she's a good worker. Her husband died recently — he was ploughman to Farmer Hotton, whose land lies outside the village on the Sawbury road — and she's got to get out of the farm cottage. Hotton's done his best for her, let her stay on there for an extra week or two till she finds something else, but he needs the cottage now for his new man. She's tramped all over the place asking for work, but there's none to be had. And she has a young daughter too, Hetty.'

'Can she not move to another district?' Sarah didn't feel able to hire two maids.

'If she tries to move away from Broadhurst, the other parishes will send her back here, so that she doesn't fall on their poor rates. And if she has to go into the poorhouse, they'll sell off all her furniture and take her daughter away from her. They put all able-bodied children over five out into service, so as not to have the expense of feeding them.'

'That's cruel.'

'Well, at least that way they eat better than they would in the poorhouse. I wouldn't feed my pigs on what they give those poor wretches. Hannah's terrified of going inside, but it's a harsh world for a widow with no family to help her. In the old days, my family could have done something, but now...' He shrugged.

Sarah chose her words carefully. 'I would be happy to see this woman, if you let her know. How old is the child?'

'I'm not sure. Nine or ten.'

'I couldn't pay the child any wages, but tell Mrs Blair to bring her daughter with her. The little girl could no doubt earn her keep by helping in small ways — if the

75

woman seems suitable, that is.' Sarah knew what it was like to be nearly destitute.

Once inside, she unpacked her purchases, listened to Mary oohing and aahing over such abundance, then limped slowly up to her room lighting her way with one of the new wax candles she'd purchased, since it was growing dark now. She caressed the banister rail as she went, revelling in the pleasure of having a whole house to herself. Inside her bedroom she put down the candle and laughed aloud for sheer joy, then sat down to rest her hip.

Eventually cold drove her back down to the kitchen. She sat before the fire and asked idly, 'Do you know a woman called Hannah Blair?'

'Yes, mistress.'

'What's she like?'

'She's a hard worker,' Mary allowed, but her tone was not enthusiastic.

'But...?'

'Well... she's a bit strange, mistress! One of they wandering preachers come round a few year ago and Hannah got took up by what he said. Though she did allus hev funny ideas, allus. She picked up some more from him, though. Used to drive her Jack wild beggin' him to be saved in Christ, and he couldn't do nothin' to stop her. Once she decides on somethin', that's that.

'She goes over to Sawbury every month for a prayer meetin' with some other dangy fools. Walks five mile there an' five mile back, winter and summer. Jack wouldn't let her take the child with her, but since he died, she've took Hetty every time. She won't go to church in the village no more, but does her prayin' by herself an' sits a-readin' of the Bible on Sundays. Tried to get other folk to join her, but they got more sense.'

She paused and looked at Sarah. 'An' thass why no one won't employ her. They don't like her prayin' ways. Don't like her sharp tongue, neither. She'll say anythin' to anyone, she will, if the spirit moves her. Told Mr Sewell once as he'd burn in hell. He threatened to hev her locked away in the madhouse, but that didn't stop her. She just told him to his face she were only afraid of the wrath of the Lord, and that He would protect the righteous.'

Which defiance made Sarah rather inclined to like the woman.

Over their evening meal, she asked about growing their own food.

'I know how to grow a few vegetables and things,' said Mary, 'but nothin' fancy, like the gentry eat. Why don't you talk to Daniel Macey about it? He lives down the back still in the gardener's cottage.'

'Who is he? You didn't say anything about him before!'

Mary shrugged. 'Never thought. Don't see much of him. That Mr Jamieson knows about him, but said to leave him be. Don't pay no rent, Daniel don't, but he d'prune the fruit trees for us an' do a few other jobs around the gardens. He's gettin' old now, but he could still help out a bit, I dare say, if you wanted. An' it'd break his heart if you turned him out!'

'I've no intention of turning anyone out!'

Mary allowed herself a smile. 'Daniel wouldn't go, even if you did, I don't suppose. When his wife died, his daughter wanted him to go an' live with her, the one as married the miller in Sawbury – she's very comfortably set up – but Daniel wouldn't go to her. Says he'll hang hisself afore he'll go an' live in a dirty old town. He would, too! So his daughter d'send him a bit o' money every now an' then, an' she pays me to clean his cottage once in a while. I keep an eye on him too, so she gives me a shilling or two for that as well. Good gardener, he is, Daniel. Grow anything you can think of. But he'll only do things his own way. Didn't matter how much Old Master used to shout at him, Daniel'd go his own way.'

'You must show me where he lives, so that I can ask for his help.' Sarah sighed happily. 'What a nice lot there is to do here!'

After she'd gone to bed, she lay awake for some time, contemplating it all with relish.

—

In the middle of the following morning, there was a knock on the back door and Mary opened it to reveal Hannah Blair and her daughter Hetty. She took them through into the little parlour, where they'd lit a fire and which her new mistress was cleaning.

Sarah put her cloth down and wiped her hands on her pinafore. 'Please sit down.'

Hannah sat bolt upright facing her. 'Will Pursley said you was wanting to hire a maid of all work.' She met Sarah's eyes squarely and spoke politely, but there was nothing subservient in her tone. The little girl pressed close to her mother's side, staring about her, wide-eyed.

'Yes. Won't you tell me about yourself and your daughter? I'm sorry about the state of this room. The whole house is thick with dust and cobwebs.'

'Will Pursley told you that the Lord took my husband last month, I b'lieve, Mistress Bedham?'

'Yes. I'm sorry. My mother died last month, as well, so I can understand how you feel.'

Hannah bowed her head gravely. 'May the Lord give you comfort, mistress, as He does me!'

'Thank you.'

'And... did Will tell you that I'm one of Preacher Dawson's congregation over in Sawbury? Best you should know now, for some folk don't like Methodists.'

'Mary told me that. Do your beliefs make any difference to your work?'

'They d'make me work harder, I b'lieve. Honest work is a praise of the Lord.'

'Then I don't see that your beliefs need worry me. What you do in your own time is your own business. What sort of work can you do?'

'Anything, Mistress. They d'reckon I'm a fair cook, an' I like doing that best. But I don't mind what I do, so long as 'tis honest toil.'

'Work in the garden, scrub, go shopping in the village for me?'

'Anything you wish, mistress. An' I'm a quick learner as well, they say, if you should want me to do other things. I relish learning new skills, that I do.'

Sarah took another quick decision. 'I must be as honest with you as you've been with me, Hannah. I couldn't pay you much by way of wages at first. I'm rather short of money until my tenants recover from the cattle sickness and can pay their rents in full. I would feed you, though, and keep you clothed and make up the wages later.'

The woman's reserve suddenly cracked. She gulped and tears appeared in her eyes. 'You mean... you'll hire me?'

'Yes, if you don't mind working under those conditions. What about your daughter? I should have no objections to her coming here with you. She could do small jobs in return for her food, and she could share your bedroom.'

Tears were falling fast down Hannah Blair's gaunt cheeks. 'The Lord has indeed hearkened to my prayers,' she said huskily. 'And you'll never regret your generosity, Mistress, I promise you that.'

'Not so generous,' said Sarah, with a wry smile. 'I shall expect you to work hard.'

'You keep us together, mistress. That's generous. Most masters wouldn't take a child as well. When shall we start?'

'As soon as possible. Though you'll have to scrub out a room before there will be anywhere for you to sleep.'

Hannah stared at Sarah, then gave a decisive nod. 'I think I shall be happy working for you. I'll stay here for an hour or two now, to scrub out our room and that will give it time to dry properly.'

Joy shone in her eyes as she stood up. 'Curtsey to your new mistress, Hetty.'

So, thought Sarah later, when Hannah had left her alone and gone off to choose a room in the servants' quarters, she now had four servants, if you counted Petey and the child! It would be five if Daniel Macey agreed to continue helping in the gardens.

And two weeks ago, all she'd had in the world had been six shillings and five pence three farthings. What a miracle it all was! Surely she was meant to stay here!

Chapter 5

The next morning Sarah was cleaning out the small parlour, which she intended to use for her main sitting room. She was dressed in a loose-fitting round gown, which she had found in her grandmother's wardrobe. It was old-fashioned and rather short for her, but a boon for doing the dirty work. Her apron had been clean when she started the day, but was now distinctly grimy. She had tucked all her hair up in a mobcap, to protect it from the dust and was attacking the years' accumulation of grime with savage delight.

When she heard horses canter up the driveway and a voice shout to Petey, 'Get out of the way, imbecile!', she went over to the window to see who had invaded her peace so rudely. She was in time to see a stout, red-faced gentleman dismount from his horse and toss the reins to his groom – none other than the man called Hugh, who had attacked her the other day. Of Petey, there was now no sign. He had doubtless run away to hide.

The visitor plied the knocker so vigorously as to demonstrate a total lack of respect for the owner. Sarah's lips tightened in annoyance. How dared this man come and spoil her lovely day!

The knocker was thumped a second time and as there was no sign of Mary, Sarah decided to open the door herself. She was about to take off her apron and check her appearance in the mirror when the knocking began again, even more loudly. This made her so angry she limped across the hallway without further ado and flung open the front door.

The gentleman stormed in without waiting for an invitation. 'Tell your mistress that Squire Sewell is here and see you answer the door more pertly in future! Well, what are you waiting for? Have you lost your wits, woman? Tell your mistress…'

Sarah made no attempt either to close the door or to move from where she stood. 'Please leave my house at once, sir!' she said icily. 'You were not invited to enter and I am not receiving visitors until I am more settled!'

The look of astonishment on his face would have made her laugh had she not been so angry.

However, he was not long in recovering. 'I must beg your pardon for mistaking your identity, madam, but,' his eyes flickered scornfully over her dishevelled appearance, 'you could hardly expect me to guess that *you* were a Bedham!'

'It is a matter of perfect indifference to me what you do or do not guess,' she retorted. 'And I have asked you to leave my house!'

'Your house! *Your house!* What maggot's got into your brain, woman? You are no more fit to own a place like this,' he eyed the hallway in a proprietorial manner, 'than you are to receive a gentleman caller.'

'As I have had no gentleman callers so far, I cannot be expected to judge that, but there is no doubt whatsoever that this is my house!'

His colour deepened and his expression grew even more angry. 'You'd be advised to bridle that sharp tongue of yours, madam! I'm not used to being spoken to like that!'

'If my manner offends you, the easiest solution is for you to leave my house and company.' She spoke steadily, but her heart was thumping now. What if he refused to leave? She doubted she would be strong enough to throw him out physically, though she was almost angry enough to try. But his bully was still waiting outside and would doubtless come to his aid.

'I see what your game is!' Sewell exclaimed suddenly, thumping his thigh with the butt of his riding crop. 'You hope to raise the price by pretending to live here. Well, it won't work! No one else would want this ruin, so you'll *have* to sell to me in the end. The offer I made to that lawyer fellow was a fair one and I shall not raise it, so you may stop this farcical pretence at once! The house is as good as sold to me and you shall not go back on your word!'

It was a moment before she could frame a reply. 'Have you run quite mad, sir? I haven't accepted any offer for this house!'

'I have a piece of paper here from what-d'ye-call-um, Jamieson, that lawyer fellow in London – written only last year and saying he was sure the new owner would be happy to accept my offer.' He brandished a paper in her face.

By now, she was convinced it was a madman she was dealing with and was afraid he would offer her violence. From the dubious safety of the other side of the hall, she repeated as coolly as she could manage, 'Mr Jamieson did suggest selling the house, but I told him I had no intention of doing so.'

Sewell's face grew even redder and he began slapping the riding crop on the palm of one hand to emphasise his words. 'You are trying my patience too far!'

'And you are trying mine, sir. I repeat: please leave my house.'

'How dare you speak to me like that? Who do you think you are?' He stepped forward menacingly, the riding crop raised as if he would hit her. She looked round hastily for something to defend herself with.

A voice spoke at the back of the hallway. 'Are you having trouble, Mistress Bedham?' Will stepped out of the shadows to range himself at her side.

'I might have known I'd find *you* here!' exclaimed Sewell.

Sarah took a deep breath and resisted the temptation to clutch Mr Pursley's arm. 'I was just asking this… this gentleman to leave. He appears to be deaf.'

'Nothing easier. You heard what the lady said, Sewell. The door is this way.' Will moved forward, only to be slashed at with the crop.

'Damn your impudence! Don't you dare touch me! I'll have you up before the magistrates for this!'

'In which case, sir, I shall be happy to bear witness that Mr Pursley was protecting me and that *you* attacked *him*.' Sarah stepped forward again.

'You'll regret this, both of you!'

Outside his bully moved forward, but at the crunching of feet on the gravel, Sewell looked quickly sideways and waved one hand to indicate that Hugh should stay back.

The more Sewell blustered, the calmer Will seemed to become. He folded his arms and waited, his expression menacing but restrained. 'I could become a lot more impudent than that,' he said softly, 'given any further provocation.'

Sarah was afraid the dark fire burning in Will Pursley's eyes might lead him to do something rash, and stood ready to throw herself between the two men. However, after choking back some further insult and glaring at her, Sewell started to move towards the front door, covering his retreat with threats and bluster.

'You shall hear from my lawyer, Mistress Bedham. Hah! Bedham, indeed! How do we know who you really are? I shall take the matter further! You're probably an impostor, so it's no use talking to you anyway. But you shall not cheat me of what is mine! A slut like you can have no connection with the Bedhams, whatever bits of paper you may have got hold of! I dare say you were a maidservant of theirs, if truth be told – or someone's whore.'

As Will growled in his throat and took two hasty steps forward, Sarah grabbed his arm.

Sewell moved hastily through the door.

Will tugged his arm away from Sarah and went to stand in the doorway, arms folded. He watched as the two men mounted their horses and rode off. As a final petty gesture, Sewell deliberately rode through the piles of weeds Petey had pulled up, scattering them across the driveway.

The noise of the horses' hoofs died away down the drive. Sarah turned to her rescuer and said faintly, 'That man must be quite deranged! How can he possibly believe he has a right to buy this house – or that I am an impostor?

My identity was verified most carefully by the lawyer in London.'

Feeling concerned about the treatment she had received and the pallor of her face, Will gestured to the small parlour. 'I think you'd better come and sit down for a minute or two, Mistress Bedham. It's a shock the first time you meet Sewell and hear him rant on like that.'

'It certainly is a shock! I was beginning to fear that he was going to attack me.'

'Oh, I don't think he'd do that. He usually leaves the actual violence to his two henchmen.'

'Is he always so... like that?' She became conscious of his arm around her shoulders, the warmth and strength of it, and paused to look up at him and give him a grateful half-smile. Suddenly she felt rather shy, and breathless, and was glad when he guided her to a chair and stepped back again, not seeming aware of the confusion into which his closeness had thrown her.

She missed his arm round her shoulders when he moved away and went to stand on the other side of the fire, for since her mother's death there had been no one to touch her. She saw him look across at her anxiously and tried to pull herself together. She wasn't so foolish as to tremble for hours because a brutal man had threatened her – but oh, she was foolish enough to be thrown all a-tremble by a kind man's strong arm, she now found.

'Sewell gets into a fury when he's denied something he wants,' Will went on. 'Like when he wanted my family's farm – for a damned pleasure garden!'

'Why do people trust him enough to borrow money from him, then?' she wondered.

There was silence until Will said softly, 'I don't believe my father did borrow money from him. He'd no need to do so and he'd always hated the very idea of borrowing. He'd have gone without rather than borrow – and from such a man, too. No, I've thought it through many times, and it's just not possible.'

She stared at him, arrested. 'You truly believe that?'

'Aye. But I'd be grateful if you didn't repeat what I said to anyone else.' He didn't know why he'd told her, come to that, except he felt at ease with her, as if he could say anything and she'd understand.

She was frowning, then said slowly, as if thinking aloud, 'My uncle also had debts to Mr Sewell.'

'So it seems.'

All the air seemed to vanish from the room and she had trouble breathing as she tried to come to terms with all that this implied. 'Why has no one stopped him?' she asked at last. 'Or at least, challenged him?'

'Because he's rich. And cunning. Even I would have thought it my father's signature on the bills. But one of these days I shall be in a position to see that Sewell gets his just deserts. I cannot forget what he did to us, because my mother still weeps over it.'

Will hadn't raised his voice, but the chill hatred in it made Sarah shiver.

He noticed, paused for a moment, then spoke more calmly. 'Please rest for a few minutes, Mistress Bedham.'

Before she could do so, she caught sight of herself in the mirror on the chimney breast. 'Oh dear! I hadn't realised what a mess I was in! No wonder he thought I was a maidservant!' And she wished Will hadn't seen her looking like this, either. She'd never bothered much about her appearance, but he made her want to.

Oh dear, she was being foolish again!

He smiled reassuringly at her. 'It'd have made little difference. A woman on her own is fair game to a brute like him.' He watched curiously as she pulled off the mobcap and pinned up her soft, straight hair again.

She flushed under his scrutiny. 'You, too, catch me at a disadvantage, Mr Pursley.'

His face resumed its guarded look. ''Tis no disadvantage to be caught working. I've no time for idle folk. But if it's not convenient to speak to me now, I can always come back later.'

Her sense of humour betrayed her. 'I'm like to be even dirtier by then, sir. Won't you sit down?'

'Thank you.' He dropped onto a chair, looking tired suddenly.

'Did you buy your cattle?'

'Aye. Fine beasts. I'll soon have them in top shape. It's about them I've come to see you.'

'Me? But I know nothing about cattle.'

His scowl was back. 'Cattle sickness has broken out again in the village. If I leave my new beasts to graze free on the common with the others, they might catch it too. Besides... I don't want Hotton's stringy bull mounting my new cows. I don't like his get.'

She blinked at this blunt talk, but realised it wasn't meant to offend, so didn't take issue with him.

'So I came to ask you – would you let me keep my cows in your park? There's a wall round it, do you see, and the grass here near the house grows lushly. We could fence off an area for them to graze. Then, if you would let me, I'd fence round the home farm properly or plant a quickset hedge. A lot of folk are doing that now, enclosing, they call it. Then I'll be able to choose the sort of cattle I breed and the crops I grow, and not have them spoiled by other folk's beasts and weeds. We had our own enclosed meadows at Hay Nook Farm.'

Sarah noticed how his taciturnity vanished when it came to agricultural matters, for on that subject he had the confidence that came with expertise, plus a love of his subject.

When she didn't say anything, he went on desperately, 'I couldn't pay you in money, but I could pay you in kind – milk, butter, eggs, my mother's cheese.' His voice cracked and he broke off, furious with himself for betraying his desperation.

So much passion, and all for his land and stock, she thought.

Unable to think clearly with his gaze fixed so hungrily upon her, she stood up and went over to look out of the window. What would people think of her if she allowed cattle to graze in the home park or on the lawns in front of the house? Well, she knew what Mr Sewell thought of her already and she didn't care, so why should she care about what strangers thought? Besides, the benefits would be considerable – free milk, butter and eggs, he'd said. The less she had to spend on food, the more she'd have to spend on the house. And that roof was in desperate need of repair. The rain was coming in in several places and had already done considerable damage.

Her eyes lit up, as an idea came to her and she turned to face him. 'I don't see any reason why you shouldn't keep your cows here.'

He let out his breath in a great whoosh. 'You mean…
you'll agree?'

'On certain conditions, yes.'

'Conditions?' His voice became wary again.

'Not unreasonable ones, I hope. Are you good at
repairing things, Mr Pursley?'

'You have to be, on a farm. I like working with wood,
I will admit.'

'I like wood too,' she confessed. 'I like polishing it,
making it shine.' She laughed. 'And that's a good thing,
because there's a house full of furniture and panelling here
that needs polishing. No one has touched most of it for
years.'

He nodded. If she'd talked about music or poetry, he'd
have retreated, because he had no time for poetry and was
almost tone-deaf. But making wooden things shine, yes,
he could appreciate the pleasure in that. 'What are your
conditions?'

'That you'll help me with some temporary repairs to
the house.'

His face, which had been apprehensive, cleared
instantly. 'Oh, yes, I can do that! As long as you leave
me to do it in my own time, whenever I have an hour to
spare. It couldn't take priority over looking after the farm,
but I could make time every now and then. Would that
do?'

'That would be quite acceptable.'

'And the home farm?' he prompted. 'Will you let me
put a fence or a quickset hedge round it? As owner, you
have the legal right to do that. I used to think enclo-
sure was a devil's trick and I argued with Parson many
a time, but now I've seen how disease can spread when

the grazing's open, destroying all a man's built up, well, I've changed my mind. If we'd still been at our farm, I'd not have lost my other cattle.'

He gave a short, bitter laugh. 'First time I've ever agreed with Sewell about anything! He'd stare if he heard me say that. He's wanted to enclose the village land for years, but your grandfather wouldn't agree. Mr Rogers says it needs an Act of Parliament and you have to have four-fifths of the owners or copyholders in agreement to do it. You still own two-fifths, even though your grandfather sold so much, so Sewell can't do anything without you. Old Squire wouldn't hear of enclosing or changing anything, but perhaps you'll feel differently?'

'Would it not be expensive to fence the land?'

'Yes. I can't afford a proper fence. But I could put in a hedge and reinforce it with dead branches and such till it grew. If you'll give me the run of your woods and fallen trees, that is?'

'As long as there's enough left for our firewood.'

He laughed. 'You've enough firewood there to last you a hundred years. I'll gather you a load from time to time, if you like. Those woods have been neglected for years, and there's all sorts of useful stuff lying around.'

There is was again, this reliance on the produce of your own land, instead of the need to buy things. 'Tell me frankly, Mr Pursley. Was my grandfather a bad landlord?'

'Well, he wasn't as caring as he could have been. Not about the condition of the land, anyway. After your uncle died, your grandfather seemed to lose interest in the estate. Said he needed the money for other things.'

'Perhaps I ought to think in a more businesslike way and *sell* you some wood?' she asked, her humour surfacing again, now that her mother was no longer there to tell her that such remarks were not ladylike.

He grinned back at her, then seemed to recollect who she was and grew stiffer again. 'I don't think that would be worth your while. But I mustn't bore you.'

'I'm not bored, Mr Pursley. I find such matters interesting. And anyway, I must learn all I can about country ways, if I'm to live here. I shall enjoy doing that. In London there was nothing much else to do but read or talk, and I often grew bored.' She felt disloyal to her mother, admitting that, but it was true. She had sometimes felt like screaming with the frustration of their narrow life, not to mention her mother's strict standards about what a lady could and could not do.

She looked around her now, beaming. 'Here there are so many things to do that I hardly know where to start and I haven't been bored once!'

What sort of life had the poor woman led, then? Will wondered. He admired her will to work, he did indeed.

There was a sudden downpour of rain outside and that broke the spell. 'Oh dear!' Sarah exclaimed anxiously. 'I must go up and check the attics. Mary's put some bowls up there to catch the worst of the leaks, and they may need emptying.'

'I'll come with you and find out what needs doing.' He led the way out of the room at a brisk pace, intent on the job in hand and not on the social niceties of allowing a lady to go first. She had difficulty in keeping up and he turned to wait for her at the top of the stairs. 'I'm sorry! I forgot about your lameness.'

She thought it one of the nicest things anyone had said to her in a long time. Most people were all too aware of her lameness and stared at her when she moved, or else averted their gaze, which was just as bad. To have forgotten it completely meant — well, it surely meant that it didn't matter to him.

Rain was already trickling in through parts of the roof and they worked together to empty the motley collection of bowls and containers out of a sheltered dormer window.

'I hadn't realised how bad things were!' he exclaimed. 'How could a man let his home get into such a state? If I had a place of my own, I'd not have wasted my money on casks of wine and fancy waistcoats, I'd have...' He remembered that he was talking about her grandfather and stopped abruptly.

'You don't offend me,' she said softly. 'Nor would I!'

When they had finished, he declined an offer of refreshment. 'No, I've too much to do. I'll bring the cattle straight over when I get them tomorrow, if I may, so I'll have to mend those gates today. But don't worry. I'll not forget the repairs to your roof. There's quite a bit I can do at very little cost, except for my time. And if you could spare just a little money for some dressed wood, well, I could do even more.'

'I might be able to do that,' she said cautiously.

He hesitated, then looked at her sideways, emboldened enough by the rapport that had grown between them to make another request. 'I'll need proper shelter for the beasts. My barn burnt down recently.' He didn't say it was common knowledge that Sewell's men had done it, but had added it mentally to the list of his grievances. 'Your stables aren't being used. They're a bit ramshackle, but the beasts would be warm enough in there. I could do a few repairs to them as well, so that'd help us both.'

She smiled again. 'Use them, Mr Pursley, use them. I shall enjoy the fresh milk and I shall be grateful for any repairs you can do. And please don't hesitate to ask me if you see any other ways in which we could be of mutual help.'

He looked her in the eyes, then, as if trying to understand whether she really meant what she said. He must have realised that she did, for he nodded in that decisive way of his which she was beginning to recognise. 'Very well. And… thank you, Mistress Bedham. I'll not forget your generosity.'

He didn't waste any more time on words, but set off at once to get to work. She stood by the window of her bedroom, watching him stride off through the leafless woods. He didn't even seem to notice that it was still raining. She touched the window frame, running her fingers down the wood.

The feeling of having come home was so very strong.

And her pleasure in Will's company was equally strong. Face flushed at that thought, she hurried down the stairs and set to work on her parlour again.

–

A little later Hannah Blair arrived, with half her worldly goods piled on Mistress Bell's handcart. Her daughter, Hetty, was helping young Ned Bell to push it, the pair of them laughing over something.

With Petey's aid, Hannah soon had her things unloaded and then sent Ned and Hetty back for the rest, the smaller things. When she came to ask what she should do, Sarah set her to cleaning the hallway and stairs. Later, the children came back with the rest of the Blairs' belongings and Sarah had the happy thought of setting little Hetty to supervise Petey's efforts to weed the drive, for that morning he had pulled up some of the few remaining ornamental plants by mistake. Hetty nodded solemnly and they left her in charge of him.

'Will she be all right?' Sarah wondered aloud. She turned to Hannah. 'She won't be frightened of him?'

'She's not frightened of any of God's creatures, my Hetty isn't,' replied Hannah serenely. 'And they sense that, for they come to her when they run from others. And what is that poor soul out there, but one of God's creatures?'

And so it proved. Petey quickly grew devoted to the little girl and would have followed her everywhere had he been allowed. With her to guide him, he proved capable of many more tasks than previously, so Sarah was soon able to reassure Hannah that her daughter was more than earning her keep. As was Hannah.

Sarah had never been so happy in her whole life.

—

After the main meal of the day, which they took at the usual hour of two, Sarah asked Mary to show her where Daniel Macey lived and went off to try to recruit the final member of her staff. She had hardly begun to explore the grounds as yet, because they were so overgrown and she was afraid of falling over in the muddy conditions.

A narrow, well-defined path led from the back of the stables through the woods to a clearing where a small cottage stood in a neat garden. Even now, there were a few early snowdrops blooming and some evergreen bushes to take the eye from the leafless trees. In many of the bare patches of earth, new shoots were pushing their way through the soil, a promise of the yearly renewal of life.

'He d'keep his garden better than his house,' grumbled Mary. 'Daniel! Daniel Macey! Where be you?'

'Round back,' called a voice.

'New mistress be come to see you,' called Mary.

'Well, she won't see me from there, will she? You'll hev to bring her round here.'

Mary looked at Sarah apologetically. 'He d'get more quibbly all the time. It's his age, I b'lieve.'

'I don't mind going round the back. Perhaps he's in the middle of doing something.'

'Oh, he'll be doing something, all right. Never stops doin' things to that garden of his, he don't. That's why he've lived so long. Over eighty, he is. Ain't found time to die yet!'

Cackling at her own pleasantry, Mary led the way round the house to where a very old man was digging in his vegetable patch. He was thin, but still looked remark-ably hale for his years, with a halo of white hair around a bald pate.

'You should ha' left that an' come out the front!' complained Mary. ''Tain't polite to make Mistress Sarah come round the back. This be our new mistress, Daniel, Mistress Elizabeth's daughter. And this be Daniel Macey.'

The old man eyed Sarah from under bushy white brows. 'You don't look much like your mother.'

'You mind your tongue, Daniel Macey!' exclaimed Mary, scandalised at this familiarity.

'Too old to mind me tongue,' he cackled. 'If a man can't say what he thinks when he's said goodbye to eighty, what can he do? The food don't taste so good now I've lost my teeth, the ale makes me dizzy and my wife's long dead, poor lass. Not but what I don't bid ye welcome, mistress. You look a man steady in the eye, at least.'

'Thank you,' said Sarah, rather enjoying his frankness. 'May I stay and talk to you for a while?'

'Talking's free and there's a seat over yonder. Send that silly wench back to the big house or we'll not get a word in edgewise. Never stops nattering, she don't!'

'Well!' Mary flounced off, pausing at the corner of the house to throw over her shoulder, 'Don't you put up with none of his rudeness, mistress!'

Daniel ignored this jibe and went on digging slowly and carefully, not wasting a movement. Sarah simply sat for a few minutes watching him. 'Your garden's beautiful,' she said at last.

He nodded in acknowledgement of this compliment, but didn't waste any breath on a reply. When he came to the end of the row, he leaned on his spade and looked at her. 'Be you really going to stay on at the Manor? They d'say so in the village.'

'Yes. And I wondered — if you had time — if you would help me grow some vegetables. Petey can do the heavy digging for you, but I don't know anything about gardening. I would pay you, of course.'

'Mmm. Thass an idea.' He paused and eyed her sideways from a pair of still bright blue eyes, 'I don't need money, but I never could get the hang o' cookin'. Messin' around in a kitchen is women's work. I'd welcome some proper vittles reg'lar like. Mind, I'll not help you fill the garden up with fancy rockeries an' statues. I don't like statues! Nasty, heathen things, statues are, folk with no clothes on! What folks want to put 'em in their gardens

97

for, I've never knowed. *He* bought some statues once. Dangy things got broke one stormy night, they did.'

As he chortled softly to himself, she smiled, guessing that the breakages had not been accidental. She waited patiently for him to finish enjoying his memory of old mischiefs before speaking. 'I've neither the money nor the inclination to purchase statues, but if we could grow some food, well, the less I have to buy, the more money I'll have left for repairs.'

He nodded approvingly. 'Sensible, that. You're like your grandmother. And yes, I'll help you, mistress, and glad to.' He wiped his dirty hands on the side of his breeches and solemnly shook hands with her to seal the bargain. 'Now,' he said, looking round with satisfaction, 'this be all the digging I can do for today. We'd better go an' see what's left in that old kitchen garden of yours so I can decide what's needed, hadn't we?'

As they began to walk, he cackled again. 'Eh, what wi' your lameness an' my rheumatiz, we make a good pair walkin' together, don't we?'

And she found herself chuckling with him. It didn't seem to matter to these people that she was lame, though it had always been a secret shame to her when urchins shouted after her in the street.

So now, she thought later, as she strolled back to the house after exploring the vegetable garden with Daniel, she had five servants, she who had always had everything to do for herself. Five servants, a great wreck of a house and an extremely hostile neighbour.

A shiver ran down her spine at the thought of Mr Sewell. She was sure she hadn't heard the last of him. Then she lifted her chin. Let him do his worst! She wasn't alone any more.

A stray memory of the way Will Pursley had protected her today, of his earnest face gazing at her across the fireplace, sent her smiling into sleep that night.

Chapter 6

Two hours later Sarah was woken up by something. She lay for a moment, trying to gather her wits, then sat up in shock as she heard the sound again. It sounded like someone moving about downstairs.

She sat bolt upright, her heart thudding, as she realised there *was* someone downstairs!. There was no one to call to for help, so she would have to go and investigate. Well, she'd done that before now, in one or two of their lodging houses. Sliding out of bed, she swung her cloak over her white nightgown and looked round for something heavy to carry, in case she was attacked. Her heart thudding, she picked up one of the pewter candlesticks and hefted it in her hand. Yes, that would do!

Taking a deep breath, she opened the door and crept down the dark stairs in her bare feet. The noises seemed to be coming from the big parlour. Who could it be? Surely everyone in the village knew that there was nothing worth stealing at the Manor?

Then she smelled burning. Without thinking of her own safety, she threw open the door of the parlour, screaming at the top of her voice for Hannah and Mary. In the dimness she saw two figures crouched over a pile of what looked like smouldering twigs near one of the chairs. They weren't going to set fire to her house! Still acting on sheer instinct, she rushed across at them, brandishing the candlestick.

As they tried to grab hold of her, she caught one of them a glancing blow on the head and heard him yelp then swear. The other seized her arm. She screamed again and swung the candlestick, but the men pushed her over. As the flames shot higher, one of them tried to muffle her mouth and hold her back, but she managed to bite him and scream again.

There were voices coming from the hallway now, shouting incoherently. When figures appeared at the door, the men let go of Sarah and dived for the window. By the time she stood up, they were outside and she could hear their feet crunching down the gravel driveway.

Her attention was now focused on the fire. Swinging the cloak off her shoulders, she threw it over the flames in one swift movement and began to stamp out the blaze beneath it. There was an acrid smell of burning wool, but the flames were soon smothered. Hannah had rushed to her side to help, but Mary stood frozen by the door, and Petey could be heard whimpering somewhere down the hallway.

There was a patter of footsteps and Hetty appeared in the doorway carrying a lit candle. As she moved forward, it flickered in the draft from the open window, but still threw enough light for the two women to check there was no one else lurking in the room.

'Good child!' Hannah went to pull the sash window down. She turned to take the candle, lighting another for Sarah then starting to examine the damage. 'Not as bad as I'd feared. We'll need to replace two or three floorboards and the chair is damaged, but that's all. What happened here, mistress?'

'I heard a noise and came to investigate. Two men were in here – they must have broken in… I think they were trying to set the house on fire. Luckily, I'm a light sleeper.'

'Whatever would anyone want to do that for?' gasped Mary, still clutching the doorpost.

There was silence as Sarah and Hannah looked at each other. 'Why indeed?' asked Sarah slowly.

'*Thou shalt not covet thy neighbour's house,*' quoted Hannah. Her eyes met Sarah's and she shook her head slowly from side to side in disapproval.

There was no mistaking her meaning.

'He doesn't want the house, just the land. And we cannot be sure it was his men, so we'd better not make any accusations. It was too dark for me to see them clearly.'

'Who else could it be, mistress? This isn't a lawless district. I've never heard of a robbery round here, no, nor anything else much, 'cept a bit o' poaching.'

'But we have no proof,' Sarah repeated quietly, 'so we can do nothing.'

'What be you sayin'?' quavered Mary.

Sarah didn't try to explain. If Mary hadn't guessed who was behind this incursion, best to leave her in ignorance. 'There's nothing more to be done now,' she said sooth-ingly. 'I don't think they'll be back, but I shall sleep down here for the rest of the night – just in case.'

'I'll bide with you, mistress,' announced Hannah. 'You can't stay here on your own.'

'Thank you.' Sarah sat down on a chair, the delayed shock making her legs feel suddenly shaky.

'We need a dog, mistress,' Hannah declared. 'Ted Haplin's got some pups from his bitch Nan. Good dog, she is, cleverest I've ever seen. We could get one, two even.'

'A pup wouldn't be much protection,' objected Sarah.

'No, but it'd give us warning if anyone came prowling round. And pups soon grow into dogs. 'Specially Nan's pups. She's big and strong, she is.'

'Petey's afeared o' dogs,' said Mary, who was still hovering in the doorway, her arm around her son.

Standing trembling beside her, he nodded his head vigorously in agreement.

'Petey wouldn't be afraid of a baby dog, would you Petey?' asked Hetty, going over to pat his arm.

'Dogs bite you,' declared Petey, rolling his eyes.

'Baby dogs don't bite,' said Hetty reassuringly. 'I'll show you how to make friends with a dog, Petey. Dogs are nice if you treat them kindly.'

He didn't appear convinced.

'Mary, you and your son may as well get back to bed,' Sarah said, wanting to think things through. 'No use losing all your sleep.'

'I'll take you to bed, Hetty,' Hannah told her daughter. 'Then I'll go and get some blankets for us, Mistress Sarah. We might as well make ourselves comfortable and you're shivering now.'

When she'd gone, Sarah sat worrying. Was there nothing that man wouldn't do to get hold of her house? Apparently not. 'He'll have to kill me first,' she vowed. Then shivered again. Surely he wouldn't go to such lengths?

But a memory of his angry face made her think he might.

–

Hannah insisted Sarah return to her bedroom once it was fully light. 'Now that the others are up and about now, we'll know if anyone comes to the house.'

The bed looked so inviting Sarah lay down for an hour's rest, feeling exhausted. There had been no more disturbances, but she'd not been comfortable on the armchair and had started awake at intervals thinking she heard intruders.

She woke some time later, amazed that she'd gone back to sleep so easily. Getting up, she pulled back the bed curtains, then the window draperies, gazing in pride at the room as the light flooded in. Everything was clean now, with window panes that twinkled when the sun shone on them and furniture gleaming with a first polishing of beeswax and elbow grease. If there were worn patches in the carpet and hangings, it mattered little to her, for they were still grander than anything she'd ever known, and anyway, a little judicious rearrangement of the furniture had hidden the worst of the carpet's holes.

She smiled as she swung her feet over the side of the bed, easing her stiff hip carefully into movement until her joints loosened up.

Downstairs she found Hannah at work in the kitchen and Hetty sitting at one end of the wooden table. The little girl stared solemnly at Sarah with wide blue eyes as she took a bite of a thick slice of bread. Like her mother she was dressed in dark clothes, with a mobcap hiding her curls and a voluminous bibbed pinafore over her dress.

The two of them looked neat and alert, as if they hadn't had a disturbed night.

'Where's your manners, child?' scolded Hannah. 'Up and curtsey to the mistress!'

Sarah waved one hand dismissively. 'There's no need for her to do that.'

But the child was already off her stool and bobbing a curtsey, after which she stood and waited for further instructions from her mother, her head on one side, her expression alert and interested.

'She must learn her manners, Mistress Sarah,' Hannah insisted. 'Finish your breakfast now, child, then you can go and help Daniel and Petey – if the mistress doesn't want you to do anything else, that is.' She looked questioningly at Sarah.

'No, no! Daniel is anxious to get some ground dug and seeds planted as soon as possible, and I can't see him being very patient with Petey.'

Hannah pulled out a stool and gestured to it. 'I didn't expect for you to be up yet, Mistress Sarah, after such a night. If I'd known you were awake, I'd have brought you some hot water.'

'No need. I washed in cold.'

Hannah's lips pressed into a firm line. 'No call for that. The kettle's over the hob and there's hot water always ready. 'Tis a fine, big kitchen, this. If you ring your bell when you wake from now on, I'll bring you some hot water up. Mary's told me how things should be done and I don't need telling twice!'

'Thank you. I'll remember in future,' said Sarah meekly and was rewarded with an approving nod from her stern handmaiden.

'Now, what do you eat for breakfast, mistress? I don't know your habits yet, or I'd have had that ready too.'

'The same as Hetty, a piece of bread and butter. And I'll eat it in the kitchen. I want no time wasted on people carrying my meals to and fro, and no money wasted on fancy food for me, either. I've never been rich enough to afford to be choosy, so I'll be quite happy to eat what you eat.'

She hesitated, then decided on absolute honesty. 'I need all the money I can save to repair the house, Hannah – and as well, all the help I can get from you and Mary to clean and refurbish. The only time I'll want you to wait on me is if anyone calls on me – any of the gentry, that is – and I have to offer them refreshments. Mr Jamieson thought Lord Tarnly might come, for my mother's sake. She was his god-daughter, you see. I'll show you how to set a tray for that later.'

Hannah inclined her head to signify assent, but she had no intention of feeding her mistress on the sort of slops that Petey was used to eating, any more than she intended to feed Petey like a lord.

She had assumed control of the kitchen that morning after seeing how Mary worked the previous evening. 'If it's all right with you, Mistress Sarah, I'll see to the food from now on. I like cooking and I do b'lieve I can make the food go further than Mary would, for she's careless with the leftovers. She says she's agreeable to it.'

'Very well,' agreed Sarah. 'Mary can do the washing and rough work, and anything else that's needed. Oh, and I forgot to tell you that Mr Pursley is to pasture his new cows in the home park and will provide us with milk, butter and cheese in exchange, so that'll help out considerably. But I thought we might get some hens and then we'd have our own eggs too, wouldn't we? And if you have any other ideas, please tell me!'

'Well, there be rabbits and pigeons in the woods, and fish in the river. That Ted Haplin as lives on the Waste is a feckless creature, but he'd come up and catch them for us if you let him keep a few for himself.'

'What a good idea! I'd never have thought of that! So I won't have to buy much meat, then?'

'With all this land, Mistress Sarah, you shouldn't have to buy much of any sort of food, except for flour, once the garden gets going. Not if you don't eat fancy. Though a side of bacon might come in useful till we get our own pigs.'

–

In the afternoon William Pursley arrived with his new cows. The front door was open to let in some fresh air and help dispel the musty odour that still lingered in the house. Oblivious to the cold, Sarah was polishing the oak panelling in the hallway with some beeswax obtained from Daniel Macey, who still kept a hive or two. She was humming happily to herself, standing back from time to time to admire the sheen on the fine old wood.

William stayed for a moment in the doorway, watching her approvingly, before clearing his throat to signal his presence.

'Oh, Mr Pursley! I didn't hear you come in! Isn't this wood beautiful?' Sarah gave the panel a final rub.

'It comes up nice,' he admitted.

'Did you want something?' Her mind was still on her polishing.

'I've brought the cows over. I thought... I thought maybe you'd like to see them.'

His pride in the new animals showed clearly in spite of his stiff bearing, so she said immediately, 'Oh yes. I would indeed.'

They walked out of the house together. On the lawn at the front Rob Cox, the former cowman from Hay Nook Farm, was leaning on a tall staff, watching with an air of satisfaction the six animals grazing placidly there.

'Rob lost his livelihood when we had to leave Haynook – and his cottage too,' Will Pursley said in a low voice. 'Some of the men got work elsewhere, but Rob has fallen foul of Sewell because of me, so he can't find anything permanent.'

'Mr Sewell seems to have a lot to answer for,' she replied, equally quietly. 'Is Rob coming to work for you again?'

'Not all the time. I can't afford it. But I give him a day's work whenever I can, and if you have any work about the grounds, you'll find him an honest man and a hard worker.'

The whole household had come out to see the new beasts by now. Petey stood, as always, on the periphery of the group, but he had caught the general excitement and was jigging up and down, making little noises in his throat. Hetty went over to stroke the cows' noses and they nuzzled her gently.

Sarah approached the animals with caution. They were bigger than she'd expected and were swishing their tails restlessly, making sudden movements as they got used to this new place. Fine countrywoman I am, she thought wryly, afraid of a few cows. Even Petey doesn't show any nervousness of them! She was relieved that no one seemed to notice her cautiousness. Or if they did, made no comment.

Hannah and Mary, having inspected the animals more closely, were discussing their finer points with William and the cowman.

'Nice long teats, they've got. Milk'll come easy,' said Mary knowledgeably.

Sarah blinked and averted her eyes, then resolutely brought them back again. She *must* learn not to flinch from such frank talk. 'How often do you milk them?' she asked, trying to join in the conversation.

'Twice a day, o' course,' answered Mary, unable to hide her astonishment at such a question.

'There'll be milk for you every day – just let me know how much you need,' said William, coming back to stand by Sarah's side. 'Perhaps Hetty would like to come across the yard to fetch it in the mornings?'

The child nodded solemnly.

Sarah watched him slap a cow's flank to make it move out of his way! How happy he looked today!

He looked up, caught Sarah's eyes on him and fairly beamed at her. 'It'll be nice to have more milk. My mother's a rare dairywoman, given the chance.' He moved closer to the animals, with Sarah trailing uneasily behind him. 'Look at that! Picture of health, they are. And that's how I mean to keep them. They've stood the journey well, haven't they, Rob? Mind you keep those big gates shut from now on, Petey and Hetty! I didn't want any of my animals going near the village cattle. I'll get my own bull to service them.'

After a while, Hannah shooed Mary back into the house and Rob drove the cows towards the grassy stretch at the side. He was to put up a rough fence from fallen timber out of the woods, and to start on this straight away. The cows ambled along, pulling at the sparse spring grass on what had once been the lawn.

Sarah and William were left standing together on the steps in front of the house.

'I thank you for this chance, Mistress Bedham,' he said simply. 'You won't regret it, I promise you.'

She carried the memory of his happiness with her through the rest of the day, and remembered it as she drifted into sleep. He was a fine, honest man and hard-working too. You couldn't help but admire him.

And, added a little voice inside her head, he's good-looking as well, the sort of man any woman would be pleased to associate with.

It was annoying the way such thoughts were popping into her head lately. She really must stop thinking that way. It was all very well for girls to dream, but she was no longer young and should be more sensible.

Only who could control their dreams? Not her.

–

Hannah didn't forget her promise to send a message to Ted Haplin, asking him if he still had any pups left. He turned up at the Manor with flattering promptness, a black and white pup under each arm and a large white dog at his heels. He was a small man, with a thatch of greying hair and a very pointed nose that seemed always to be sniffing the air, questing after something. He had on a shapeless coat with large sagging pockets, worn over a miscellany of patched clothes.

'Heard as you wanted a dog, mistress.'

'Yes.' Sarah stroked one of the pups' noses timidly. Dogs were still an unknown quantity to her, except for the half-starved and vicious strays that had haunted the alleys in London. But these pups were plump, bright-eyed creatures. When one began to lick her finger tentatively, she smiled and gave its head a pat.

Ted seemed in no way overawed by his company. He eyed the house with great interest. 'Hetty did say as how someone broke in last night and set a fire. Wouldn't do that if you had a dog or two about the place. This be my Nan, mistress, best guard dog I ever had. I have no trouble finding homes for her pups, but I'd be honoured if you took these two. Come from the Manor in the first place, these dogs did. My granfer was give one by your grandmother.' He set down the two wriggling creatures, which immediately began to explore their surroundings, tails up and noses busy on the floor.

Sarah stared at them, not knowing what to do.

Hannah pushed her daughter forward and little Hetty bobbed one of her curtseys. 'Please, mistress, I can see to them for you. I like dogs.' She scooped one of them up and cuddled it. It nuzzled her hand, chewing gently on one of her fingers.

Ted smiled, not a nice smile this time. 'That game-keeper of Mr Sewell's tried to get hold of a pup this time. Offered me half a guinea for it, he did, but I wouldn't let my Nan's pups go to such as he. Tried to threaten me, too, when I said no. Well, we don't threaten so easy on the Waste, mistress. We know how to look after our own.

And my Nan's got good, sharp teeth. That gamekeeper hasn't come back again.'

Sarah smiled. 'Very well, I'll take these two and thank you for them. How much do you want for them, Mr Haplin?'

'Don't want no money from you, mistress. But I'll maybe be back for one of their pups when my Nan gets too old for work. They're both bitches, these are.'

'But I can't just take them.'

'You're a Bedham, and I'm not charging a Bedham for one of my dogs.'

'Well I… I thank you kindly.'

His expression changed to a sly grin. 'I did hear tell, though, mistress, as how you wanted someone to catch a few rabbits for you. Pigeons an' game birds too, mebbe? Fish, even?'

'Yes. Hannah said you might be able to help us out.' She was as frank with him as the others. 'I couldn't pay you in coin, for I've little to spare, but you could perhaps catch some animals for yourself in return for helping us?'

He chuckled. 'Ah. I could do that, I s'pose. Seem funny, it will, though, as if I was your gamekeeper! But my Poll's partial to a nice rabbit stew or a bit of pigeon pie. An' she do be afeared I'll get took up for poaching if I nip a few creatures here and there. Not that I'd take anything from *your* woods, mistress, but Sewell's different. His gamekeeper sets mantraps an' I don't hold with them. He put a few in your woods too.'

'Mantraps! In my woods.'

'Ah. Reckoned they'd soon be his woods, he did, mebbe. But word is you're not sellin' to him.' He cocked one eyebrow at her.

'No. I'm staying here.'

He nodded. 'That'll set a few people's minds at rest.'

It seemed amazing to her that she should have the power to help people – and wonderful, too.

He clicked his fingers to his dog. 'Right then, mistress. Me and my Nan will catch your rabbits for you, and whatever else comes to hand. I'll ask Hannah to let me know what she needs. Plenty for us all.'

'And the mantraps? Could you do something about them?'

He tried – and failed – to feign innocence. 'They seem to have got themselves damaged already. Proper shame, ain't it?'

'A great shame,' she agreed with a straight face.' As she watched him saunter off down the driveway, the bitch trotting obediently at his heels, she chuckled, then turned to get better acquainted with her pups.

She really must take the time to write to Mr Jamieson and tell him she hadn't changed her mind about living here. When she had a moment or two to spare. Not today.

And as for Mr Sewell, he would just have to get used to her presence at the Manor. Ever day she spent here made her more certain she'd made the right decision. She'd found the permanent home she had always longed for.

Chapter 7

The next week passed in a blur of activity for Sarah. She soon knew every nook and cranny of the big house, though she paid only a cursory visit to the cellar, which was damp and seemed to contain nothing but wine casks and a few piles of junk. That could be sorted out later.

The furniture at the Manor was mostly old-fashioned and made of oak, but it was sound beneath its dust. And in one or two rooms, the ones her grandmother had used, there were some relatively modern pieces, more delicate in design and made of mahogany or walnut. With her servants' help, Sarah began to rearrange things, concentrating first on the small parlour which she intended to make into her own sanctum.

Hannah had been quick to learn how to set and serve a tea-tray, so that Sarah would not be ashamed to offer refreshments if someone called, and she now insisted on making up a tray every evening for her mistress, a small ritual which pleased them both.

The servants used the tea leaves a second and third time, and considered themselves lucky to get an expensive drink like tea so regularly. Like their mistress, they began to make a nightly ritual of their own tea-drinking, and all of them looked forward to that cosy final hour in front of the kitchen fire before they went to bed, when they would chat, or listen to Hannah reading from the Bible and explaining the harder words to Mary and Hetty.

In the presses, Sarah found piles of household linen, yellowed and creased, but of such excellent quality that it would last her for many years, with some mending and patching. Thank heavens she was a good needlewoman!

First, however, she set herself the task of remaking some of the old-fashioned clothes she found in the cupboards upstairs for poor Mary and her son, who were dressed in near rags. She might not be able to pay them properly, but she could see that they were decently clothed, so they were not ashamed to go to church on Sundays.

For her entertainment she turned to the small library. It contained some yellowing copies of an old newspaper entitled, 'The Ladies' Diary', carefully sewn into leather binders. More to her taste was another periodical called 'The Tatler', which promised in its opening number instruction for the general public and entertainment for the fair sex. The few books on the library shelves formed a motley collection, ranging from the most modern, 'The Country Gentleman's Vade Mecum' of 1717 to old-fashioned volumes of poetry, plays and even sermons. The pages of some books were still uncut, and she wondered why they had ever been purchased in the first place if no one had bothered to read them.

The little dogs, which Sarah christened Bella and Betty, soon made themselves at home and insisted on joining her in the parlour in the evenings, rolling about on the carpet till they fell asleep by her feet. She found them surprisingly good company, for they always came rushing to greet her when they returned from a walk with Hetty, nuzzling her with their heads until she fondled them.

She had never had anything to cuddle like this before and wondered wistfully how it must be to have a baby of your own to love. She'd often watched other women with their children and envied them. But to have a baby, you must have a husband and who would want her? She didn't let herself dwell on that matter too deeply, just enjoyed what had been granted to her – it was more than she'd ever expected, after all.

At nights the dogs slept on old blankets outside her bedchamber in the long narrow area which was part landing and part long gallery, a place for the owners to enjoy walking in winter. Twice the pups woke her by growling at something. Each time she roused the servants, and they lit candles and made a lot of noise.

After the second occasion, they were not disturbed in that fashion again, but one morning, Will Pursley found signs that someone had tried to light a fire in one of the outhouses. Luckily it hadn't spread far, because the place was so damp. After that, he arranged for two of the youths from the Waste to sleep above the stables with a fierce dog, of which there were several among its inhabitants, who were of a more independent nature than the villagers.

The animal would give warning if anyone tried to break into the outhouses again and as the youths lived in crowded conditions with their families, they were happy to have a comfortable bed of hay to themselves, and some hearty meals at the big house as a reward, not to mention permission to take rabbits from the woods.

One evening, Will Pursley came up to the house to consult Sarah about some small alterations he wished to make to the stables, so she invited him to take a dish of tea with her. Her happiness at having a guest to entertain was so transparent that Will hadn't the heart to tell her he detested the taste of tea and couldn't understand why people paid ten shillings or more a pound for the bitter stuff with its inedible leaves.

He did find, however, that he enjoyed sitting quietly by the fire in an elegant room, resting after the labours of the day. Sarah Bedham was a very undemanding companion and didn't expect him to entertain her – as Amy Barton always had. Best not to think of Amy. He was well shot of her, he supposed, but she had made him laugh – and he missed the companionship of a woman, as well as the prospect of a wife and family of his own.

The harmonious relations between Will and Sarah did not, however, last indefinitely. Mr Rogers had heard of the break-in and the other attempts to damage the Manor. He also thought Sarah was looking a little tired, so he made Will promise to keep a better eye on her and not let her exhaust herself or take any foolish risks. Inevitably this brought them into conflict.

When Will met Sarah limping back from the village, favouring her bad hip more markedly than usual and looking white with exhaustion, he attempted to remonstrate with her. And she, knowing that she shouldn't have attempted the journey on a muddy day, fired up and told him in no uncertain terms to mind his own business.

Will too had had a hard day, which had included an encounter with Sewell, who had harangued him from the safety of his coach, while his bullies watched and laughed. As Will knew that Sewell would like nothing better than a chance to have him up before the magistrate for assault, he had forced himself to walk away and ignore the gibes, even when the coachman flicked his hat off with the whip.

Now, at Sarah's sharp words, his temper flared up and his answer was in no way respectful. He concluded by pulling the heavy basket out of her hand and carrying it up to the Manor, with her fuming by his side.

'I don't need your pity!' she spat at him as they entered the small gate in the wall.

'Pity! Who'd pity a she-cat like you?' he retorted. 'It's plain sense not to try to do things that are beyond your strength.'

'I'll decide what is and is not beyond my strength! I've managed for twenty-eight years without anyone's help and I'll continue to manage for the next twenty-eight, thank you very much!'

'Well, in the country, we all help one another, so *you* will have to get used to that.'

He slammed the basket down on the front steps of the house and strode off across the garden and through the woods, while she, more exhausted than she would admit, with her hip aching furiously, picked it up and took it to the kitchen.

'That Will Pursley is a deal too high-handed for a man in his position!' she stormed. 'Who does he think he is?'

Mary eyed her mistress's angry face in amazement, and with a touch of amusement, too. 'His father were just the same. Your grandfather used to say that those Pursleys didn't know their station in life, but damned good farmers all the same and good men to hev on the land. Had a soft spot for them, he did, even after he went funny.' She clapped her hand to her mouth, belatedly remembering to whom she was talking.

Sarah couldn't help chuckling at what Mary had said, but her mood darkened again after Hannah came in and told her bluntly that she'd better go and rest, for she looked fair wore out.

'Not you too!' exclaimed Sarah. 'I've just had Will Pursley hectoring me about not doing too much!'

'Well, he was right then, wasn't he? White as a sheet, you are, mistress. I'll light the fire in the parlour and you can go in there and rest.'

'I've no intention of resting! There's too much to be done!' To assert her independence Sarah dragged herself off to make a survey of the dining-parlour and decide what needed doing there. The two servants exchanged expressive glances and went back to their tasks.

But these were small squalls which didn't spoil the sheer pleasure of living at Broadhurst for Sarah.

The letter to Mr Jamieson had been written a while back, and one day she received a stiff reply that he would honour her wishes, but still couldn't agree with her decision.

–

At the end of March it was Quarter Day and Will Pursley went off in the snow, which had brought icy winds whistling round the eaves again, to collect the rents. Very much on his dignity with Sarah after their disagreement, he came up to the Manor one evening to present his accounts and hand over the monies.

She still owned two smallish farms near Sawbury, which had some enclosed land of their own and some grazing rights to the common meadows there. The grazing was shared by Mr Sewell and Lord Tarnly's tenants and by divers other smallholders.

There were also four cottages and Mistress Bell's shop which gave her rents in the village of Broadhurst, and two houses and a shop in Sawbury itself. Mr Jamieson might consider this a much diminished inheritance, but to Sarah it was astounding that she owned so many places. She'd had to expend much of the money she'd brought with her from London on dressed wood and new tiles to repair the roof, but fortunately, the tenants of the cottages and houses had paid their rents in full. The two farmers, however, had also suffered from cattle-sickness and could pay only a portion of what they owed.

'Are they good farmers?' Sarah asked.

'Not very, but they won't listen to any advice. And someone has told them they're safe until their leases run out, whether they pay their rent or not. I think that same person has also been filling their heads with the idea of complaining about the state of their houses, for they made some very unreasonable demands, considering how much they still owe. I soon told them they could expect no improvements till they started to look after their land properly and pay their rents!'

Her shoulders sagged and she stared at him in dismay. 'Is this Mr Sewell's doing again, do you think?'

He nodded. 'His bailiff's, anyway.' He hesitated, then added, 'And I didn't mention it before, because I didn't want to worry you, but someone's pulled up part of my new hedge and a couple of time the park gates have been opened at night. They want my cows to stray, I suppose. So with your permission I'll buy a strong padlock.'

'When did this happen?'

He shrugged. 'A few days ago. Last night as well.'

'Why didn't you tell me before? Those are *my* gates! I'll pay for the padlock.'

'You've enough to do, worrying about the house. Besides, I lock my beasts up at night and we've got young Zacky Haplin and his friends keeping a watch on things.'

'I wish to be informed of such things in future. I do not care to be kept in ignorance. See that you remember that!'

'Yes, Mistress Bedham.'

His tone was mocking. She didn't know how to deal with him sometimes. And yet, in spite of his broken nights, he still found time to watch out for her going into the village and appear conveniently with his trap to drive her home. She sighed and moved her position now, unconsciously easing her aching hip, then flushed as she realised he was all too aware of why she had moved.

'What about your own rent?' she asked quickly to divert his attention from herself. 'We must come to some new agreement, because you've supplied us with food and helped us in so many ways.'

'I can pay half,' he said, stiff now with embarrassment. 'Half in coin, that is.'

'Then there is your fee for acting as my agent and collecting the other rents.' She took out a new quill, sharpened its point and uncapped the ink pot. After scratching down some figures, she shook too much sand out to dry the ink, clucking in annoyance at her own carelessness as she blew it gently off. 'I have taken into account the work you've done on my roof and windows, also the milk, butter and cheese you've supplied to the Manor – not to mention the mutton when you kill a sheep. I think we may call ourselves quits about the rest of the rent, Mr Pursley.'

His voice was rough and angry. 'I don't need your charity!'

'I'm not offering it! See for yourself.'

She tossed the piece of paper at him, scattering more sand over the other papers, then sitting drumming her fingers on the table as she waited for him to finish studying her figures.

He muttered under his breath, then looked up with another of his frowns. 'You've been overgenerous.'

'On the contrary, I've omitted the many small services you've done for us. It is I who am in *your* debt and I'm no more minded to take anyone's charity than you are!'

They sat glaring at each other across the table and in the end, conscious that she was his landlord as well as an attractive woman, Will forced himself to swallow his anger and say in his abrupt way, 'Then we'll call it quits and I'll be over tomorrow to start mending those attic windows.'

She inclined her head, accepting this compromise, and watched him stalk out of the house. She had intended to offer him a dish of tea again because when they were not quarrelling, she enjoyed his company greatly. The pile of coins he'd left behind was smaller than she'd hoped, but she had complete faith in his judgement, as well as his honesty. And when had she begun thinking of him as simply 'Will'? It wasn't seemly.

But she knew how much she depended on him. If only she'd been pretty, she might have – what was she thinking of? She tried to turn her thoughts elsewhere, but it was in vain. Every time she saw him, he seemed to lodge a little more deeply in her thoughts.

'Oh, you are a fool, Sarah Bedham!' she muttered, then realised how comfortable the new name had become on her lips and gave a wry smile.

–

One day, when Sarah and Hannah were working together on one of the dusty rooms, Hannah asked her about some rumours that were circulating in the village. 'They say you're goin' to leave Broadhurst after all, mistress, that you be short of money.'

'What? Who says that?'

''Tis common talk over the cider pots. Ted Haplin heard it and asked me if it was true. Him an' his family would be in a fine pickle if Mr Sewell took over, you see. Don't like the Waste dwellers, he don't, because they don't pay any rent to him.'

'Well the rumour isn't true! How could anyone possibly think I'd leave?'

'No one would blame you, mistress,' said Hannah, striving to be fair. ''Tis hard for a woman on her own, as I d'know, and you not raised to country ways. They say as you're missin' town life and the company you had there.'

'I'm *not* on my own and I had no other company in town than my mother. Here, I have you and Mary and Daniel…' She saw that Hannah was still frowning. 'Well, what else is there?'

Hannah gave her a long, thoughtful look. 'No other gossip, but there is something I'd like to say to you.'

'Well?'

She took a deep breath. 'Mistress Sarah, I doubt it's my place to speak such things, but there be no one else, so

I've prayed to the Lord and studied my Bible, and it came to me what I must say.'

Sarah was puzzled. 'I shall not take offence at anything you say, I promise you.'

'Well, then. Be you intending to live here all the length of your days, mistress?'

Hannah's conversation was sometimes a strange mixture of rustic speech and quotations from the Bible, Sarah thought, but the maid never spoke to no purpose, so she replied to the question.

'You know I am! The Manor has belonged to my family for many years. It's my *home* now,' her voice cracked on the word, then she whispered, 'the only real home I've ever had, Hannah.'

'And after you die – what then?'

'Die? Really, Hannah, why be so gloomy? I'm not like to die for a good few years yet!'

''Tain't bein' gloomy, mistress, 'tis using plain common sense. I'd been a-reading my Bible the other night, as they taught me at chapel, and there the answer was, starin' me in the face as clear as my own hand: Genesis, Chapter 9, First Verse, '*Be fruitful and multiply and replenish the Earth.*' What you need, Mistress Sarah, is a husband, or you cannot be fruitful and multiply. 'Tis not enough just to live out your days here. You need a helpmeet to tend your land and to provide heirs for the future.'

Sarah stood there, stunned.

As the silence continued, Hannah said anxiously, 'I pray you be not offended!'

'I'm not offended. I'm… surprised.' How could you take offence at a woman like Hannah, who was honest and sincere, and who had become her mistress's main comfort and support?

What had surprised and shocked Sarah was the sheer good sense of what Hannah had said. She did need a husband, someone who would have a vested interest in looking after her and her land. 'It's just that… marriage is not very likely. No gentleman has ever,' she coloured, 'shown an interest in me.'

The admission came painfully, for there was nothing Sarah would have liked better than to marry and have children. She would believe herself resigned to her spinsterhood, but then something would remind her of her longing for children and always, it was like touching a fresh wound. It had been worse since she came here and – she admitted it to herself at least – since she met Will. 'I learned years ago, Hannah, how unattractive I am to gentlemen. Who would want to marry me?'

'I weren't talkin' of love matches, Mistress Sarah. I don't hold with that sort of carnal love, anyway. I were talkin' of bargains, fair honest bargains. Nor I weren't talkin' of gentlemen, neither. A fine gentleman would be no use to you in this. You've got land, do you see, even if it is in bad heart, and there's many a man would be glad to take you, yes and treat you decently, for the sake of it. If you be not too proud to wed a farmer.'

Sarah pressed both her hands to her hot cheeks.

'Oh, Hannah, don't! I… It's just not possible.'

'I must speak out, mistress. The Lord has put the words into my heart and I must say them for Him, if I suffer for it after. You have a kind soul and that do shine in your face. It's only young girls without dowries as need to be pretty, and that's a fact! Folks round here generally think carefully what they be doin' when they decide to get wed. They look for a wife as'll be a helpmeet to them, or a husband as'll be a good provider.'

She let that sink in, then added more softly, 'You mustn't hold yourself too cheap. You've got a lot to offer a man. And besides – you look better now you're eating well – as long as you don't work too hard, that is. Everyone's noticed. Your hair fair shines in the sunlight. Lovely, it is.'

Sarah avoided her eyes and fiddled with her apron, embarrassed by this plain speaking, but unable to stop listening, nonetheless.

'So, mistress, we must look round for the right man for you.' Hannah nodded her head briskly. 'And that, mistress, is what needed saying, so I'll hold my tongue now and leave you to think on it.' She returned to her scrubbing.

Sarah went to wash the windows in the library, but her thoughts weren't on her work, and when Hannah came in and offered to finish them for her, she nodded and wandered out into the garden, needing to be on her own for a time.

In the distance she could see old Daniel Macey directing Petey and Hetty's efforts, so she turned in another direction, making her way as best she could along the overgrown paths. Bella appeared and started to follow her, making little sallies into the shrubbery and emerging with sticks to be tossed and earth on her nose. The two dogs were growing fast and already they reached Sarah's knees, promising to be as large as their mother one day.

Hannah's words kept echoing in her mind as she walked. 'What you d'need, Mistress Sarah, is a husband.' *A husband!* Perhaps some man – Sarah carefully refrained from thinking who – might marry her for the sake of the land. No, no, what was she thinking of? The very idea was ridiculous! She was lame and too tall. Men didn't find her attractive. But – there were men who hungered for land.

Will Pursley's face rose again before her eyes and she moaned as embarrassment flooded her cheeks with heat. He would never... She couldn't bear the humiliation of even suggesting it and... Oh, why was she thinking like this?

Turning round abruptly, she called to the dog and returned to the house, where she immersed herself in work and gave herself no more time to think. All day long she kept her body busy and tried to occupy her thoughts with practical plans for the future improvement of the main rooms.

But that night she tossed and turned for hours, and couldn't get Hannah's words from her brain. She *did* have a duty to her family's home and land. What would happen to Broadhurst after she died if she didn't give it an heir?

It wasn't too late for that! Not yet.

–

The next few days passed in such furious activity on Sarah's part that Hannah kept looking at her thoughtfully.

They must do something about the other rooms, declared Sarah.

They couldn't leave the garden at the front of the house any longer in such a wild tangle. What would people think if they came to call? she demanded the next day, hands on hips, frown on her face.

She spent the whole of one day collecting the broken metal household equipment together. These must be taken to Thad the Blacksmith to be repaired. So the flat-irons, candle-snuffers, toasting forks, bedwarmers and other tools of everyday life were despatched and Sarah turned to find another task.

But nothing she did stopped her thoughts returning to what Hannah had said, and the phrase, *Be fruitful and multiply and replenish the earth* kept repeating itself in her brain – and in her heart, too.

Even Will had once said that she really needed a husband.

–

By the second Sunday in April, Mr Rogers was at last well enough to hold a service, and everyone in the village, gentry and common folk alike, dressed in their best and made their way to church on a fine, but windy day.

Will and his mother insisted on driving Sarah there and when they arrived, the churchwarden, Thad Honeyfield, ceremonially escorted her to the Bedham pew, where she was left to sit in solitary splendour. The Sewells were in the front pew on the other side of the church and behind them sat two elderly ladies, who must be the Misses Serring. Mr Rogers had mentioned them, saying they would soon be returning from visiting their niece in Wells.

Sarah couldn't help being conscious of the scowls Mr Sewell cast in her direction, but didn't let that deter her from studying his family. Mistress Sewell was a small, faded-looking woman, who threw Sarah a quick, apologetic glance and then kept her eyes on her prayer book. Beside her sat a thin-faced young man, the son no doubt, and beyond him their daughter, a buxom girl with a high colour and elaborate clothes more suited to a rout party than a Sunday visit to a country church. The young woman stared curiously at Sarah until her mother nudged her and tapped the prayer book on her lap.

Mr Rogers preached a brief sermon on the text of loving your neighbour, during which Mr Sewell yawned audibly. The sermon was liberally interspersed with Latin tags, which were beyond most of the congregation, but they sat there stolidly, only moving to cuff any child who dared to fidget. There was no village choir or means of making music, but Thad Honeyfield led the singing of a hymn in a rich bass voice and everyone joined in with great enthusiasm, if not agreement about the key to sing in.

At the end of the service Mr Sewell moved rapidly from his place to follow the parson down the aisle, dragging his shrinking wife on his arm. Sarah couldn't understand why the congregation gasped and muttered at this, and it had to be explained to her later. Everyone knew it was for Thad, as churchwarden, to open the pew gates and then the Bedhams should lead the way out.

Outside, the Sewells didn't linger, but Mr Rogers stood in the porch and introduced Sarah to the Misses Serring, who were eager for an opportunity to meet their new neighbour. They twittered over her for a while, which she endured as patiently as she could, accepting an invitation to take tea with them with a stifled sigh, because she found them over-fussy.

She didn't deem the question of precedence worth making a fuss about, but the villagers thought otherwise. On the following Sunday, Thad Honeyfield was waiting as the service drew to an end. He managed to hold the gate of the Sewells' pew closed as the parson made his way down the aisle, so that Sarah was forced to leave her pew first. There was a general nodding of heads in approval and folk smiled at her as she led the way self-consciously out of the church.

Again the Sewells did not linger but climbed into their carriage and were driven straight off home, but the other folk stopped to chat.

Having taken tea with the two old ladies, Sarah felt obliged to invite them to visit her at the Manor on the following Tuesday, though she didn't take much pleasure in their company. They seemed to fill their days with a quantity of useless activities and to lavish their otherwise unwanted affections upon a fat and elderly dog and a disdainful grey cat.

Would she too become like them when she grew older if she never married? And what *would* become of the Manor when she died?

She clicked her tongue in exasperation at herself. Hannah's words seemed to have coloured her thinking about everything, even two harmless old ladies who were making overtures of friendship.

–

The following week, the weather broke again and it rained for three days without stopping. The farmers might be glad of it, but Sarah fretted at her incarceration. When the fourth day dawned clear but cloudy, she decided to walk to the village and make a few purchases.

Hannah warned her that the going would be heavy, but shrugged her shoulders when her mistress insisted that she needed the exercise. If Mistress Sarah wished to make herself suffer, she would do it whatever anyone said.

But the mud was worse than Sarah had expected and her bad hip and leg were aching before she even got to the village. And to make matters worse, both Mr Rogers and Mistress Jenks were out, so she couldn't stop at the parsonage for her usual rest. Stoically she began to limp home with her basket, regretting her obstinacy now and concentrating all her efforts on not falling.

Will Pursley appeared as if by magic at the end of the lane and this time she didn't protest when he took the heavy basket from her and set it down by the side of the road. But when he swung her into his arms, she gasped in surprise.

'Put me down at once!'

He ignored her request and began to carry her up the pathway to the home farm.

'You seem hell bent on killing yourself!' he stated, with his usual bluntness. 'You're as white as those walls with the pain of that hip! Why do you *do* it?'

'I didn't realise that it would be quite so bad – and Mr Rogers was out, so I couldn't have a rest there,' she replied in a low voice, embarrassed to find that she felt more like bursting into tears than arguing with him over his high-handed behaviour. She blinked the tears away and leaned her head against his chest, feeling his heart beating and hearing his deep breaths as he carried her into the cottage. How safe it felt in his arms! How strong he was!

He kicked the door open and shouted for his mother as he deposited Sarah on the sofa. 'Mother, Mistress Bedham has very foolishly over-tired herself again. Give her a cup of tea while I fetch her basket of shopping. After I finish clearing the gutters, I'll harness the pony and drive her back to the Manor. It's a good thing I was up on the roof and saw her.'

'I'd have managed!' Sarah threw at him. 'I've told you before I don't want your pity!'

'*Pity!* It's not pity you need, but a good scolding to try to get some sense into you. You've more than yourself to consider now. What would folk round here do if anything happened to you? They'd be completely at Sewell's mercy then!'

'Will! Hold your tongue, do!' Mistress Pursley pushed him out of the house and he went, still muttering under his breath about 'stubborn fools, who won't admit their own limitations'. His mother turned and said apologetically to Sarah, 'He means well, my Will, but he was never one to coat the truth with honey. Don't let him upset you.'

'I'm afraid he was right. This time, anyway.'

'Well, it's water under the bridge, now, my dear. I dare say you felt cooped up after all that rain. I'll tell you what, I'll mull you some of my own cider. That's the best thing there is to warm you up, never mind tea. You lean your head back and rest for a while, and I'll make us both a tankard, then, when he's finished, Will shall drive you home, like he said.'

Sarah nodded, still close to tears. She let Mistress Pursley fuss over her and drank the mulled cider obediently, holding the warm pewter tankard gratefully between fingers that still trembled a little.

She thanked Will stiffly when he later deposited her at the front door of the Manor. He carried the basket inside for her in silence, telling Hannah to see if she could talk her stubborn fool of a mistress into lying down for a rest.

Fuming, Sarah watched him stride out, but when he'd driven off, she burst into tears and allowed Hannah to fill a warming-pan with hot coals and pass it over her bed.

'It's none of Mr Pursley's business and he can keep his high-handed behaviour for those who like that sort of thing,' she declared. But oh, how she wished she hadn't been born lame. How ugly she must look, limping like that.

'Soft-hearted, he is, Will Pursley,' said Hannah, 'for all he tries to hide it. He means well and if you ask me, it was a good thing that fool Amy Barton did turn him down after he lost Hay Nook Farm. She's a hard piece, for all she's so pretty, and she'd have made him a bad wife, as Jamie Yarrow is finding out to his cost. Proper hen-pecked, he is now, as anyone can see.'

'Was Mr Pursley betrothed, then?' Sarah was unable to conceal her interest.

'Ah. He was for a time. But she wouldn't marry a poor man, wouldn't Amy, so she broke it off when he was told to leave the farm. The very next day she sent her father to tell him, the heartless jade. He took it hard, coming on top of everything else.'

She looked sideways at her mistress and added, 'He's a good farmer, is Will Pursley, best in the district. And Parson do set a lot of store by him too. Make a good husband, he would!'

'I'm too tired to gossip,' declared Sarah, and cut off the conversation by rolling over and closing her eyes. But her thoughts didn't stop twisting about inside her head. Would he even consider it? Dare she ask him? Oh, no, it was not to be thought of. She would die of humiliation if he turned her down.

No, she didn't dare risk it. Definitely not.

But if he were to accept…?

Chapter 8

'Mistress! Mistress! Come quick! Someone hev opened up the gates and let in one o' they cows from the village!' Mary came rushing into the house, shrieking the news. 'Jack Boddy's Tinker, it be. Come quick! Will Pursley be chasin' her now, tryin' to drive her away.'

She saw with satisfaction that she had an attentive audience and indulged her taste for dramatic gloom still further. 'Likely all his cows will hev took the cattle sickness from her an' we'll lose the whole herd!'

'Oh, no!' Sarah slipped her iron pattens on over her house shoes to lift her out of the mud, and limped out with the others to see what she could do to help. Her quarrel of the previous day with Will was completely forgotten, as well as her embarrassment at the thoughts he aroused in her, for she knew how bad this could be for him.

She found the cows milling about on the grass near the yard and a strange animal, a scrawny red-brown beast, tied up in a corner of the yard lowing miserably, while Will stood with hands on hips scowling at it.

He turned towards her. 'You should be resting today. And don't try to come over here. It's slippery.'

'I heard about the cow and wanted to know if we could do anything to help you.'

He came across to join her, his fists clenched by his sides, anger in every line of his body. 'It's a good thing Robin built that inner fence around my cows. Otherwise we might be in trouble. This was done on purpose, you know. I came over to fetch the cows for milking and found the small gate open. I closed it myself last night. I'm always careful about it.'

He drew in a breath rough with anger. 'This has got to be more of Sewell's work. His men must have had a hard job persuading that poor beast to walk though the small gate, for she's always been skittish.'

'Are you sure? Why should he persist in this vindictiveness? Could it not be just... just an accident?' Her voice tailed away.

'I told you. I closed the gate myself last night. And anyway, the padlock was sawn through. This was no accident; it was planned. Sewell told me when he turned me off the farm that he wanted me out of the neighbourhood. *I'll not rest till I've got rid of you*, he said. I've never forgotten his words – or his tone! And he's driven others away, once he's set his mind to it.'

She placed her hand on his arm. 'I'm so sorry! But he won't be able to drive you away from your home and job because I shan't listen to anything he says.'

He patted her hand absent-mindedly, clasping it for a moment in his warm hand. 'Sewell's trying to get at both of us this way. Don't mistake it, he's taken against *you* as well and he won't stop till he's got what he wants – or until he's dead.'

'Can't anyone stop him? There must be something we can do!'

He let out a snort of bitter laughter. 'Tell me what? We have no proof and no prospect of obtaining any, he's such a cunning devil. And if I did make a complaint against him, who would listen to me? Sewell turned me off his farm two years ago. They'd say it was spite on my part.'

He let go of her hand and gripped the frame of the back door, his knuckles white with the pressure, as he added in a low voice, 'And besides, he's gentry; I'm not. That makes a difference.'

'Could I not do the complaining, then? This is my land, after all.'

He let out a soft noise, an approving murmur. Smiling at her, he patted her hand once again, staring but saying nothing.

She could only stare back at him, for this touch had sent a warm feeling running through her whole body.

After a minute or so, he shook his head, like a man waking himself up. 'They'd not listen to you, either, Mistress Bedham. You're a newcomer and a lady. What do you know about such things? And what proof have you, either? Sewell's got a nasty little lawyer in Sawbury, who looks after his interests and would probably sue you for slander if you tried to do anything. He delights in lawsuits, that man does. And in inventing debts.'

'But… is the justice of the peace on his side too? That's Lord Tarnly, isn't it? Surely he's not a friend of that man?'

'Lord Tarnly's fair enough and he doesn't seem to think much of Sewell – well, that's what folk say. He doesn't invite the Sewells over to visit, as he does the other gentry. But he'd not take action against him on just your word.' He spoke factually, not meaning to insult her.

'But we could at least tell him what we suspect and…'

He shook his head. 'Mistress Bedham, believe me, it's no use wasting our time. We can only keep a better watch on the beasts in future. I'll order another padlock for the side gate this very day.' He left her and went over to fasten a leading rope round the frightened cow's neck.

She watched him gentling the animal, her heart aching for his helplessness in the face of these attacks.

Will looked across at her. The yard was full of people, but he spoke only to her. 'I'd better return this poor creature to its owner, I suppose.'

She could see that even in his distress, his hands were careful as he tugged it gently into movement.

'Mary, you can see to the other cows this morning, can't you? You're a good milker. But take care that you wash your hands and the udders properly! My mother has scalded out the pails already.'

Bridling with imperfectly concealed pleasure at this compliment from a man who did not give them lightly, Mary marched across to the cows and slapped the nearest one on the rump. 'Come on, my little lovie. Come and let Mary milk you.'

It occurred to Sarah, as she watched Will disappear across the meadow, that no one ever disputed Will's orders – even on her land. She smiled wryly. He was a good master, but a firm one. Would he make a good husband, too?

If only she had some idea of how he might feel about the idea, she might put it to the test? If she could only pluck up the courage.

–

But Mr Sewell had not yet finished making mischief. On the very next day a carriage with a crest on its doors drove up to the Manor and a footman jumped down from his perch at the rear to rap on the front door of the house. Hannah, who answered it, demonstrated how much she had learned from her new mistress in a very short space of time by showing in the three visitors with calm confidence.

Two embarrassed-looking gentlemen hovered in the doorway of Sarah's parlour, as if they did not wish to enter. The third visitor was Sam Poulter, who stood shuffling his feet in the hallway behind them, looking everywhere but at Sarah. She had expected the visitor to be some lady come to call upon her, but this was obviously an official deputation of some sort.

What now?

She stood up instinctively to face them, wondering what they wanted and not reassured by their demeanour. 'Please come in, gentlemen.'

They moved forward and the minute he entered the room, Sam Poulter burst into speech. 'This weren't my idea, mistress. I didn't want to come a-botherin' of you. Nor I don't believe what that man says!'

The elder of the two gentlemen gestured to him impatiently. 'Quiet, fellow! You're here in your official capacity as Constable of this parish. Introduce us, since you have already met the lady, then leave us to conduct this interview.'

Sam muttered something under his breath and looked apologetically at Sarah. 'This is Lord Tarnly, mistress, and this is Dr Shadderby. They've come over from Sawbury to see you.'

Both gentlemen bowed gravely.

Sarah inclined her head. 'Will you not sit down?' When they were installed on two armchairs, she waited to see what they wanted.

Lord Tarnly cleared his throat. 'Er... you claim to be Sarah Bedham, daughter of Elizabeth Mortonby, née Bedham, I believe?'

Sarah stiffened. *Claim to be!* What did he mean by that? 'I take exception to that remark, sir! I *am* Sarah Bedham, and why you are offering me such an insult, I cannot imagine!' She glared across at them.

Lord Tarnly made a hrumphing noise in his throat. Whatever the rights and wrongs of the case, it was immediately obvious to him that he was dealing with a gentlewoman. And now he, who had always prided himself on his considerate dealings with the weaker sex, must offer this strange lady further insults. He cursed Sewell mentally. The fellow was a trickster and was after something, even if he had dressed this complaint up in legal terms.

Sarah waited to be enlightened, tapping her foot impatiently. The doctor avoided everyone's eyes and gazed alternately out of the window then back at his feet, as if dissociating himself from the whole business, whilst poor Sam continued to shuffle his feet by the door and mutter under his breath.

'I am... ahem... I am here in my capacity as Justice of the Peace,' stated Lord Tarnly, taking refuge in formality, 'to... er... to investigate certain complaints that have... er... been laid against you.'

Sarah felt icily calm, having no doubt in her mind as to who had laid the complaints, though on what grounds she could not imagine. She stared at his lordship unwinkingly, leaving him to flounder on through his explanation.

'The... ahem... the complainant alleges that you are... er... well, an impostor, and that you have... er... fraudulently taken possession of this house and land, which he had an agreement to purchase. We are here to make preliminary enquiries into the matter, to see whether there is a case to be answered.'

She said nothing, for she did not trust herself to speak, but anger churned inside her. Will was right! Sewell was trying to find other ways to harm her!

'And,' Lord Henry continued, doggedly doing his duty, but finding it even more distasteful than he had expected, 'the complainant further alleges that you are... ahem... not in full possession of your mental faculties. The... er... the doctor is here to testify as to your... your rationality.' His face was scarlet with embarrassment by now, for he had never had to offer such an insult to a lady in his entire life.

Sarah felt quite sick with fury, but this was not the time to lose control of herself. 'I begin, sir, to weary of Mr Sewell's interference in my life. I shall furnish you with the name and address of Mr Jamieson, my family's lawyer in London. *He* is quite satisfied as to my identity. And if you will excuse me for a moment, I can show you a copy of the deposition made by Mr Peabody, my mother's lawyer in London, who has known me all my life.'

She limped from the room, returning with Hannah in tow, to give her moral support. 'I should prefer, gentleman,' Sarah stated, with icy calm, 'to have my housekeeper present as witness to this... impertinence.'

Hannah, not subservient and overawed by her company like Sam, was furious that anyone should dare lay a complaint against her mistress. She stationed herself behind Sarah's chair, folded her arms and stared accusingly at these people who had come on the Devil's business.

Sarah handed the deposition to Hannah. 'Pray give this to Lord Tarnly.'

Hannah marched across the room and slapped it into his hand, with no respect for his status.

Scarlet-faced, he studied it, then stood up to pass it to the doctor.

'Ahem!' said his lordship, trying a more cunning approach, just to be certain, for he did not wish to have to return on a similar errand if that damned weasly lawyer of Sewell's complained about how they had done this. 'I was... er... acquainted with your mother. Tall woman with fair hair, a bit like yours.'

Was that the best he could do? thought Sarah scornfully. 'My mother, sir – as you must be well aware, since you were her godfather – was a short woman, with dark hair. I have here her locket, which *you* gave to her on her sixteenth birthday.' She unfastened it from her neck and held it out.

Hannah took it from her and passed it to his lordship in disapproving silence.

He took it in his hands, recognising it at once. His expression grew sad as he studied the face inside it. To think that pretty little Elizabeth, whom he had known from birth, was dead before him!

'Hrrumph. That's certainly the locket I gave my god-daughter. No doubt at all about that.'

Sarah decided it would be wise to supply him with further proof. 'Moreover, I remember my mother telling me many things about you. You were Master of Hounds and you used to ride a big grey called Captain, which would dance for a piece of sugar loaf.'

He could only gape at her and finger the locket again.

'My mother, sir, often used to reminisce about her youth and I believe I have heard tales about most of the people she knew. Am I correct so far?'

'Well… er… ahem… yes.'

'Pray question me further. We don't wish to leave any doubt in Mr Sewell's mind, do we?'

'No need for that, ma'am. I am convinced of your identity.' He produced a large handkerchief and mopped his brow. 'Fully convinced.'

Sarah turned to the doctor. 'Have you no questions to ask me, sir? If you are here to question my sanity, then pray proceed! For I have better things to do with the rest of my day, I promise you, and would prefer to settle this ridiculous business quickly.'

It was the doctor's turn to display extreme embarrassment. 'Been observing you, madam… er… Mistress Bedham, I should say, from the moment we arrived.'

'And, have you come to any conclusions about my mental capacities, sir?'

'I have no doubts about either your sanity or your breeding, Mistress Bedham. You seem a remarkably lucid young woman and have coped admirably with a difficult situation.'

'Thank you.'

He bowed slightly. 'My name's Shadderby. Surgeon *and* physician. At your service any time. Teeth pulled, draughts concocted, only the best leeches used.' He bowed again, ignoring his lordship, and walked out of the room. He had no intention of further antagonising a potential client.

He was followed with alacrity by Sam Poulter, who had already been made aware of his Prue's displeasure about this attack on Mistress Elizabeth's daughter. Not that he'd had any choice about coming, he thought aggrievedly. He *was* the village Constable, after all. But Prue wouldn't take that into account, would she? When something upset her, she just let fly. He was in for an uncomfortable evening, he had no doubt.

Left alone with his icily polite hostess, Lord Henry begged Mistress Bedham to accept his apologies and to believe that he had only been doing his duty, however distasteful. 'Thought it best to inquire informally into the matter, before allowin' anyone to take official steps. Save us all a dashed lot of trouble. But regret the inconvenience. Deeply regret it. Trust you'll accept my apologies and take no offence. Pray believe that you have my very best wishes for your future here.'

Sarah bowed her head slightly and requested Hannah to show the gentlemen out.

-

'By Jove,' Lord Henry told his wife that same evening over supper, 'damme if I didn't know her for a Bedham almost from the first – without that damned deposition or the locket! Cool as ice, she was, and had a look of her great-grandfather. Remember him well. She could have been his sister today – well, I know he didn't have one, but if he had had… What's that? Oh, she's a great tall maypole of a woman. Not pretty, though not ugly, either – no style at all in her dress, and lame into the bargain. Had to admire her courage, though. Didn't flinch, didn't weep and wail. Set us in our places good and proper. What?'

He blew out an angry puff of air. 'No, *of course* she's a gentlewoman. Saw that at a glance. Her behaviour throughout showed excellent breeding. She made me feel dashed uncomfortable, I can tell you! By George, she certainly did that!' He shuddered at the memory and paused for a moment to wipe his brow.

'That Sewell fellow ranted and raved like a madman when he came to lay the complaint before me. Shouting and threatening *me*. Never did take to him. Common fellow! Ugly customer, too. Treats his dependants harshly. No sense of duty. Well, this is one trick he didn't win, as I was pleased to inform him. What? Oh yes, I visited him after I'd left her. Thought it needed doing at once before he took the law into his own hands.'

As he was getting into bed, he burst out laughing. 'Damned if Mistress Bedham didn't rout us, horse and foot,' he told his wife. 'Shouldn't object to you calling on her sometime, my dear. In fact, be grateful if you would. Owe her a bit of recognition by way of an apology.'

'She *is* Elizabeth Bedham's daughter, then?'

'Not a doubt of it!'

'Then of course I shall call! I don't expect to enjoy the visit, but you have never found me lacking in the common courtesies, I trust, Henry?'

'Certainly not, my love! Besides, her mother *was* my god-daughter. Feel a bit guilty that I never tried to find out what happened to Elizabeth. Make it up to the daughter a bit, eh?'

When Will heard about Lord Tarnly's visit, he hurried to the Manor to see how Sarah was, angry that she should have been treated like that and expecting to find her upset. She should not have had to face them alone. He realised in mild surprise that he had started to think of her by her first name. Well, it suited her better than the stiffness of 'Mistress Bedham' and she wasn't one to stand on ceremony.

However, when he arrived he found her triumphant, eager to share both her anger at being questioned like that and her pride in how she had dealt with the situation.

They shared a pot of tea and sat comfortably together by the fire, for the evenings were still chilly.

When the conversation languished, she said diffidently, 'Is there a small conveyance in the stables that I could learn to drive? And would it cost a great deal to buy a horse? I'm finding it hard to walk into the village and sometimes it'd be nice to go into Sawbury to do some shopping. Or Hannah might use it in inclement weather to go to that chapel of hers.'

He nodded slowly. 'I should have thought of that myself.'

'You don't think… It's not an extravagance, is it?'

'No. There is a small gig you could use. We could hire Rob for a day to set that in order. And…' he considered the question of a suitable animal, which must be quiet and easy for an inexperienced lady to drive. For a moment he could think of none, then he remembered that his friend and fellow farmer, Edmund Bertil, had spoken of selling an ageing mare which was not up to the hard work he needed. Edmund wouldn't want much for it, Will was sure, and it'd be perfect for Sarah to learn on.

Within two days, the gig was washed and made safe, and the lessons commenced. He found her an eager pupil, and an apt one. 'You're doing well. You need to practise, but you'll soon have the hang of it, I'm sure.'

She glowed with pleasure at his compliment and thought how wonderful it was to sit up there and let the horse do the work – not that she intended to drive the old mare too hard. 'I could go out with Hannah sometimes, couldn't I?'

'Oh, yes. She's capable enough. But don't go out on your own yet. I'll come over and give you another lesson or two first.'

She watched him stride away, her eyes bright with happiness, caught sight of her own face in a mirror and gave a shamefaced laugh. 'You must be careful not to let this go to your head!' she told her reflection, wagging one finger at it. 'He is just being kind.'

'You get on well with Will Pursley,' Hannah said pointedly that evening.

Sarah didn't respond. She and Will did deal well together – most of the time, anyway.

But to go beyond that, did she dare even think about it? Not yet, not until she had got to know him better. It would help if he gave her some sign that he would not be averse to... a closer relationship.

Chapter 9

Before Lady Tarnly could pay the promised visit to Broadlands, Sarah did something which turned Mr Sewell puce with fury and sent his wife cowering to her bed, to avoid his fits of violence against anyone and anything which lay in his path.

The days following the incident with the cow continued intermittently rainy and, mindful of the difficulties she'd had last time she walked into the village after a wet spell, Sarah sent Hannah to market for her. She set Mary to work in the wash-house, where the copper boiler gave off a comforting steamy heat, and told Petey to help Daniel in the gardens, for once without Hetty's supervision, as the child loved market day and always accompanied her mother to help carry their purchases back.

Alone in the house, Sarah tried to settle to her accounts, for she was husbanding every farthing and keeping a firm check on how she spent her money. She sometimes thought the villagers would end up calling her Old Scrope, as Mary said they had nicknamed her grandfather, because after his son's death he had apparently complained at every farthing, or scrope, to use an old-fashioned word, he had to spend on things other than his own comforts.

Well, let them call her that if they wanted; all she cared about in the short term was husbanding her money and repairing the roof. With Will Pursley's help, the worst of the leaks had been stopped, but so much remained to be done to make the house sound again that sometimes she despaired of ever managing it.

Having finished the accounts, she grew restless. After being cooped up in the house for days, she was tired of sitting down, tired of polishing, and sick of cleaning out cupboards, too. On a sudden whim, she decided to go and explore the cellars, where someone really ought to investigate the assorted piles of junk. Hannah said if they got a cat or two to keep the mice down, they could use the cellar for storing hams and preserves. It was the coolest place in the house.

Sarah hesitated at the top of the steps, which were steep, then mentally dismissed an image of Will frowning at her and began to make her way down. She moved slowly and carefully, holding her candle high in one hand to light her way. Shadows danced across the walls to greet her as the flame flickered in the draughts.

When she was only half way down, however, something that squeaked and scuttled from beneath her feet made her jump and cry out in panic. As she moved, she caught her shoe in the hem of her dress, flailed her arms wildly for a moment, then lost her balance and tumbled down the stairs.

Only the rats heard the thump as she bumped her head against the stone wall and landed at the foot of the steps in an unconscious heap.

It was some time before Mary, the first stage of her washing completed, came back to the house and went round to check the fires. Even then she wouldn't have discovered the accident had Bella not stood whining at the open cellar door until Mary felt obliged to go and investigate, if only to quieten that dratted animal.

Taking a candle from the parlour, which happened to be the nearest room, she lit it at the fire and, grumbling audibly about 'dogs as is favoured till they don't know they're dogs', she descended the steps.

When she discovered the unconscious body of her mistress lying on the floor in the damp and darkness of the cellar, she screeched with shock and almost dropped the candle. Sucking a finger burnt by the hot wax she had spilt on it, she cautiously approached the body, whimpering to herself and calling Sarah's name.

When she discovered that Mistress Sarah was still alive, she cried out, 'Thank goodness! Thank goodness!' and continued to repeat the words under her breath, because any sound was comforting in the darkness of the cellars.

She tried to rouse her mistress, but when Sarah didn't stir the 'Thank goodness!' gave way to 'Lord ha' mercy!' and an occasional 'Dear bless us all! What next?'

None of Mary's rough remedies had any effect and her mistress remained unconscious so, weeping and sniffling, she decided to send Petey to the Pursleys for help. She went outside and yelled across the gardens till he came shambling back to the house, but it took a while to get the idea into his head that he must fetch Master Pursley and not return to his work with Daniel. She watched him set off through the woods at a stumbling run, then returned to the cellar.

It being market day, only Will was at home, for his mother had driven the cart into the village, taking Hannah and her daughter with her for company and protection. Will was so much alarmed by Petey's incoherent gabblings, which included the words 'mistress is hurt', that he was quite easily persuaded to follow him up to the big house.

Once there, Petey dragged him towards the cellar, still mouthing incoherently, and Mary, hearing their footsteps, set up a loud wail of distress, which was echoed by the whining of the two dogs. Will hurried down the steps to find Sarah still stretched out on the cold stone floor, only partly conscious, with Mary weeping over her.

His heart nearly stopped at the sight, for he thought at first Sarah was dead. And to think of the great house without her, to think of never sitting quietly enjoying her company again – no, the very idea was anathema.

Then she stirred and groaned, and he muttered, 'Thank goodness'.

Scolding Mary for leaving her mistress lying there chilled and damp without even a blanket to cover her, he enlisted Petey's help to carry Sarah up to the bedroom. She was so cold and pale he couldn't at first think what to do, except to chafe her hand and stroke her hair gently back from her forehead, whispering her name as he did so.

'She's a-goin' to die, ent she?' moaned Mary. 'Oh, Lord ha' mercy on us all! What will me an' Petey do then?'

'Of course she's not going to die! Don't be so foolish!' But he was worried about Sarah's stillness and pallor, and wished desperately that his mother or some other sensible woman was there to help.

'She's very cold,' he said, thinking aloud. He turned to find Mary still standing there wringing her hands. 'Stop your wailing, woman, and do something useful!'

Mary hiccuped to a halt and gaped at him. 'What shall I do, then, Master Pursley?'

'We need to warm her up. Go and put a brick to heat on the kitchen fire, then get this bedroom fire lit!'

Mary's face cleared. She brought up some burning embers from the kitchen fire on a shovel to kindle the wood laid ready in the grate, then, when that was alight, looked trustingly at Will for further instructions.

'The brick?'

'It's heating on the fire.'

'Go and fetch some brandy, then – if there's any left!'

'Oh, ah, there's still some left. Old Squire didn't hev time to finish that last barrel. Hardly started it, he had, when he died an' nobody's touched it since.' Well, Mary and Daniel had shared a small jug of it at Christmas-tide, but she wasn't going to admit to that, especially with Will Pursley looking so upset and stern. She went away to get some.

As he watched anxiously over Sarah, Will thought he could detect a little more colour in her cheeks. 'Wake up,' he murmured, pressing her cold hand between his two warm ones, then feeling her forehead again.

She stirred against him, just a small movement, but it sent hope shooting through him.

When Mary plonked a decanter of brandy and a rather dusty glass down on the table and again stood waiting for instructions, he ground his teeth at her lack of initiative.

She suddenly exclaimed, 'Oh, dear Lord, I've left the washing a-boiling in the copper!' and ran out of the room.

'She's nearly as simple as her son!' he muttered to himself, as he tucked the blankets carefully round the still figure on the bed.

Too frightened by Sarah's pallor to leave her to Mary's inept care while he sought help, he decided he would have to remain with her. Once or twice he moved across to put more wood on the fire or stare out of the window and wish capable Hannah would return. Or his mother.

But there was only him.

As he passed the glass, he picked it up and stared at it, then dusted it carefully on a corner of the sheet, swinging round suddenly as Sarah moved again and moaned softly.

When she opened her eyes a minute later, this time seeming aware of what was going on around her, he groaned aloud in relief.

The first thing Sarah saw was Will Pursley's face leaning anxiously over her. She tried to speak, but her mouth felt numb and wouldn't obey her. Her eyes betrayed her panic.

'It's all right,' he said reassuringly. 'You fell down the cellar steps and knocked yourself unconscious. You've banged your head and I think you've also hurt your ankle, for it's swollen. Lie still and let your body come to itself.'

She began to shiver. 'C-cold,' she managed to croak.

He moved away from her, but kept talking, as if he sensed she found the sound of his voice comforting. 'That fool of a Mary left you lying on the damp cellar floor, didn't even think to bring you a blanket. It's to be hoped you haven't taken a chill.'

She heard the sound of something being poured into a glass and was glad when he reappeared beside her.

'I've poured you some brandy. It'll warm you up.'

Her body was beginning to obey her again. 'Oh no, thank you. I don't...'

He put the glass down, lifted her into a sitting position and then held the brandy to her lips. 'Drink it! This is no time for your foolishness, Sarah. Do as I say!'

He wasn't even aware that he'd used her first name, but she was. As she leaned against his chest, she found herself sipping, then choking as the fiery liquid slid down her throat. She made a feeble effort to free herself from his hold, but her head swam so much that she was forced to continue leaning against him again for support.

It was bliss to be held like this in his arms, for whatever reason.

When he bade her stay quiet and let the brandy do its work, she murmured her agreement.

He began to chafe one of her hands in his big warm one. More bliss.

'How are you feeling now?' he asked after some quiet moments had passed.

'Much better. Thank you.'

'Shall I let you lie down?'

'No. Please don't move. I'm very comfortable like this.'

So was he. He gazed down at her lovely hair, her soft pink lips, and treacherous thoughts began to slip into his mind. How would it feel to touch that creamy skin or even kiss those lips? He tried to tell himself not to do this, but he couldn't stop his thoughts lingering on the warm body nestled against him. He liked having her in his arms. It was as simple as that. But he had no right to feel like this. She was gentry and he wasn't.

'I'll stay with you until Hannah gets back, then,' he said. 'Mary's slow-witted and you aren't yourself yet. I was wondering whether we should we send for Doctor Shadderby. Your face is still very pale!'

She clutched his hand. 'Oh, no! Please don't! He'll only bleed me! That's all doctors ever do, well, that or give you a purge. I hate to be bled. I'll be all right once I'm warm again.'

As he himself hadn't much confidence in doctors, either, he didn't press the point.

Mary came in with a hot brick wrapped in flannel and showed a disposition to linger and comment loudly on how terrible bad her mistress was looking.

When he saw how her loud voice was making Sarah wince, Will sent the woman away to put another brick on to warm, ordering her to wait in the kitchen till he rang for her. Sarah's pallor still worried him, though so he bullied her into drinking another glass of brandy.

This time, she enjoyed its fiery warmth and the lazy feeling it gave her afterwards. That feeling crept into her head, too, and tempted her into allowing her secret thoughts out of hiding. She glanced up at Will and found him staring down at her. Under the heady influence of the brandy, the solution to her problems seemed suddenly so obvious and straightforward, requiring only a few words from her, that she wondered why she hadn't done something about it before.

'Mr Pursley,' she said, 'Are your... um, affections engaged with anyone?'

He gaped down at her. 'I beg your pardon?'

'I don't know how else to put it. Are you... courting anyone... a woman, I mean?'

'What's that got to do with anything?' he asked in bewilderment. Perhaps the blow to her head had affected her brain. And yet, her eyes were as steady and clear as ever. Lovely eyes they were.

'Please… would you mind answering me? It's very important.'

Because she still looked so wan, he decided to humour her. 'Of course I'm not courting anyone!' He couldn't prevent the bitterness creeping in. 'What have I got to offer a woman? I'm short of money and will be for years. *You* should know that better than anyone!'

'That's good.'

'Good? That I'm short of money!'

'No.' She could feel herself flushing as she said, 'That you're not courting anyone, I mean.'

'Sarah, what is the point of all this? Are you sure you're—'

She rushed into speech before she lost her courage. 'The point, Mr Pursley, is that I need a husband and… and you need land. So I think it would be a good solution to both our problems if you and I were to get married.' She was mildly pleased with the way she had expressed herself, and deeply anxious lest he scorn her, so she said nothing else.

'What?'

He sounded so incredulous she felt impelled to add, 'Not, of course, if you find my… my person displeasing.'

He laid her back against the pillows and sat where he could see her face, eyeing her suspiciously. But she didn't look as if she had run mad. Then his glance fell on the glass and he realised what had happened. 'It's the brandy! It's gone to your head!' Only, why should that make her ask him to marry her?

'Oh, no! Though I do feel it has given me the courage to speak. I see now why they call people who have been drinking too much "pot-valiant".'

His face became wooden and his eyes turned dark and stormy. 'Well, then, I care not for your drunken jest, Mistress Bedham.'

She clutched at his arm. ''Tis no jest, but an honest offer and… and I think you should consider my suggestion very carefully, Wi–Mr Pursley. It would be a… a good bargain on both sides, don't you see? I have the Manor, but I lack the skill to manage my land properly or the means to pay a bailiff. You have no land, but many skills. It's very obvious, really.'

He sat like one graven from stone, his face betraying nothing of his thoughts, his eyes as dark as pools of deep, still water.

Since he had neither ridiculed her nor rejected the suggestion out of hand, Sarah felt encouraged to continue. 'I am lame – and I believe I'm a year or two older than you – but I'm *not* too old to bear children. And in spite of my bad hip, I enjoy excellent health.' Honesty compelled her to add, 'Though I do get tired sometimes when I have to do a lot of walking.'

'What put this wild idea into your head?' he asked roughly. 'A lady like you doesn't marry a common farmer like me! And so you'll agree once the brandy's worn off!'

She felt tears well in her eyes. 'No, I won't. But I know I'm not pretty or—' Her voice failed her, but she remembered suddenly that he had once quite forgotten her lameness! 'I've been here long enough now to realise what a difficult task it will be to rebuild this estate. So you see, I'm only offering you a lifetime of hard work. And… does the owning of a piece of land outweigh my… my personal disadvantages?'

It took him a minute to realise what she meant. How could she think so badly of herself? 'Don't talk like that! You may be lame and taller than... than is usual for a lady, but I'm tall, too, and you're a fine, healthy-looking woman. Why... you aren't even pock-marked and your hair is,' he reached out to touch a strand and his voice softened, 'a lovely colour.'

She felt suddenly breathless and hopeful, and could feel herself blushing furiously. 'Then you... you don't find me... too plain?'

'No!' He sounded angry. 'And I don't like to hear you talk so ill of yourself!' He searched desperately for words, for he had never been one to whom glib phrases came easily. 'It's not *that* I'm worried about – but well, you've had a knock on the head and two glasses of brandy, so you aren't thinking straight. You'll be embarrassed about this tomorrow and regret what you've said.'

'I shan't be embarrassed, and I'll only be regretful if you reject my offer.'

Her tone was quiet and firm, and she was starting to sound more like herself again. He frowned at her. Did she truly mean this, then? Dare he – he drew in a breath – think of accepting?

'I've been trying to work out what to do for days, ever since Hannah told me I needed a husband. I do. I need one quite desperately, Will.'

'I'm no gentleman!' he said, desperate that she should realise the implications of what she was asking. 'I don't even talk right!'

'I'm twenty-eight years old, I'm plain and I'm lame.'

'Stop *saying* that, Sarah! I've told you – it doesn't matter to me that you're lame! I had a lame cow once that produced the best cream of any. And you're not plain.' His voice softened involuntarily. 'Not at all plain in my eyes.'

She blinked at this simile, then decided that comparing her to the cow was another of his lop-sided compliments and smiled at him. 'So?'

'You *do* mean it, don't you?' His voice was barely more than a whisper. He turned abruptly and walked over to the window, needing to be out of sight of her wide grey eyes to think clearly.

The vision of himself as master of all swam temptingly before him. No one – absolutely no one – could then take his land away from him then! And the vision of himself married to her followed it almost immediately – he and Sarah sharing their lives, chatting quietly together in the evenings, lying cosily together in the huge bed behind him. He didn't know which vision appealed to him more. Only… how could a man like him marry the Old Squire's granddaughter?

He turned to look at her and she smiled hesitantly, as if in encouragement. He tried to think his way through this carefully. She would be bound to despise him and his rough ways – but then he remembered how, lady or no lady, he'd found her scrubbing floors or washing windows, humming happily to herself, her hands red and rough.

And he'd enjoyed the way she nestled trustingly against him just now.

She closed her eyes again and lay back on the pillows with a sigh. He had seen her look exhausted sometimes and try to favour her bad side, or rub her hip furtively when she thought no one was looking. It must ache, but she never complained and she tried not to let it hinder her. If only he could believe that she meant this offer, that he would not be doing her an injustice in accepting it he might… Aye, accepting it! He was sorely tempted. He would ask nothing better of life than to be the master of his own acres – and to marry a woman like her!

From the bed Sarah stole another glance sideways. *Oh, please!* she prayed, more fervently than she had ever prayed for anything in her whole life before, *please let him accept!*

He walked slowly across to sit beside the bed, taking her hand again. 'Are you quite sure you mean it, Sarah?'

'Absolutely certain.'

Still he hesitated. 'I have to confess that I'm very tempted to accept. It would be a… a fine bargain indeed for me. And I would be happy to have *you* as my wife. I… respect you greatly – what you are doing here – everything.' He waved one hand to encompass the room, the house, as well as her, but couldn't find any other words to express his feelings for her. 'But have you thought this through? As your husband, I would own everything. Are you not afraid of that?'

'No, I'm not afraid,' she said softly. 'You would love the Manor as I do and serve it far better than ever I could.'

He closed his eyes, then opened them again as the solution came to him. 'I'll go and ask Mr Rogers about this and if *he* sees no objections and… and you are still of the same mind tomorrow, then,' he took a deep breath, 'I'll do it gladly.'

Sarah swallowed convulsively. How could she bear to wait until the next day for his answer? But then, instinctively, she knew she must wait, must give him all the time he needed. He was being very generous in giving her this chance to reconsider and in consulting the parson. She must be equally generous with him. 'Yes, that would be best,' she agreed. 'It'll give you time to think about it, too.'

'Nay, I need no time,' he said harshly, staring at her with a fierce expression on his face. 'For me it would be more than I've ever dared dream of. To be master of my own land! What more could a man ask?'

'Or woman. That's why I won't sell Broadlands, why I must do my best for it.'

'If we marry, I won't force my attentions on you,' he offered.

She flushed. 'But I want children. It's one of my main reasons for marrying. So if the idea of... of sharing a bed with me does not displease you, that should be part of the bargain. Else what will become of everything when we die?'

'You... would not mind that?'

'No.' Her voice grew as fierce as his. 'I *want* children! I've always wanted children. I just thought I would never have the opportunity, that no one would ever—' She let the words trail away.

He took her hand gently, raising it to his lips. 'I think you should rest now,' he said quietly, 'And I must go and puzzle it all out, think what's right... for both of us.' He saw disappointment in her eyes. 'I'm not a man to rush into things, Sarah, especially something as important as this.'

'I hope you won't change your mind, Will,' she whispered.

'I hope *you* won't, either.'

Those words comforted her greatly after he had gone, but she slept very little that night. Her head ached and her thoughts went round and round in the same circles.

She couldn't see any reason for Mr Rogers to raise objections to their marrying. He knew Will's worth as well as anyone and seemed fond of him, too. But until she heard for certain that the Parson had given his approval, she wouldn't be able to rest easily.

And for a woman who was contemplating a marriage of convenience, a mere bargain between two people, her heart beat very fast at the thought of becoming Will Pursley's wife.

–

The following morning, as soon as he had seen the cows milked and turned out to graze, Will washed and changed into his Sunday clothes.

'Is something wrong, son?' his mother asked anxiously.

'No.'

'But why are you wearing your good Sunday clothes on a Friday?'

'I have to go and see Parson.'

'But...'

'Mother, I can't stop now. I'll tell you why afterwards.' He didn't give her any more chance to question him, but strode out of the house and got the cart out.

If Mr Rogers was surprised to receive a visit from his protégé so early in the morning on a weekday, he didn't show it, but made Will welcome in his usual kindly way. 'What can I do for you, my dear boy? I hope nothing's wrong? Your new beasts haven't taken the sickness, have they?'

'No. No, nothing's wrong exactly, but I... I need your advice.' He explained what had happened.

Parson stared at him. 'Bless me! This *is* a surprise!'

162

'Aye. She surprised me too.'

'But you like the idea?'

'I should have my own land.' Will explained simply. 'And... I like Sarah. We deal comfortably with one another.' He smiled reluctantly and added, 'When we're not quarrelling over her trying to do too much, that is. It's just –will *you* just speak to her first? Make sure that she really means it? I shouldn't like her to regret it afterwards.'

'What does your mother think of the idea?'

'I haven't told her. Time enough for that when things are settled. She wouldn't know what to say about it, anyway.'

'You don't think you should ask her advice as well, though?' pursued the parson, feeling the responsibility sit a little heavily upon his frail shoulders.

'No. My mother's not a thinking woman. She's the best dairywoman I've ever seen, but I wouldn't ask her advice about this. So if you're agreeable, I'll drive you over to the Manor now and you can talk to Sarah.'

He wasn't aware that he kept calling her by her first name, and smiling as he said it, but Parson noticed and drew his own conclusions. 'Very well.'

The short journey passed in near silence. Will's face was now wearing its dark, brooding expression and the parson was holding an internal dialogue with himself, which occasionally caused him to mutter something under his breath.

–

Sarah refused to stay in bed that morning and hobbled downstairs with Hannah's help. She promised to spend the day sewing quietly in her little parlour, for there was an abundance of things to be mended and she had also promised to alter some more old clothes to fit Mary, so that they could persuade the old woman into more regular washing of her person.

Though Sarah didn't admit this to herself, from the parlour windows one had a good view of the driveway, so if she sat there, visitors wouldn't be able to take her by surprise.

She watched, heart in mouth, as Will drove up to the house, helped the parson down and then went back to loosen the horse's reins, so that it could crop the grass at the edge of the drive. She could tell nothing from his expression. What had he and Parson decided? She watched as Mr Rogers came towards the house and Will started to pace up and down near the trap.

Hannah showed Mr Rogers in and Sarah drew a deep breath as she faced him.

'My dear Sarah, Will told me about your accident. How are you feeling today? No, don't get up! Should you be downstairs so soon after your fall? You look rather pale.'

Mr Rogers clasped her hand in his and stood looking down at her searchingly. These two young people were both dear to him, almost like the children he had never had, and he must ensure they were making a wise decision.

She couldn't bear to waste time on trivialities. 'Has Will spoken to you about my proposal?' Her cheeks were flaming as she said that word.

'Yes. He wants me to talk to you – to discuss the question of marriage.'

'He will agree, though?'

'Yes. If you are still of the same mind, my dear. He doesn't want you to regret this later.' He took the seat she indicated.

She couldn't hold back a long, shuddering sigh of relief. She'd been terrified Will would change his mind.

Mr Rogers steepled his hands and stared at her over them. 'I can't conceal from you that the news came as a great surprise to me. Are you... um, quite sure it's the right thing to do?'

'One can never be completely sure of anything, can one, my dear sir? But I'm very sure that I need a husband – and that I'd like it to be Will.'

'And why him? Should you not rather look for a man of your own station in life?'

'A gentleman, you mean?' She shrugged. 'A gentleman would expect the estate to support *him* – at least, the only sort of gentleman who would consent to take a woman like me to wife! And it can't. There is less than a hundred pounds a year coming in now and the whole place is so run down... No!' Her tone carried conviction. 'A gentleman would be of no use whatsoever to me. And a man who owned his own land already would care more about that than mine. But Will Pursley is heartsick for a place of his own and would, I think, give his whole life to restoring my estate. He is – not uneducated – thanks to you, my dear sir, and,' she lowered her eyes, blushing hotly now, 'I think he is... a fine-looking man, whose company I enjoy.'

He was convinced more by her blush and the way her voice softened as she said Will's name than by any of her careful reasoning. Coming across the room, he took hold of both her hands and smiled down at her, then bent and kissed her cheek. 'I'll go and call him in, then, and you shall both have my blessing.'

He found Will raking the slimy mess of plants from the pond, working with furious concentration, heedless of his good clothes. When he heard the sound of footsteps on the gravel, he made no move towards the parson, just stood there, rake in hand. 'Well?'

'She hasn't changed her mind and I shall be happy to call the banns for you as soon as you like, my son.'

Will's face lit up in a way that gladdened the heart of the kindly old man. He hadn't seen his young friend look so happy since before his father's death.

'Well… aren't you going to go to her?' he prompted. 'She's waiting.'

Will threw away the rake and ran across to the house, entering the door with a sense of ownership that made him feel like weeping, strong man though he was. He barely checked his step, but strode into the little parlour and went to take her hand in a fierce grip. 'I'm glad,' he said simply. 'When shall we be wed, then, Sarah?'

Her face was radiant. 'As soon as you like.' But she had to add, 'Will… you're quite sure about this?'

'Aye, I'm sure. Very sure. And you?'

'Oh, yes!'

A voice spoke behind them. 'Then let me give you my blessing, dear children, and I'll call the banns on Sunday for the first time.'

But Mr Rogers had to take out his handkerchief and blew his nose very loudly to hide his emotion before he could begin speaking, for their joy seemed to light up the whole room.

Chapter 10

The village church seemed more crowded than usual to Sarah that Sunday. Heads turned as she entered and stayed turned when they saw her on Will Pursley's arm. Voices buzzed like a swarm of bees as he escorted her and his mother to the Bedham pew and then sat down with them there, arms folded, staring straight ahead.

Mr Sewell's voice floated across the aisle, asking what 'that fellow' was doing at the front among his betters. Sarah was afraid Will would become angry, but he didn't seem even to hear the comment. She realised then that he was nervous, as nervous as she was, so she reached out to clasp his hand. He turned his head and as their eyes met, she smiled and after a searching glance, his eyes softened into an answering smile.

Then his mother shifted uneasily in her seat and whispered, 'Will, are you sure we should be here?'

His eyes held Sarah's for a few seconds longer, then he turned to reassure his mother. 'Of course we should. Mistress Bedham has invited us to share her pew.'

Jessie Pursley tried to smile at him and nod, for she was very proud of her tall, handsome son, but she couldn't help glancing round and wincing as she saw Mr Sewell glaring at her. And she still hadn't grown used to the idea of her Will marrying a Bedham.

She turned round to look back at a friend, who was staring at her open-mouthed. She wished she was still sitting in her usual place. All her life the front pews had belonged to the gentry and she had sat part-way towards the back. She had still not taken it in that she was to go and live with them at the Manor after his marriage, and was to be in charge of the dairy there, with Mary to help her.

Perhaps she was dreaming all this? She hoped not. Her Will looked so happy – and Mistress Bedham did, too. Only she was supposed to call her 'Sarah' now. Surely this couldn't be wrong?

It was a relief to all three of them when Mr Rogers entered the church and people turned to pay attention to him. The service began and was quite short, because he was still not well enough to hold a longer one. After one hymn, he opened the Bible and said quietly to the congregation, 'Today I will read to you from the Book of Jeremiah, Chapter 29, Verses 5 and 6:

> *Build ye houses, and dwell in them; and plant gardens, and eat the fruit of them; take ye wives, and beget sons and daughters; and take wives for your sons, and give your daughters to husbands, that they may bear sons and daughters; that ye may be increased there and not diminished.*

'And we should do likewise, my dear friends,' he finished, in his beautiful, deep voice. 'We should marry and beget children and plant gardens for ourselves, for there is no finer way of thanking the Lord for his gift of life, than to pass on that gift to our children and our children's children.'

Everyone stared at him, slightly puzzled, except for Sarah, who had her head lowered and Will, who was glancing sideways at her.

When it was seen that Mr Rogers had finished his short sermon, everyone started rustling their things together in anticipation of being dismissed.

But no! Parson held up his hand for their attention and when he had it, shocked everyone into immobility by reading out the banns for Sarah Elizabeth Anne Bedham and William James Pursley. He had to pause after he had said that, for the whole congregation gasped aloud and there was a loud buzz of comment and speculation that brought a scowl to Will's face and made Sarah blush as scarlet as a poppy in a hayfield.

Mr Rogers waited serenely for the noise to subside and then continued with the banns as if it were nothing out of the ordinary for a farmer to become betrothed to the lady of the manor.

Sarah had expected an outburst from Mr Sewell, but it did not eventuate. After the first shock, he sat looking across at her through narrowed eyes, and he silenced his son with a sharp word and a threatening gesture when that young man started to make loud, unflattering comments on the disparity of the match.

This time, the Sewells were allowed to lead the way out of the church with no let or hindrance, for Thad deemed it best to be rid of 'they troublemakers' as quickly as possible. The rest of the congregation was happy to wait their turn, for they were more interested in staring at Will and Sarah than in getting out of the church.

It was agony for Sarah to limp along the aisle on Will's arm past rows of staring people, especially as her ankle was still sore and made her gait even more clumsy than usual.

Outside in the churchyard he paused and said, 'We have to face them sometime, Sarah. Let it be now.' So the three of them remained near the door and people paused beside them to offer congratulations and stare at Sarah as if she had two heads and belonged in a raree show.

Fortunately her status saved them from too many prying questions, while Will's protective stance and the way he kept exchanging glances with his betrothed lent colour to the idea that this was more than just a marriage of convenience.

And it was, for Sarah at least. During the night, as she had lain happily wakeful contemplating the future, she had admitted to herself at last that she loved Will Pursley, and had done for a while. She thought he was getting fond of her, too, and was happy with their bargain, but she couldn't imagine him loving her as she loved him.

But still, she did wish he loved her, couldn't help that.

–

On the following Tuesday, the warm sunny weather tempted Sarah to leave her work and drive herself out along the lanes nearby. This was the first time she'd been out on her own, but Will had said she should be safe now handling a gentle horse like Lally, and all she needed was practice. Hannah, too, approved of her going out and had supervised the harnessing of the old horse in person.

Sarah didn't realise that her servants were in alliance with Will to prevent her working too hard, and wanted to get her out into the good fresh air that was putting more colour in her cheeks and sparkle in her eyes.

She let Lally clop along the lanes at her own slow pace, staying near the Manor and taking the same route as on her other excursions, happy simply to be out of doors. After a while, she followed a small lane which she knew led back to the main Sawbury road, from whence she could easily make her way home. She was feeling very pleased at how well she had coped and even humming under her breath as the horse made its way placidly along under some trees.

Then they turned a bend and Lally slowed down of her own accord because a carriage was blocking the way at a small cross-roads. With a sinking heart, Sarah recognised the Sewell equipage. Hugh and Izzy were standing nearby and as soon as he saw her, Hugh came striding across. She looked round, feeling suddenly nervous, but there was no space to turn the gig.

This time the one called Hugh spoke to her politely enough. 'Excuse me, mistress, but Mr Sewell would like a word with you.' He held out a hand to help her down, but she shook her head.

'If Mr Sewell wishes to speak to me, then let him get out of his carriage to do so. I see no need to leave my vehicle.'

He reached up and grabbed her arm. 'Mr Sewell told me to fetch you,' he said, ignoring what she had said and dragging her from her seat.

'But the horse!'

'That old bag of bones won't run away!' He set her down and, still holding her arm, walked her across to the carriage. She didn't attempt to struggle any more, because the man was too strong and she had no wish to be dragged before Mr Sewell in an undignified scuffle. Besides, she couldn't believe that even Sewell would offer her violence in broad daylight so close to her home. Rumour said he left the actual violence to his henchmen, apart from slashing at people with his cane when he was angry.

At the carriage, Izzy opened the door and gestured to her to get in. She hung back.

'Pray join us for a moment, Mistress Bedham.' Sewell's voice came from inside the vehicle.

When Sarah saw that Mistress Sewell was with her husband in the carriage, she sighed in relief. He would definitely not have brought his wife with him if he'd intended to do her any harm.

He sat smiling, clearly enjoying the sight of her discomfort. 'You haven't met my wife yet, have you? Not formally, that is?'

'No. Er... how do you do, Mistress Sewell?'

'W... Well, I thank you,' whispered the woman in the corner. She was pale and had the air of a hunted rabbit. Her eyes flickered to and fro from Sarah to her husband, but she said nothing further.

An ungentle hand poked Sarah in the back and she had no choice but to climb into the carriage or engage in a scuffle.

'There now, isn't that cosy?' asked Mr Sewell, in his rather grating voice. 'A real neighbourly gathering, eh?'

'What do you want, sir?' asked Sarah. 'I am expected at home.'

'Oh, I'm sure you can spare us a moment or two of your precious time first.'

The carriage door slammed shut and Sarah couldn't conceal her nervousness.

'No need to worry, Mistress Bedham. I mean you no harm, but I thought you might not speak to me willingly – or in private – which is why I accosted you here. And I brought Mrs Sewell with me so that you would feel more at ease. But my wife is susceptible to draughts, are you not, my dear Rosemary? We cannot have her catching another cold, can we?' His smile was almost a snarl and Sarah felt sorry for the poor shrinking woman in the corner. 'Is that not so, my dear?' he repeated.

'Yes, Matthew.' But Mistress Sewell's voice was a mere whisper and she didn't meet Sarah's eyes.

'Well, sir?' demanded Sarah. 'What is it you wish to say to me in private?'

He looked at her, not a kindly look, but not a hostile one either – more like a man appraising a new horse. 'I underestimated you, Mistress Bedham,' he said at last. 'I have to admit that I definitely underestimated you.'

'In what way, sir?'

'I underestimated your intelligence and shrewdness? When I called upon you, I was completely misled by your appearance. Well, now I see your game more clearly and I salute you for your perspicacity.'

She was puzzled, but tried not to let it show. 'I am playing no game, sir. I am merely settling into my new home and life.'

'Oh, come, Mistress Bedham. There's no need to keep up the pretence any longer! You want more than just a house, I can see that now. You want – shall we call it lifelong security?'

She looked at him in honest puzzlement, but he didn't notice that, though his wife did and bleated out a 'Matthew, pray...'

'Be quiet, you fool!'

She shuddered and closed her eyes.

'Well, Mistress Bedham, you shall have your lifelong security. You've played your cards well. The cowman was a masterly touch. But we can do better for you than that. I have no objection to a daughter-in-law who has all her wits about her, not when she comes endowed with what I want most as her dowry.'

Sarah was by now convinced that Mr Sewell had run mad, and his wife's behaviour only lent credence to this idea, for Mistress Sewell had buried her face in her hands.

'I don't understand you, sir,' Sarah said flatly when it became obvious that he was waiting for her to speak.

'Now you do disappoint me! There are times to keep up a pretence and times to speak openly. I've been very frank with you. Pray do me the same courtesy.'

Sarah could only frown at him.

'My son is, I believe, much more presentable than the cowman, if a little young. He is quite willing to marry you. The estates would match up nicely. You would get the security you want and I would get the land at no cost, or very little, anyway.'

Sarah gazed at him in astonishment as his meaning sank in. 'Am I to take it... Do you mean that you believe my engagement to Mr Pursley to be merely a ploy?'

'What else could it be? A lady does not marry a cowman!' But now it was his turn to frown at her, for something in her tone didn't ring true with the picture he'd painted in his own mind of her character and intentions.

'It was no ploy,' Sarah said slowly and clearly, 'And I wouldn't marry a son of yours if he was the last man on earth. Nor do I intend to give you my inheritance.'

She made as if to get up and leave, but he pushed her back, ignoring his wife's bleated, 'Matthew... *please!*'

'You are a fool, after all!' he spat at Sarah. 'And will live to regret that decision.' He opened the door and the same brute who had dragged her from the trap appeared instantly. 'Get out!' he snarled at Sarah. 'Hugh, you'll have to...'

A cough from the other side of the road suddenly made Mr Sewell aware that they were not alone. He turned his head and his men spun round, but both froze into stillness as they saw Ted and Joe Haplin standing there, guns cocked and expressions menacing.

'Be you all right, Mistress Sarah?' called Ted, his eyes never leaving the two men and his finger steady on the trigger of his gun.

'Yes.' But Sarah was taking no risks. She got out of the carriage as quickly as she could, abandoning dignity in favour of a flurry of petticoats and a rapid departure before Sewell could do anything to detain her.

Ted waved his gun towards one of the men, who had begun to inch forward. 'Get back, you... 'less you want to have a little accident!' He clicked his tongue disapprovingly. 'Some folk can't stand still for a minute can they, Joe? Want any help there, mistress?'

'No!' Sarah climbed up awkwardly into the gig and picked up the reins, as well as the whip she never needed to use on old Lally.

'I wonder, mistress, if you'd do us the favour of driving us back with you?' Ted asked. 'My poor brother's that tired. Not been well lately, he hasn't, poor old Joe. Had a lot of disturbed nights.'

Joe grinned broadly, looking the picture of health.

'Very nervous, he is, as well – 'specially about people what might make sudden moves. I do hope they drive that carriage gently and slowly out of our way, or Joe might pull the trigger of his gun by mistake. He's that edgy today! We wouldn't like any accidents to happen, would we?'

The coachman was quick to take a hint and moved the carriage slowly along the lane to a broader place which would allow the others to pass, leaving Hugh and Izzy standing on their own.

'There,' said Ted admiringly. 'Did that all nice and gentle, didn't he? Not as stupid as he looks. Not quite. Now, mistress, if you please?'

Sarah edged the gig slowly past the coach and the Haplins swung up into it, one at a time. Ted gave a click of his tongue and Lally began trotting towards her home and stables.

Once they had rounded the bend, Ted took the reins from Sarah's hands, which had suddenly started to tremble. 'You're all right now, Mistress Bedham. We'll see you safe home.'

She took a deep breath. 'Thank you, Ted. I'm very grateful. How did you know I needed help?'

He spat and rubbed his nose. 'Didn't know it were you, mistress. Thought it were Will when I saw that gig standing near the coach without a driver an' them two grinning at one another beside it. Will Pursley wouldn't willingly get into a coach to hobnob with Sewell, so I reckoned someone must ha' forced him.'

'Ah,' put in Joe. 'Them two bully-boys is headin' for trouble, one way or another. Folks'll not stand for much more of Sewell's nasty ways. And if them timid fools what live in the village is afeared to do somethin', us folk from the Waste aren't!' For him this was a long speech and the implied threat left them all silent and thoughtful.

They drove on for a moment or two, then Ted asked in a more normal tone, 'You sure you're all right, mistress? You d'look a mite pale still.'

'Yes. I'm all right. But Ted...'

'Yes, mistress?'

'I think I would rather you didn't mention to Will that I had this encounter with Mr Sewell.'

'D'you reckon that's wise, mistress?'

'I don't know if it's wise or not, but it's what I prefer. He might get angry and do something which would put him at risk.'

Ted spat again. 'All right. Hear that, our Joe?'

'Ah. But best not go out driving on your own again, mistress. 'Less you're just going into the village, that is. Can't lie in wait for you on that little lane, can they? Not with Will's farm nearby and Santo ready to snap at them.'

'I'll be most careful in future.' She couldn't prevent another shudder.

When they got to the Manor gates, the two Haplins saw her through, then melted into the woods, leaving her thoughtful.

–

The following week, when the banns were read for a second time, there was an expectant hush, but not the same fuss. As far as the villagers were concerned, Will

Pursley had made a shrewd move, getting himself a wife rich in the thing that mattered most – land – and good luck to him!

When the service was over, there were a few grins at the way Will and Thad had Sarah and Mistress Pursley out of the pew before the Sewells could move. Sewell's face was ruddy, not only with impotent fury at their taking precedence, but also from years of heavy drinking. However, even he didn't like to make a scene in church.

The sight of his anger made the villagers dig each other in the ribs on the way out. They chortled over it all afterwards, though not when Sewell or his bully-boys could see them, for he had a nasty way of avenging what he saw as insults to himself, did Mr Sewell. But as the villagers told each other gleefully after church, and at intervals during the next few days, it were as good as a summer fair, all this were!

–

That week, Lady Tarnly came to call on Sarah. She was a white-haired old lady of little height or style, but much self-consequence, and she brought one of her married daughters along with her to lend her support. She wasn't sure she wished for this acquaintance, but her husband had insisted she pay the visit. Henry seemed to have taken quite a fancy to Mistress Sarah, and his wife knew that once he'd decided upon something, he'd stick to it through thick and thin.

It was always easier in the long run to do as he wished in small matters, she had long ago decided. Besides, she did have some curiosity to meet the woman herself.

There was also the question of Mistress Bedham's projected marriage to be looked into. Lord Tarnly had had what he called a 'damned impertinent letter' from that fellow Sewell, saying the new owner of Broadhurst had contracted to marry a common cowman, and if that didn't prove that she'd taken leave of her senses, he didn't know what would!

Lady Tarnly had been instructed by her husband to inquire into the matter as soon as possible, to see if there were any truth in it. She sighed as the coach stopped in front of the manor. What Henry thought *she* could do about it, even if what Sewell said were true, she didn't know!

In the event, her ladyship was pleasantly surprised by Mistress Bedham, and even her daughter, now Lady Wiltherton, allowed afterwards that the new owner was 'passable well bred'.

Lady Tarnly left Broadhurst quite in charity with Sarah. A sensible woman. Perfectly frank about her marriage and the reasons for it. No foolish airs and graces. Her ladyship considered that, given the very obvious problems at the Manor, the proposed marriage was an eminently practical solution and therefore to be commended.

If more people cut their coats according to their cloth, there would be a lot less unhappiness in the world, her ladyship often declared, and did not scruple to tell her tenants as much when she caught them being wasteful or extravagant. In fact, it was one of her most cherished beliefs that one should live within one's means. She herself had never spent a farthing above her husband's income, never gambled more than she could afford, however fashionable gaming might be, and always paid her tradesmen's bills within the sixmonth.

And what's more, the man wasn't a cowman at all, but a farmer whom Henry knew, for she remembered him helping Mr Pursley after Sewell threw him off his farm.

If she and her husband did not disdain the company of those who worked the land, then why should this Sewell fellow? Besides, it was quite fashionable to take an interest in agricultural improvement. Lord Tarnly held annual open days for the tenants of his farms, who were encouraged to visit the home farm, which his youngest son, who acted as their land agent, was managing in the most modern way.

Lady Tarnly couldn't say that she was fascinated by the breeding lines of cattle and sheep, but it was common sense to get the best out of your land, and it was the duty of the nobility to set an example to the lower orders.

When his wife returned and admitted that he was right about Mistress Bedham, who had clearly been raised as a lady, and who was doing a very sensible thing for one with such a sadly limited inheritance, Lord Tarnly slapped his thigh and let out a great roar of laughter.

'Didn't I tell you? Didn't I, by Jove? Knew you'd like poor Elizabeth's daughter? Breeding will out, whether it's man or beast! Breeding will always out! And what about this marriage, then?'

'Mr Sewell has, as usual, twisted the truth. The man in question is a yeoman farmer, not a cowman. You know him. His name is William Pursley.'

'Pursley, eh? Of course I know him. He's not a cowman! Knew the father, too. Comes from good farming stock. Family's been in the district as long as we have. Fallen on hard times lately, thanks to Sewell. Father hung himself when he got into debt with Sewell, then Sewell turned this young fellow off the farm and knocked it down. Damn shame, that!' He brooded for a moment, then recovered and guffawed again, 'No wonder Sewell's hoppin' mad!'

'That man's opinions are a matter of the utmost indifference to me. He is ill bred and I would never agree to receive him here, even for you, Henry.'

'Knew a Bedham wouldn't marry a common cowman!' he crowed again, only half listening to her. 'One in the eye for Sewell, that!'

'Yes, dear. Now...'

He wasn't listening. 'I believe we should attend the weddin' ourselves, m'dear. What d'ye say, eh? Give the couple our open support and approval, what?'

Now it was Lady Tarnly's turn to frown. 'No one has invited us to attend, Henry. And we don't even know that there'll be any festivities to attend. It might be a very simple affair.'

'Nonsense! People always celebrate a weddin'. And pish to invitations! I'll drop Mistress Sarah a line myself, or ride over there one day, if you're too nice to do it.'

'Do you not think she might be offended?'

'Not she! Sensible sort of woman. I'll tell her I've heard of the match and approve of it. Offer to give her away, for her mother's sake. That'll make Sewell look sick as a horse. And if I drop her a hint that our support will help Pursley to get accepted by the county gentry, I dare say she'll jump at my offer. She'll know what it's worth to be accepted by the Tarnlys, even if Pursley don't.'

Chapter 11

On the Wednesday of the following week, another carriage turned into the driveway of Broadhurst Manor, a dusty vehicle with tired horses, which had obviously come a long way.

Will, who was working in the grounds, didn't like the look of this. He didn't know what Sarah might have to face now, but was determined not to leave her to confront whoever it was on her own. Face grim, he ran over to the house, entering the back way and demanding water to wash his hands and a cloth to rub the mud off his shoes. At once, if you please!

By the time Hannah went to answer the front doorbell, which had now been repaired, he had finished his rapid ablutions and slipped into Sarah's parlour. 'I don't know who it is, but you're not facing them on your own!'

She gave him her wide, calm smile and said simply, 'Thank you, Will.'

They turned together towards the door.

'Mr Jamieson to see you, mistress,' announced Hannah, as Sarah had taught her.

Sarah's face cleared and she limped quickly across to the figure in the doorway. 'My dear Mr Jamieson! Whatever brings you down to Dorset? I hope there's nothing wrong? Hannah, fetch us a tea-tray, will you? No, I remember, you don't like tea, do you, sir? Claret, then, and some glasses, please, Hannah.' She only hoped the wine they'd found would be palatable.

Mr Jamieson shook her hand and retained it in his as he eyed her searchingly. 'You look very well, my dear,' he said, in a distinct tone of surprise. 'And the house too! You have wrought miracles!'

'I *am* well, sir, as you see.' But he was frowning suspiciously at Will and she couldn't have that. She held out her hand to bring him over to join them. 'And I'm very happy to be able to present Mr William Pursley to you. No, you know him already, do you not? But what you will not know is that Will and I are betrothed.'

The two men shook hands stiffly and Sarah saw with dismay that Mr Jamieson was very much on his dignity. She gestured to a chair. 'Won't you sit down, sir, and rest after your journey? Hannah will be along in a moment with refreshments. Will, you'll take a glass of wine with us, won't you?'

It was a command, not a suggestion. He nodded.

Sarah waited until they were all seated, then turned to her visitor. 'Now, my dear sir, pray tell me what brings you to these parts?'

Mr Jamieson decided to be blunt. 'I received a letter telling me of your proposed marriage. What the writer had to say worried me, so I felt I must come down to see you about it.' The look he cast upon Will was distinctly unfriendly. 'Er... I would prefer to speak to you alone, if you please, my dear Mistress Sarah.'

'I'm not leaving her to face things on her own!' declared Will at once. 'She's had enough people upsetting her!'

Sarah was rather more diplomatic. 'I'd prefer Will to stay. We have no secrets from one other. What letter are you talking about? Who can have been writing to you about me? I gather you haven't yet received my own letter telling you about our coming marriage?' As if she couldn't guess who'd written! Only one man would have the temerity.

'I received a letter from Matthew Sewell. Paid for in advance, too. He is, I understand, Squire of this village, now that your grandfather is dead, and he's worried about you, my dear, as was I when I read his letter. He says... let me see...' He fumbled in his pocket.

'He says I have taken leave of my senses and am about to squander my inheritance upon a farmer,' Sarah finished for him, trying for a light, joking tone, to spare Will. 'Am I correct?'

'Well... er... yes. Though he said it was a... a cowman. He didn't mention Mr Pursley by name. I hadn't realised it was him you were to marry.'

She could sense that her betrothed was almost ready to explode. Indeed, she was feeling extremely angry herself. But they would gain nothing, least of all Mr Jamieson's approval, by ranting and raving. 'Is there no limit to the man's effrontery?' she asked as calmly as she could. 'Lady Tarnly tells me he wrote to her husband in a similar vein. Lord Tarnly calls Mr Sewell "that damned impudent upstart of a tea-merchant", I gather.'

'Lady Tarnly tells you?' Mr Jamieson asked quickly, not slow to pick up the implications of this.

'Yes, sir. I have made one or two acquaintances in the district. Lord and Lady Tarnly have been kind enough to call on me, and his lordship offered only a few days ago to give me away at my wedding. He was my mother's godfather, you know.'

'He has offered to do that?'

'Yes. Hasn't he, Will?'

'Aye.' Will was still glowering, because it was plain to him that Mr Jamieson was hostile to the idea of him marrying Sarah, and Will didn't know how to deal with him, since he could see both sides of the question and knew some would rightly call it a mismatch.

'Then he – Lord Tarnly approves of the match, unequal though it is?'

'Yes indeed, sir.'

'And Scwell is not the Squire of Broadhurst, either,' put in Will, for this point had grated upon him as much as anything. No person of sense would consider a fellow like Sewell to be Squire! Only think of all the trouble and unhappiness he'd caused in the village! Only think of the ruffians who served him! It was a Squire's job to look after his people, not cause trouble.

'But why did he do it, then?' worried Mr Jamieson.

'Because Sewell hates me and has tried to run me out of the village – and I suppose because he wants to get hold of Sarah's land, to add to his estate, and that will not be possible if she marries me. And when he wants something, that man won't take no for an answer, but uses any means he can to obtain it.'

'Mr Sewell told me when I first came here that Broad-hurst was already promised to him,' Sarah added, 'because of a letter you wrote to him.'

'Promised to him? But that's ridiculous!' exclaimed Mr Jamieson, diverted from the question of Sarah's marriage. 'At no time did I have the authority to accept it without the owner's consent, and so I told him. He can't possibly believe that it was *promised* to him!'

'Well, he does. He is a man of choleric disposition and little rationality, and he's much disliked in the district for his overbearing ways. Did you not meet him when you came down here after my grandfather's death?'

'No. He was away in Bristol, I believe. But… to say the estate was promised to him! It was no such thing!' Mr Jamieson's indignation was so great that his speech was punctuated by angry little puffs of air, but he was still looking suspiciously at Will and added, 'Be that as it may, my dear Sarah, I am not happy to see you rush into an… er… unequal marriage.'

''Tis a fair bargain,' declared Will. 'Else I wouldn't have agreed to it.' He put his arm protectively around Sarah's shoulders and she leaned against him, looking happy and comfortable.

Mr Jamieson jerked. 'Agreed! What do you mean, *agreed!* Sarah, surely that does not mean that you…?'

Sarah smiled across at him, a smile of such radiance that the ageing lawyer blinked at the way it transformed her face, which he had previously considered rather plain.

'Yes, sir. It was I who asked Will to marry me, not the other way around. And had to work hard to persuade him to it, as well!'

She could see that he was beginning to come round and said coaxingly. 'We have made a good bargain, my dear sir, I do truly believe that. I have land, but not the skill to make the best of it. Will has the skill, but not the land. Why, you said yourself that I couldn't hope to manage this place without a husband!'

'But you hardly know Mr Pursley. Surely you should wait until you get better acquainted to marry.'

'I am twenty-eight. If we are to have children, I cannot afford to wait. And my land cannot afford to wait for heirs, either.'

Mr Jamieson opened his mouth, then shut it again, feeling this subject to be too delicate for him to discuss.

'Dear sir,' she said coaxingly, 'I get on very well with Will and I *want* to marry him! In fact, we have set the wedding for next week.'

There was silence and Sarah grew anxious as she saw the frown on Mr Jamieson's face.

'Then you and Mr Pursley had better hear the other condition of your grandfather's will,' he said at last.

'Condition?' she whispered, white-faced. 'What other condition did he make?' Was she to lose her only chance of a husband now?

'That if you marry, your husband must take the name of Bedham, or the inheritance will be forfeited.'

She said nothing, greatly relieved that it was no worse, but she looked anxiously at Will, who would be most affected by this condition. His face had taken on its dark, closed look.

'Can a man do that?' he asked at last. 'Can he just change his name and take another?'

'Yes,' answered Mr Jamieson. 'Though it's best done properly. There will be a Justice of the Peace in the district, no doubt. It would be better to make a formal declaration before him. But there would be no difficulty. Mistress Bedham changed her name in order to inherit Broadhurst and her husband must do the same. These were the late Squire's conditions.'

But they weren't really listening to him. They were engrossed in each other.

'Shall you do it, Will?' Sarah asked hesitantly.

He patted her hand and his dark features lightened briefly into a near smile. 'Aye, Sarah, I shall. If I set my hand to a task, then I do not give up so easily. But all the same, it's hard for a man to lose his name. I shall be the last of the Pursleys now.'

Her hand went out to touch his for a moment. 'Thank you, Will.'

Then she became brisk again and turned back to the lawyer. 'Are there any other conditions of which you have not informed me, sir?'

'No. That's the only one. I'm sorry, my dear. I really should have told you before, but I thought... I thought there would be no need.' He broke off, embarrassed to realise how unflattering to her this explanation was.

She smiled slightly, knowing perfectly well that he hadn't told her because he hadn't considered her likely to marry. But this thought no longer had the power to hurt her, for now she had Will. 'Then if that is settled, will you please stay for the wedding? Mr Rogers has been a good friend to us both and Lord Tarnly has been very kind, offering to give me away, but I would prefer it if... would *you* give me away instead, my dear sir? You seem as near as I can get now to family.'

He smiled back at her, won over in spite of himself. 'I'm honoured that you ask me, my dear Sarah. And I would be happy to stand in place of a father to you – though I must warn you that I have no experience in giving people away.' And, he thought, we shall just have to hope that this marriage works out well for her. At least, if I have a few days here, I shall be able to sound the fellow out a bit more and draw up proper settlements to protect her interests. Pursley has always seemed a dour, surly type to me, but he is reputed to be a good farmer, and I have found him scrupulously honest.'

'Thank you, Mr Jamieson,' she said gratefully. 'And now, here's Hannah with the wine. Will, you'll take a glass with us, won't you?'

'Er… no. You know I'm not one for drinking wine, especially in the middle of the day, with half my work yet to be done. If you're all right now, Sarah, I'll go and show the men where to water their animals. There is no stable-boy here, you see, Mr Jamieson.'

'Bless me, I'd quite forgotten the post-boys! Well, if I'm to stay, I must pay them off and send them back to Bath. They shall return for me next week.' Mr Jamieson bustled out, but Will lingered for a moment before following him.

'You're sure you'll be all right now?' he asked. 'He won't try to bully you, will he?'

'No, no. He has my welfare at heart. And he has been more kind to me than could be expected of a family lawyer. We dined together a few times before I left London. I've grown to regard him almost as an uncle.'

'He mislikes the match.'

'He will grow used to it, and anyway it's me you're marrying, not him.'

He nodded, but his expression didn't lighten.

'What is it?' she coaxed.

'I mislike the way people take me for a… a fortune hunter! 'Tis not like that between us!'

'As long as *we* know where we stand, Will, I think we need not fear malicious tongues. And Mr Jamieson's presence will lend the marriage even more respectability.' But she could see that he was still disturbed. Nothing in life was easy and straightforward, she thought wistfully, even marriage to the man you loved.

When Mr Jamieson returned a few moments later, Sarah had a smile lingering on her face and he couldn't help but realise once again how happy she was now.

As if reading his mind, Sarah turned back to him. 'It *was* a miracle, that day in London, wasn't it? I never thought to have so much – Will, the house, children perhaps, if we're really lucky. Now, pray let me give you that glass of wine and one of Hannah's little honey cakes.'

–

During the next few days, Sarah and Will were both made aware of the sharp brain behind Mr Jamieson's kindly exterior. He wanted to know all their plans and their smallest concerns, and asked shrewd questions, even about matters he knew little of, like the cattle and Will's plans for breeding better beasts. On the Saturday, he even inspected the ram and half dozen ewe-lambs Will had bought at Sawbury market.

'Why these sheep?' asked Mr Jamieson, walking round them. 'Sheep all look much alike to me, I must confess.'

Will answered confidently, sure of his ground. 'They've more meat on them, see, and shorter legs, which is a good thing. Not so scrawny as the others, and the fleece is good, too. Give me a few years and I'll have a flock worth something. Times are changing, sir. Some men are beginning to breed their farm beasts more care-fully, as they do their horses – and they keep more of them alive through the winter, too, so there can be fresh meat whenever it's wanted. I mean to be one of those new men! I mean to breed sheep and cattle that other men will pay good gold for to breed with their own flocks.'

'Hmm!'

That evening, Sarah went out, as she often did now, to watch Will drive in the cows for milking. They stood together as the placid beasts made their way into the yard and Mary, who seemed to prefer outdoor jobs, walked past them with her milking stool and pail.

'Sarah!' Will turned and gripped her arms abruptly. 'Sarah, if you should wish to change your mind – well, I wouldn't hold you to it! I know how far below you I am. Your lawyer – you can see that he's worried, and…'

To his surprise, she flung her arms round his neck. 'Don't talk like that, Will! Don't ever talk like that! I need you in so many ways! I shall always worry that I've forced *you* into a marriage that is distasteful. What have I to offer a man? I'm not even pretty!' And she burst into tears.

'Sarah! Sarah!' He lifted her face from his shoulder and kissed her on the mouth for the first time, kissed her good and long. 'How you do go on about not being pretty!' he said when he drew away, smiling down at her. He shook her slightly to emphasise his words. 'I like your face well enough, I promise you. And I like your company, too. I believe we shall do very well together.' Then he patted her on the shoulder and walked back to his cows.

She watched him go, not trying to guard her expression for once. If he turned, she was sure he would see clearly written on her face all the love she felt for him. Raising one finger to her lips she touched them gently. He had kissed her, lingered on the kiss, too. She hoped he would do that often. He made her feel – happy inside when he touched her.

She laughed softly at herself and went back to her work, feeling much happier.

–

On the Sunday, Mr Jamieson escorted Sarah to church, and if his dignity suffered from riding there in Will's farm cart, he didn't let his feelings about that show.

'Have you no carriage?' he asked Sarah when they returned.

'Oh, yes, two of them – but no horses, apart from dear Lally, whom Will found for me.'

He could only shake his head in disapproval.

That evening, he produced a property settlement, carefully drawn up to ensure that Broadhurst Manor and the other bits of land or cottages were held in trust for Sarah, giving her absolute freedom to choose her inheritor. She protested that there was no need to protect her from Will, but her betrothed also read the document through carefully, asking for explanations of the words he didn't understand and pronounced it a good idea.

This pleased Mr Jamieson greatly. The marriage might turn out quite well after all. Pursley was certainly not stupid, and could read and write better than some lords that Mr Jamieson had dealt with.

At Sarah's urging, however, another clause was added, bequeathing the land to Will if she should die without heirs of her body. She would never allow anyone to take his land from him again.

That generosity brought Will near to tears when he found out, so that he couldn't speak for a moment, only clasp her hand tightly and swallow hard.

—

The wedding took place on the first Wednesday in June. The morning dawned fine and sunny, with the promise of a hot day to follow. Only occasional clouds drifted across the sky and trailed their shadows over the fields. The birds and insects came out to enjoy the sunshine, and chirped or hummed a distant chorus that followed Sarah throughout the day, forming a counterpoint to the joy which was singing through her veins and overflowing into everything she said and did.

Always after that, throughout her whole life, she would be reminded by a particularly fine summer's day of her wedding and of the happiness she had felt as she was driven to the church, with the future stretching before her, all rosy with promise.

Mary came up to the bedroom to fill the wooden tub with warm water as soon as she heard Sarah stirring. 'It be a fine day, mistress,' she announced unnecessarily, beaming all over her round face, 'An' we all d'wish you joy in your marriage.'

'Thank you, Mary.'

Sarah washed herself, dressed as far as her stays, chemise and petticoats, and pulled a house gown over them till it should be time to finish dressing and leave for the church. The wedding was set for ten in the morning and it was only seven o'clock by the time she had finished. How would she manage to fill the hours till it was time to leave?

There being no sound from Mr Jamieson's bedroom, she wandered down to the kitchen. Mary squeaked and rushed to close the back door. "Tis bad luck to sight your man afore the weddin'!' she warned. 'And Will Pursley is still around.'

'Bad luck!' scoffed Hannah. 'That's a pagan idea, Mary, and you should beg the Lord's forgiveness for ever uttering it!'

"Tis, too, bad luck!' muttered Mary under her breath, but she didn't pursue the matter, for Hannah had a very sharp way with her at times. Furtively, Mary made a sign to ward away evil and went back to her work.

'I don't feel very hungry,' Sarah protested, as a platter of food was placed in front of her.

Hannah spoke firmly. 'You need to break your fast, mistress, or you'll be feeling faint before the morning's over. Come now, try a bit of this nice crusty bread with some honey on it. You can't beat honey for settling the nerves,' she threw challengingly at Mary, in case the other woman got the idea that she, Hannah, subscribed to the silly customs that folk with no more sense followed on their wedding day, such as eating honey for fertility.

Sarah dutifully nibbled at the bread, but it might have been baked from sawdust for all she could taste. Several chunks of it were gobbled down by Bella and Betty under the table when Hannah's back was turned, and Mary so far forgot her place as to wink at her mistress to show that she could keep that little secret.

Politely, but just as firmly, Hannah refused her mistress's offer of help in the kitchen, and suggested that Mistress Sarah go and sit in the little parlour to rest until it should be time to get ready. With dragging feet, Sarah went to fidget over a piece of sewing, setting in stitches so crooked that she had to pull them out again when next she took up her work.

At half past eight, Mr Jamieson joined her in the parlour and consumed a hearty breakfast of roast beef, bread and hard-boiled eggs on the little table by the window. The sight of the food made Sarah shudder, but she managed to make tolerably sensible replies to his attempts at conversation – at least, she thought she had done, though he looked at her strangely once or twice.

At nine o'clock, she thankfully escaped up to her bedroom to finish making her toilette. Hannah came up soon afterwards to bring her a posy of choice blooms that Daniel had picked for her from his garden, and to see if she needed any help. She didn't, but was glad of Hannah's company, because foolish fantasies, like Will changing his mind at the last minute, seemed to fly away in the face of her maid's sturdy common sense.

The lilac silk dress looked quite elegant, Sarah thought, twisting and turning in front of the mirror. How lucky she'd been to find ribbons in one of her grandmother's trunks, so that she could make herself a neck band. Round the edges of her bodice was heavy lace, also her grand-mother's, brought up carefully and lovingly by Mary, who was good at laundry work. It edged her sleeves, too, and she shook one arm to watch if fall delicately around into place. Her full skirts were spread wide over well-starched petticoats, for lack of a hoop.

But oh, her hair was as fine and flyaway as ever, and wisps of it would drift down from under the fine lawn of the small new headdress she'd made for herself, fashioned rather like Lady Tarnly's, using more of the lilac ribbon to trim it.

Soon after that, the boy's halloo as he drove up to the house in the freshly washed and polished trap from The Golden Fleece brought Sarah away from the mirror and made her hurry down the stairs, panicking now lest they be late at the church and keep everyone waiting.

The sun was hot on her face. The sides of the lane were a-flutter with flowers and even the corn in the great village field seemed to be bowing her along her way. In the back of the trap, Mary's broad face beamed at the world around her, its shiny pink colour a testimonial to the thorough scrubbing she had felt the occasion to warrant. She was wearing a new dress cut down for her by Sarah from things found in the cupboard and she smoothed its brown linen folds over her knees once or twice with rough red fingers, proud to look so fine. She wished Petey could have come too, but going into the village would have upset him and he would be better off with Daniel.

Beside her Hetty jigged up and down with excitement and even Hannah wore a pleased expression on her gaunt face, for she felt that the Lord's will was being done and that His plan showed a tender, fatherly care for His daughter, Sarah, who, in Hannah's stern estimation, fully deserved this chance of happiness. For once, Hannah was happy to visit the Established Church.

Everything was peaceful on the village green, though more people than usual had found business there in order to catch a glimpse of the bridal party. Hugh and Izzy had been observed earlier lingering in the vicinity of the church, preventing anyone from going inside. They had been cracking coarse jokes and looking as if they intended to create a disturbance.

When Will arrived, they slipped behind some gravestones, butwhen Lord Tarnly's carriage drew up, they left, knowing their master would not wish to offend his lordship, much as Mr Sewell had wanted the wedding disrupted.

After they had gone, a few of the village women crept into the back of the church to watch the ceremony.

As Sarah limped down the aisle, one or two of them turned to smile and nod at her, which heartened her greatly. Part way down the church sat the Parson's housekeeper, Mistress Jenks, rigidly upright, and Prue Poulter beside her, smiling fondly. At the front, in the Bedham pew, sat Lord and Lady Tarnly and a very nervous Jessie Pursley, who had begged in vain not to be forced to hobnob with these august personages.

In front of the altar stood Will, and as soon as he saw her, his stern expression lightened. He was dressed in his dark Sunday best, for lack of any more festive garments, but wore the new shirt of fine linen which she had sewn for him. Beside him stood Mr Rogers, who smiled encouragingly down the aisle at her.

What was she hesitating for? This was what she wanted more than anything. Taking a deep breath, she began to move slowly forward on the lawyer's arm, walking with as even a gait as she could manage.

'You're sure of this?' Mr Jamieson whispered to her as they started to move, for he could feel her fingers trembling.

'Oh, yes, I'm very sure! I'm just a little nervous. I don't like to be the centre of attention.'

'You look very fine today, my dear.' She had surprised him, for her hair was gleaming like best honey in the sunlight, and her skin flushed slightly, in a way that made her look younger, somehow. And that lace framed her neck and face very prettily. He had always liked lace against a woman's soft skin.

As they reached the front of the church, Will turned to stand facing Sarah and they gave each other shy half-smiles.

She began to feel a little better then. How handsome he looked! To think that such a man was marrying her! How happy her mother would have been for her.

Her nervousness made Will feel protective towards her, for the hand he was clasping was quivering! He realised suddenly that she was more important than the land, much more important. A woman like her would be friend, help-meet and lover – all that a man needed. This one would not desert him if times turned bad. He squeezed her hand gently as he spoke his first words of response and smiled at her again as he finished them.

She too spoke firmly and with confidence the words which would bind them together for life, and when the ceremony was over and she heard Mr Rogers pronounce them man and wife, her heart swelled with joy.

Will whispered his personal promise. 'I shall look after you, Sarah, for all the days of my life.'

'And I you, Will.'

Again they gazed at one another, neither attempting to move, then the people at the back of the church cheered, reminding them that they were not yet alone. Lord and Lady Tarnly were smiling at them benignly, Mistress Pursley was wiping away a tear, but was also smiling, and Mr Jamieson was blowing his nose vigorously to hide his emotion.

Afterwards they were all invited to dine at the parsonage, where Mistress Jenks had surpassed herself and prepared a meal that would not have shamed royalty.

Lord and Lady Tarnly were very gracious. ('We are become quite democratic and hobnob with farmers and all classes of person in their own homes,' Lady Tarnly later wrote to one of her daughters.)

My lord, a noted trencherman, didn't worry about who was there, he was too busy doing full justice to everything that was set before him.

Mistress Pursley sat mumchance, completely overawed by this exalted company, but enjoying the sight of her Will, looking so handsome and mixing with the gentry as if he'd been born to it. If only his father had lived to see this day! How proud her Fred would have been!

After the meal Mr Rogers made a little speech, rather rambling, for even two glasses of wine had gone to his head, and Lord Henry made another one, very jovial, for he had drunk several glasses of claret, was well-fed and felt benevolent towards the newly-wed couple. He wound up by proposing a toast to their health and wishing them a long life together, many good romps in their marital bed, and a large family to prove it. He guffawed heartily as he said this, ignoring his wife's frowns.

('Your father made his usual wedding jokes, to the embarrassment of all concerned,' wrote Lady Tarnly, embellishing the statement with a blot. 'The poor bride blushed scarlet, but the groom took them in good part.')

It seemed strange to Jessie Pursley to hear her Will addressed as Mr Bedham, when he had been christened

Will Pursley in the very same church where he had just got wed, but she supposed she must try to get used to that, too. And she must get Daphne Jenks to give her the recipe for those tartlets – honey and almonds, she'd guess – *very* light and toothsome! She had noticed that Lord Tarnly, nobleman or not, had gobbled down a full half dozen of them like a greedy little boy. It made her feel more at ease to see such a human weakness in one of his rank.

Eventually, the festivities started flagging and Will began to talk about getting home.

'I would enjoy a stroll after such a good meal,' Mr Jamieson declared. 'Mistress Pursley, may I invite you to accompany me back to the Manor on foot? It would be delightful to take the air, would it not?

That would leave the newly-wed couple some time to themselves, he thought complacently, as he watched them make preparations to leave.

'I hope they're happy together,' he said when they had driven away.

Mr Rogers smiled after them. 'I'm sure they will be.'

Which sentiments were echoed by everyone present.

–

After some discussion over a pot of cider in The Golden Fleece, Hugh and Izzy made their way towards the Manor, to see what mischief they could wreak there, but before they had even reached the gates, Ted Haplin materialised from behind some bushes, his gun cocked. One of his sons stood behind him, similarly prepared for trouble.

'Lost your way, hev you?' Ted inquired sweetly.

'Just takin' a walk,' snapped Eb. 'It's a public lane, ain't it?'

'No, 'tain't! This be Bedham land, so you can just take your walks somewhere else in future. You're not welcome here, an' a watch'll be kep' over things from now on. Fond of Mistress Sarah, we are. Fond of a bit of peace, too.'

His dog, who stood nearly waist high, growled behind him. 'Thass right, Nan, lass, you tell 'em!' He grinned evilly. 'Nice strong teeth, she has, my Nan. Keeps 'em sharp, a-chewin' on bones. Crunches them bones up like they was made of piecrust, she does.'

The two men retreated.

–

When Matthew Sewell heard that Lord and Lady Tarnly had attended the cowman's wedding, when they would scarce give *him* the time of day, he was furious. And at the thought that they had even stayed for the wedding feast at the parsonage, he grew so angry that Mistress Sewell took to her bed again with the megrims and remained there for a whole week.

The servants at Marsh Bottom had a very hard time of it, with cuffs and blows scattered around on the slightest pretext, and even Sewell's two henchmen not immune to his anger.

'What if that woman produces an heir?' he said to his son. 'It is not to be borne. I will not *allow* it to happen!' His fists clenched at the mere thought.

'Do we really need their land?' Edward asked. 'After all, our estate is bigger than theirs, now.'

'I not only need their land, I want them out of the village. I'll have no other family trying to lord it over me. Some of those clods still consider Bedhams to be members of the squirearchy, and will not grant me my rightful title until I remove them, lock, stock and barrel.'

'But… you can't do that. It'd mean…' His voice faded away.

'I can do what I please, you poltroon! Might is right and always will be.'

'But—'

His father's face grew even redder. 'Hold your tongue, you blithering fool! How are we ever to be accepted in the county if we do not have land – and *more land* than others? I'm doing this for you, but I don't know why I bother. Fine heir I've got myself. Too dull-witted to understand anything, you are. Get out of my sight, damn you! And somebody bring me the rum.'

Edward was pleased to leave him, going to sulk in his room and finger the fine clothes he'd rather be wearing in a town. He'd never wanted to live in the country and longed for city life. He wanted fine clothes and witty company, not talk of cows and crops. But when had his father ever asked any of them what they wanted? His father only *told* them what to do. And was even now planning his sister's marriage to an elderly but rich widower whom she detested.

But one day, even his father would die and then Edward would sell this place. That thought was his greatest comfort.

Several days later, Hugh came up with an idea that raised his master's spirits greatly, an idea which horrified Edward and set his mother weeping with fear.

Chapter 12

'I think it all went very well, don't you?' Sarah asked Will as they drove out of the village.

'Aye, I suppose so. But it's a lot of fuss over nothing, I reckon.'

She felt hurt and couldn't hide it. 'Would you call our wedding nothing?' she asked in a small, tight voice.

He noticed how upset she was and berated himself for speaking so clumsily. He let the horse slow down – something Lally was not loathe to do – as he answered. 'I call the fuss and show nothing, not the promises we made, Sarah. It's what we do with our lives together that counts now, how we keep our bargain and spend our days together.'

'Well, I enjoyed the fuss, myself,' she muttered. 'Once the ceremony was over, that is. That was an ordeal to me, everyone staring at me!'

'Aye. I could feel your hand trembling.' He captured the hand and raised it to his lips.

She found it hard to breathe and it was a good thing Lally now knew her own way home, because Will had completely forgotten to watch the road and was contemplating the strong firm hand of his wife instead. 'I like your hands. They're capable, those are. I look forward to seeing them holding my son one day.'

Warmth spread through her. 'Oh, Will, so do I!'

As they approached the Manor, Ted Haplin stepped forward to greet them and open the gates.

'Any problems while we were away?' Will asked.

'Nothing we couldn't handle.'

Sarah looked from one to the other in dismay. 'Why should there be trouble?' When he didn't answer, she said in a firm voice, 'I wish to know, Will. You are not to hide these things from me.'

'Oh, we were just taking precautions,' he told her. 'In case certain gentlemen found the thought of an unattended house tempting.'

She turned to Ted. 'And... did they?'

He cleared his throat. 'They got as far as these gates, then they saw us.'

All colour left her cheeks and her expression was so stricken that both men exchanged unhappy glances.

It was Ted who saved the day. 'Got something for you, Mistress.' He went behind some bushes and came out with a little plant wrapped in sacking. 'My Poll sent you this, for a wedding day present. It has yellow flowers in early spring and she thought if you planted it in your gardens it might remind you of today.'

Sarah's smile returned. 'How kind of her! Please thank her for us.'

Will clicked to the horse and it began to move on.

Ted watched them go, his expression losing its geniality as soon as they were out of sight. 'There's trouble ahead for those two,' he told his son. 'I can feel it in my bones. If you see any of Sewell's men sneaking around, you're to tell me at once, you hear?'

'Yes, Da.'

'Or any strangers... *any at all!*'

'Yes, Da.'

When they got to the Manor, the bridal couple unloaded their presents. 'I never thought to receive anything today,' Sarah said, picking up the clock, which Lord and Lady Tarnly had given them and which she had carried carefully on her knee, not trusting it to the back of the trap.

In the parlour, she unpacked the other presents from Mrs Jenks' a fine new shopping basket containing several jars of her best preserves. There was a silver tray from Mr Jamieson, who had gone into Sawbury by himself one day to buy it and had cunningly left it at Mr Rogers' house on the way back, so that it should remain a secret until the wedding day. Parson had given them a pair of very pretty silver candlesticks which had once belonged to his mother.

'Presents are well enough,' said Will, 'And 'tis a kindly thought to give us something, but I shan't need a clock to tell me it's time to rise in the morning or to milk the cows, *or* when I'm hungry for my dinner. And,' he drew Sarah close, 'I shan't need a clock to tell me when to kiss my wife.'

She gave him her lips willingly. 'I shall try to make you happy, Will,' she promised as they drew apart. She loved the feel of his strong body against hers. She loved his beautiful, serious eyes, which changed to deepest black when something angered him, but which were luminously brown today, like chestnut shells. As his hands lingered on her shoulders, then slid slowly down her body pulling it close to him, she gasped and arched instinctively against him. She had often watched those hands caress one of his animals and wished they were touching her, but the reality was far better than the dream.

Colour flooded her cheeks at the direction her thoughts were taking, but she didn't pretend that she wasn't enjoying this.

'I think we'll go to bed early tonight, madam wife,' he said softly.

She was beyond speech, for he was still caressing her, so she nodded and when he paused, she leaned forward to give him another kiss and run her fingers down his cheek.

The rest of the wedding day passed in a strange mixture of everyday chores and the sometimes awkward companionship of two people who hardly know each other's ways. Will went out to check on the cows, but left the care of them to Mary and the others, it being such a special day and him in his best clothes still.

Sarah went to oversee preparations for a light supper, but found herself shooed back to her husband by Hannah. So she and Will went for a stroll round the gardens instead, discussing how they might improve them and where to plant Mrs Haplin's bush.

In fact, since neither bride and groom were used to sitting idle, they were both much relieved when the evening drew to a close, with its final ritual of the tea-tray.

'Will you take a dish of tea, Will?'

He hesitated. 'Well, I… No. I thank you, Sarah. Truth to tell, I've small liking for tea. 'Tis thin, bitter stuff.'

'But you've taken tea with me several times!'

'Ah. Yes, well… that was for the pleasure of your company. Only now we shall be living together,' he gave one of the rare smiles that lit up his face, 'I shan't have any need for excuses.'

She felt a warm glow inside to think that he had enjoyed her company so much as to drink something he disliked. 'Would you prefer a glass of wine, then?'

'Nay, I'm no tipplepot. What I do like in the evening, though, is a pot of ale or cider, mulled in winter. My mother will be able to brew ale and cider for us now – she gets a fine sharp taste to them both. Better than what they serve at The Golden Fleece, to my mind.'

Sarah rang for Hannah and commanded a pot of cider for Mr Pur... er... Bedham, stumbling a little over his new name. To hide her embarrassment, she concentrated on pouring a dish of tea for herself, not knowing what to say next.

How little she knew about her husband! She stole a glance at him. He was slouched in a chair, his hands in his pockets, staring into the empty fireplace. He didn't look unhappy, though; he looked relaxed, at peace with himself and his surroundings. She wondered if Will liked to chat in the evenings, or if he preferred to sit quietly. What did he eat for breakfast? What did he look like when he was asleep? Her mind shied away from that thought, for the wedding-night still lay ahead of her.

As if he could feel her gaze upon him, Will turned towards her. 'I like this room. Do you sit in here every evening?'

'Yes.'

'That's good. I shall enjoy that.' He sighed, the long, slow sigh of a man relaxing after a hard day.

She couldn't think of anything to say, so she rested her head against her chair back, occasionally moving it to take a sip of tea. For several minutes there was only the sound of the new clock ticking on the mantelpiece, a dog barking somewhere in the distance and the branches of the trees swishing outside in the light breeze. There was no need to force conversation, she realised with relief. Sometimes, silence could be just as pleasant, if it were shared.

'What time do you like to go to bed, Sarah?'

'What? Oh, I don't mind. Whenever suits you. You'll have to rise early, won't you?'

'Aye.'

'So you won't want to be late.' She finished her tea, put the dish down and took a deep breath, 'Perhaps we should retire now.'

'Retire.' He tested the word on his tongue. 'Is that what you call it when you go to bed?'

'Er... yes.'

He gave her a slow smile. 'Let's retire, then.'

Sarah led the way upstairs, sheltering the candle flame carefully against the drafts that swirled round the old house even on calm days.

In the bedroom doorway, on this first night, he stopped and looked round with the same satisfaction he had shown over her parlour. 'It's a rare fine room, is this. I never thought I'd be sleeping in Squire's bed.'

'For most of my life, I've had to share a room with my mother. In the last year or two, we didn't have much money, and we had to live and sleep in the one room. I still lie in bed here and marvel that it's all mine – all ours now,' she amended hastily. The last thing she wanted was to make him feel dependent upon her benevolence.

He was still deep in his own thoughts. 'I always forget... that you used to be poor, I mean.'

'Very poor. I've gone hungry at times to save money – especially at the end, when my mother needed the laudanum.'

That caught his full attention. He stepped forward and put his arms round her. 'Well, you shall never go hungry again, Sarah. I'm a good enough farmer to promise you that.' As she leaned against him, he asked diffidently, 'Would you rather wait until we know one another better to become man and wife? We don't have to do anything tonight but sleep, if that's what you'd prefer.'

She didn't even have to think about it. 'No. I wish to be your proper wife, Will.'

He kissed her cheek very gently. 'Then get you ready for bed, my dear.'

She nodded, then remembered that she had not yet shown him the rest of the details of how things were arranged. 'I nearly forgot to tell you where things are. Over here is my dressing room.'

He walked across and raised the candle to peer into it. 'I see. You keep your clothes and things in here.'

'Yes. And over the other side is your dressing room.'

He walked back and stared into an almost identical room. 'To think of it – one each, and just for keeping clothes in! There's folk as have only one room for themselves, and their animals must share even that.'

She waited a moment or two, then said, 'Well, I'll get ready for bed now.' But for all her brave words, her heart was beating rapidly and her throat was dry with apprehension.

Will watched her limp over to her own dressing room. Poor Sarah, she did look nervous. He must deal gently with her. He strolled back into the small room that was his and couldn't help grinning. His few garments looked lonely in the great clothes press, for they didn't even half fill the space. How elegant it all was here at the manor! He stroked the wood of the press doors. Fine workmanship there.

He found a ewer of warm water standing on a small table, with a basin and towel beside it. This was what it was like to have servants to tend your needs. As he took off his clothes, folded or hung them, washed his person and dried himself on the towel laid beside the basin, he had to admit that it made your skin feel nice, all this washing. Would she like the feel of his skin, as he already liked the feel of hers?

He pulled on the new nightshirt his mother had made for him, which someone had also laid ready, then a problem arose. Would Sarah expect him to wear a nightcap? His mother had insisted on providing one. He couldn't abide the things, no, nor wigs, neither – though the gentry seemed to wear things on their head all the time. What was wrong with their own hair? Would Sarah expect him to shave his hair off and wear a silly contraption of scratchy horsehair in its place? He didn't think he could face that, not under any circumstances, any more than he could put on a silly nightcap now.

When he went back into the bedroom, she was sitting up in bed, wearing a white nightgown and a frilled nightcap on her head, her hands clasped around her knees, her expression solemn. Carefully he carried his candle over to the vacant side of the bed and set it down next to the tinder box.

'Ready?'

She nodded and blew her candle out. He watched her slide stiffly down in the bed, nervousness showing in every line of her body. He climbed in beside her, wet his fingers and pinched his own candle out, hearing her draw in a trembling breath.

'Will, I don't really know what to... what to do.' The words came in a rush, before he'd even had time to lie down.

'Ah, but I do,' he said gently. He took her in his arms, untied her nightcap and tossed it aside, then stroked her hair. 'Lovely hair,' he whispered. 'I've always wanted to stroke it. Soft as silk, it is, and the colour of new honey.' In the darkness, tender words were not nearly as hard to find.

'Do you... do you really think so?'

'I wouldn't say so, else.'

'Oh, Will, no one has ever said such nice things to me as you do!'

That made him realise how sparse compliments must have been in her life, for he knew himself to be no word-smith. Poor Sarah! He must do his best to make her feel comfortable with him.

She sighed and nestled against him, so he began to caress her body gently. 'I shan't hurt you, my lass. Let me show you what to do.' He began to trace the lines of her body, caressing each curve until she was gasping and writhing. He kissed her until he could wait no longer and she was as pliant as wax in his hands.

And when he entered her body and she cried out, not in pain but in pleasure, he smiled in triumph before allowing himself his own release. It was far better between them than he had expected.

Afterwards, he kissed her on the cheek. 'You're my wife in every way now, lass. Eh, what's this?' For she was weeping.

'I was so afraid I'd disappoint you,' she confessed.

He rocked her a little and shushed her gently. One thing led to another and he found himself enjoying a second congress that night. Well, it had been a long time since his body had had any relief, and she seemed to enjoy it, too.

'I think we are very well suited indeed,' he told her afterwards. 'Not all find pleasure in this act – especially when first wed.'

She fell asleep in his arms, her breaths soft against his chest. He lay awake a while longer, thinking over his day and saying a little prayer that life would deal kindly with them.

—

Mr Jamieson left for London again two days later with a sense of relief. Really, when you thought about it, marriage was the best thing that could have happened to Sarah. A woman on her own was a prey to fortune hunters and thieves. Now, her inheritance was tied up safely and she had a husband to look after her and her property. And though Will Bedham might be a simple yeoman farmer, he was an honest enough fellow, at least, a hard worker and clearly cared for her.

Both Will and Sarah had begged Mr Jamieson to return for more visits, and he rather thought he might do that. He had no close relatives left and it was pleasant sometimes to leave the heat and dust of the city. Besides, he had grown fond of dear Sarah and intended to keep a close eye on her and her affairs from now on.

–

Will found it extremely pleasant to live at the big house. There was something about having spacious rooms and willing servants that made a man feel good. He enjoyed coming in after a day's toil to find a ewer of warm water waiting for him in his dressing room. He grew quite used to changing into what he called 'indoor clothes' in the evenings.

It was good, too, to dine with his smiling wife in the cosiness of the parlour. They took their evening meal late, when the day's work was done, not at a fashionable hour in the afternoon. Sometimes, his mother would join them, but she was not yet fully at ease with Sarah, or with her own position here. More often she would make her excuses and stay with Hannah in the kitchen, for the two of them had struck up a friendship.

After supper, Will would sit with Sarah and discuss the day's small happenings, or read one of the books from the library, or a newspaper that the parson had passed on to them. With the latter, he would read out the interesting bits to his wife and could be sure her comments would be sensible.

After Mr Jamieson's departure, he discussed their daily finances with Sarah and was relieved to find her capable of handling the accounts. 'I'll leave that to you, then.'

'I thought you might wish to take over the money side of things yourself,' she said.

'Is that what you want me to do? Tell me the truth, now! Always tell me the truth!'

'Well… I don't mind how we arrange it, actually, Will. As long as you're content. But I do enjoy dealing with figures, I must admit.'

'Well, I don't enjoy casting accounts. I work long hours and should be pleased to have such things taken off my hands. My mother always handled those things in our house, but we cannot ask her to do that here.'

She nodded agreement. Their life was settling down into pleasant patterns, and the only thing that was wanting was for him to say he loved her. He *showed* he cared about her in many ways, but she hankered after the words – and until he did say them, she didn't dare express her own love fully, though it seemed to overflow into every aspect of her life – always there, always a thought of Will behind every action.

They now started in earnest on the more major repairs Will considered vital. He haggled with the timber merchant in Sawbury for beams to replace those gone rotten, finding a barter which would benefit them both, by ceding to the timber merchant the right to cut down a certain number of trees in exchange for the required dressed timber, those trees to be chosen only by mutual consent and not to be taken from places where their loss would be seen from the house.

After that, Will summoned Joe Haplin from the Waste, for Joe was good with his hands, and set him on at day rates, under his own careful supervision, to repair the roof. 'A proper carpenter would want fresh timber for everything,' he told Sarah, 'but Joe's used to making do. There are old planks and pieces of wood lying around all over the place in the barns – I never saw such waste! – so we'll collect them and barter for others, and only buy what we're forced to.'

For nearly a month, the daylight hours were filled with the sound of hammering, sawing and banging, but no one minded that, because everyone at the big house was busy for as long as the summer daylight lasted. Those working outdoors were galvanised into a variety of new tasks by Will or in the dairy by Jessie Pursley, and those brought in from the village to help indoors were urged on by a fearsome alliance of Sarah and Hannah Blair.

In late July came the haymaking and this year found the home fields rich with lush grass, for there had been a happy alternation of sun and showers that had set everything growing rapidly. Not content with reaping the fields, Will culled as much hay again, if of an inferior quality, from the bits of land around the house and from odd clearings in the woods. This time he hired Ted's sons to do it, which pleased Poll greatly.

After the haymaking was over and the ricks built, they held a modest celebration for the labourers and their families in one of the tumble-down barns, though it was the strangest haymaking supper in living memory, and had its sad side, too, because only half the village was able to attend, those bound to Mr Sewell having been strictly warned to keep away from any festivities at Broadhurst.

Mr Sewell flouted custom and held no haymaking celebrations at Marsh Bottom, for he considered them a waste of time and money. This caused considerable ill-feeling among those whose labour was tied to him, but no one dared say so. They arranged a surreptitious celebration of their own in The Golden Fleece, but it wasn't the same.

In September there was the harvest to be gathered in, always one of the most significant events of the year. If the harvest failed, people went hungry and the weaker ones died. This year, it was a good harvest and the sale of the surplus wheat produced by Will brought in a welcome purse of golden guineas to fill the Bedhams' empty coffers and pay for new tiles for the roof.

This year at harvest tide, said the villager elders, meeting in solemn assembly in church, they would follow the old customs to the letter, so that no more bad times should come to them. It didn't do to neglect the proper ceremonies and customs.

Even Mr Sewell couldn't persuade them otherwise, so he scornfully granted them permission to do as they wished.

'Ah,' said Thad Honeyfield, newly appointed to the select group which made the important decisions about crops for the common fields and when to sow them, 'even that old devil has to bend sometimes.'

They shushed him quickly. It was one thing to insist on sticking to their customs, another to utter insults aloud about a man who repaid with violence anyone who displeased him.

'One day...' said Thad.

'Ah, one day,' they agreed in whispers, 'but not yet, so hush up, lad.'

After the last sheaf of Will's wheat had been loaded on the wagon, the villagers formed a procession to escort it to the barn at the manor. Mr Rogers led the procession, carrying a beautifully-carved crucifix to placate the Christian God, and old Richard Bennifer followed him, playing his fiddle all the way to drive away evil pagan spirits.

Sarah gave no credence to the idea that following the old customs would ward off evil, but she saw no harm in people who had worked so hard enjoying a little light relaxation, and she allowed them to enthrone her on the cart with a child on her knee, and drive the corn home in style.

Afterwards, on Jessie Pursley's advice, she supplied the villagers with a barrel of cider to quench their thirst and a hearty meal in token of the plenty they had brought in from the fields.

'And that,' said the elders, 'Is how a harvest had oughter be celebrated. Real gentry look after their folk.'

–

Of course, Sarah and Will had their disagreements from time to time. That was inevitable, for in spite of their quiet ways, they were both strong-willed. Many of their quarrels came about because Sarah insisted on overtaxing herself. Now that he was her husband, Will didn't hesitate to tell her when he thought she was being foolish.

He came in one day to find her toiling in the library, which she had been longing to restore. He knew she'd already spent a hard morning in the kitchen, helping Hannah to preserve fruit for the winter, and could see that she was tired.

'You've done enough physical labour for today, my lass.'

'I want to finish this room.'

He removed the damp cloth from her reddened hands, and retained one in his own, examining it. 'There's no need for you to get your hands in such a state. Leave the rough jobs to the servants.'

'I *like* doing things myself. I *want* to take my share of the work.'

'Well, I don't like you over-tiring yourself, and what's more, I'm not having it!'

'I shall do as I like! You work all the hours of daylight – and more. Shall I sit at my ease and leave everything to others?'

'Aye. When it comes to toiling like a scrubbing maid, at least!'

She tried to tug her hand away and failed. 'I'll decide for myself what I shall and shall not do, thank you very much!'

'Not if you don't show more sense!'

'Who do you think you are?'

'Your husband.' He threw the wet cloth into a corner and pulled her from the library.

She tried to resist, but he was too strong, and she could only drag along behind him, still protesting. He threw open the door of her parlour and pushed her in. Then, as she stumbled, he grabbed her, to stop her falling.

'You're a plaguey headstrong wench! Why will you not look after yourself?' Finding her closeness exciting, he pulled her into his arms and gave her a hearty kiss.

She felt suddenly weak and clung to him. 'I don't like to leave everything to you, Will.'

'You don't leave everything to me! You work beyond your strength. Who can do more? Now, will you sit down and rest, or must I tie you to a chair?'

She coloured. 'Well, I am a little tired...' She lifted a hand to stroke his cheek and her smile was a promise of pleasures to come.

Another time, when she proved recalcitrant, he simply picked her up and carried her into the parlour, where he dumped her none too gently into a chair and threatened to stand over her to make sure she rested. When she answered back sharply, he lost his temper and threw her bucket and cleaning implements out of the front door.

'If I have any more of this foolishness, I'll carry you up to the bedroom and lock you in!'

'If you touch me...'

'You'll what?' He grinned at her, enjoying the way he could bring colour to her cheeks, or make her suddenly gasp and falter in her arguments, by kissing her.

Gradually the sound reason behind his arguments, not to mention his forceful way of making his point, won him his way.

'Why don't you use your needle instead, mistress?' Hannah asked one day, more tactful than Will about preventing Sarah from working too hard. 'You're a skilled needlewoman and there's so much mending and refurbishing needs doing. Master won't be able to complain about you doing that.'

Sarah stared at her, then nodded. 'I suppose so.'

And there was another reason for her to take things more easily, a reason which made her smile and lay one hand on her still flat belly. She was beginning to suspect that their love-making had already had results. She didn't dare say anything yet, and Will seemed not to have noticed, but it seemed likely that she was with child.

Oh, the joy of that thought!

Chapter 13

Matthew Sewell continued to brood on what his enemies were doing – for by marrying Will Pursley, Sarah had become an outright foe in his eyes.

When Izzy came to report one day a pile of broken mantraps dumped on the boundaries of Sewell land, Matthew nearly choked on his rage.

'Shall we make another try to burn the place down?' Izzy offered.

'And fail again? And prove to everyone that I'm behind this? No, you shall not! You two are known as my men, so we must find others to undertake what is needed – but first we must lull them into a belief that we've given up.' His lips bared in a snarl which showed yellowing teeth, certain gaps in their ranks testimonies to the hard fights he had had in his youth to win his way into the ranks of money and success, other gaps due to increasing age, something which also angered him.

'So what shall I do with the traps, master?'

'Leave them be.'

He sent Hugh over to Poole the following week, ostensibly on business, but in reality to recruit men from the docks, always a fruitful source in these cases. The men were to stand ready to come when summoned to take action.

In the meantime, he continued his efforts to find another husband for his daughter, since she'd annoyed the first man he'd chosen. He was determined to make an alliance for her that would have him accepted into the ranks of the gentry.

''Tis a father's right to find his daughter a husband,' he mother said whenever she complained.

'A father who cared about his daughter's happiness would look for a man who would be kind to her, though, not one who can scarce dodder from bedchamber to table!'

'Shh! You know we can do nothing against his wishes, only hope and pray for your happiness.'

Which made her daughter even more sulky and chancy-tempered.

–

When he returned to London, Mr Jamieson didn't forget the Bedhams. Always a devotee of the bookshops, he now sought out volumes he thought might be of interest to his young friends in the country and sent them down to Broadhurst as surprise presents.

Sarah's first gift was called 'The Complete City and Country Cook' and was accompanied by a finely-bound volume of blank paper upon which she might inscribe her own household hints and receipts.

She gazed at them both in delight. Here, in clear black and white, was a treasure-trove of useful information, not only of receipts for delicious new dishes, but also of hints on how best to preserve food, details of the brewing of small ale, and the concocting of simples and medicines – and even instructions for making such luxuries as lotions to keep the skin soft and the hands white. This, together with her grandmother's receipt book, would help her run her home more efficiently. She shared its riches with Hannah, who had hitherto read only the Bible and was at first reluctant to waste her hard-earned reading skills on anything else.

Mistress Pursley also spelled laboriously through the pages of the two books. 'To think on it!' she declared several times. 'To think of them writing all those things down to make a book! I never thought much of books afore, thought they was just wasters of time, but I was wrong and I'm not ashamed to admit it.'

Will's first present from Mr Jamieson was a treatise on agriculture by a Mr Jethro Tull. He was as delighted with that as Sarah was with her book, for the ideas expounded in it fell on fertile ground. He studied the book until he knew it by heart, poring over the woodcuts of new implements and mulling over Tull's ideas about ploughing and planting.

These ideas were not all new to him, for there were always men who would experiment, and Will had listened carefully to what other farmers said after market in Sawbridge. Some of Mr Tull's new ideas seemed to make good sense to him for the conditions round Broadhurst, others offered less promise. Next year he would, he decided, try dibbling the seed in, instead of broadcasting it.

One evening he asked, 'What do you say to trying out some of the new crops on the home farm, Sarah? It wouldn't be possible on the strips we share in the village fields – those dolts won't change anything unless forced – but on the home farm we can do as we please.'

She smiled her acquiescence, feeling tireder than usual, and fell asleep in her chair, so that he had to wake her up and send her up to bed.

He stayed downstairs for a while longer, still making plans. During the slack winter months, with the help of Thad, who loved the idea of devising new tools, he would see if he could make himself a dibbler.

—

Other things were changing, too, in the district. It was at first a nine-day wonder to the villagers that Will Pursley, not content with marrying into the gentry, should also want to change his name to Bedham. But they gradually grew used to it, and Mistress Sarah was a Bedham born, after all.

Mr Sewell made no such effort. The politest terms he had for Will were 'that Pursley upstart' or 'that clod lording it at the Manor'.

When some of the villagers took what seemed to them the logical next step and began to address Will as Squire, Sewell became quite incoherent with rage. Those employed by him took care to refer to Will still as Pursley in their employer's presence, but they got themselves into tangles at other times, trying to use the correct name to suit their company.

It was all very confusing, said the village elders, and they didn't know what the world was coming to with two Squires in one village; all they knew was that it wouldn't have happened in their grandfathers' day.

Throughout that summer and autumn, Sewell and his henchmen continued a small war of attrition along the boundaries of Broadhurst, but he was still biding his time, waiting for the right moment to do more serious damage. The two bullies trespassed several times in the Manor woods, on the pretext of chasing poachers. While there, they did as much damage as they could, breaking fences, trampling down the saplings and shooting at the birds.

One day, Will caught Izzy on his property and gave him a sound thrashing, but this had only a temporary effect on the depredations. Formal complaints to Mr Sewell were ignored and Will was not yet confident enough in his new position to take the matter before Lord Tarnly.

After due consideration, however, he worked out a plan that would prevent a lot of the damage. He talked it over with Sarah first, then he went over to confer with Ted Haplin.

'I'm getting tired of Sewell's men trespassing on my land, Ted.'

'Ah. Rascals, they be. Hard to stop 'em, though. You can't be everywhere at once, can you?'

'No, but it'd help if I had some keepers.'

Ted's eyes grew wary. 'Oh? Keepers, is it now?'

'Yes. I thought of you for one. And your brother Joe for another.'

Ted gaped. 'Me?' His mouth opened and shut, and he swallowed hard. 'Me, a keeper?' he managed at last.

'Yes. Why not? You know these woods as well as anyone.'

A slow grin crept over Ted's sharp features and he ran a hand through his greying hair, ruffling it still further. 'Adone-do! Who'd ever ha' thought of such a thing? Me, a gamekeeper? I usually been on the other side o' the fence!'

'Then it's about time you reformed your ways, for I'll not have you or anyone else poaching in my woods! Well, give me an answer! I can't stand here all day. Will you do it or not?'

Ted rubbed his head again. Such a rapid decision was difficult, but he was always one to seize an advantage. 'Could be. You goin' to build me a keeper's cottage, an' all?'

Will scowled. 'You know how we're fixed at the Manor, Ted. I've little money to spare after fixing the roof.'

'Can't be a keeper without a cottage,' insisted Ted and walked away laughing.

Will came back to him two days later. 'I've been looking over the old gatekeeper's lodge. The walls are still sound and there's plenty of good timber left in the roof. Wouldn't take us more than a few days to set it to rights and then we could get the thatcher and glazier in. You could whitewash the walls yourself and after that, you'd have your cottage. Mind, I can't pay you any money wages till times are better, but there are four rooms in that cottage and a big garden. Why, it's more than twice the size of what you've got here. I'd let you shoot enough rabbits for the pot – and a few extra to sell. Later, when things settle down, we'll talk about money wages.'

'Hev to think about that,' said Ted, hiding his exultation at the prospect of such lavish accommodation.

Will ground his teeth in exasperation. He was afire to set things to rights and the slightest delay made him angry. 'Just tell me whether you'll do it or not.'

'What about our Joe?'

'I was coming to that. There are some ruined cottages on the other side of the woods. You could get enough stuff from the others to make at least one of them good.

And I'd let Joe take up a bit of land round it and shoot for the pot same as you.'

Ted nodded and spat on the ground to emphasise his approval. 'Aye, Squire, I'll do it! My Poll will be fair set up about that, she will. Been goin' on at me lately, she has, about our cottage here bein' too small and...'

'What did you call me?'

'Squire.'

'I'm no Squire!'

'You're a Bedham now,' Ted pointed out, not without a certain malicious satisfaction. 'And Bedhams is allus Squires round here.'

'Don't be ridiculous, man!' And Will left hurriedly, before Ted could say that word again, stopping a few yards away to toss over his shoulder, 'You and Poll can meet me at the cottage at noon!'

Ted stood and watched him leave, chuckling to himself at the effect his words had had. 'You ain't got no choice about it, Will, my lad,' he said aloud, 'No choice at all! You're the Squire now, whether you like it or not.'

Then his wife called out to ask him with heavy sarcasm how much longer he intended to stand out there talking to himself like an idiot at a fair, and her with no firewood in the house, so he hurried off to acquaint her with their coming rise in the world. Poll was always a mite touchy when she was near her time, and stronger men than Ted Haplin had quailed before her anger, but this news turned her sweet as a young dove in spring.

–

When Sarah told Will that she thought she was with child, she saw tears rise in his eyes. 'Are you... pleased?' she asked.

For answer, he hugged her close and buried his face in her soft hair. 'Nothing could please me more, nothing!' he said when he'd recovered from his unmanly weakness. 'You've given me everything a man could desire.'

She had completely stopped trying to flout Will's orders that she was to do no heavy work, because she was afraid of doing anything to harm the child. She felt well enough, apart from a slight queasiness in the mornings, which usually wore off by ten o'clock and which Jessie said was only to be expected, but she had to admit to herself that she was somewhat anxious about what lay before her. Twenty-nine was old to be having one's first child, very old indeed to be facing such a dangerous experience. She knew as well as anyone the risks women ran every time they gave birth.

So when Will suggested casually one day that it might be as well to consult Dr Shadderby, because they didn't want to take any chances, she agreed without the protests he had expected. Will was no fool. 'Worried?' he asked.

'A little,' she admitted. 'At my age...' She shrugged and left the sentence unfinished, but he took her meaning at once.

'If you were a cow, I should have no worries.'

She gaped at him. 'Sh-shouldn't you?'

'No, none at all. You're built nice and broad. It's the narrow ones who usually have the trouble. I'd never buy a cow that's narrow-built. I shouldn't think women are all that different when it comes to calv... er... giving birth.'

She burst out laughing. 'Then 'tis a pity I'm not a cow!' But his words gave her comfort nonetheless. And the doctor also made her feel more confident, for he gave her an examination, then said the same thing, though he couched it in much more delicate terms.

Since Sarah had never had anything to do with babies and pregnancy, it was to Mistress Pursley that she turned for information and advice. Together the two women calculated the probable arrival date of the baby. Unasked, Jessie brought out the remains of Will's baby clothes, which would serve as patterns for new ones, if nothing else. She also explained, with a countrywoman's frankness, exactly what to expect, and advised Sarah to go and watch some of the farm animals giving birth if she wanted to see what it was all about.

The best midwife in the village was Mistress Bell and Jessie advised Sarah not to waste more good money on a doctor, but to trust herself to one who knew first-hand what it was like to give birth.

'Men don't know about birthing!' she scoffed. 'How can they?'

But Will disagreed with this and commanded every member of the household, on pain of instant dismissal, to send for him the instant anything started. He would then ride over to fetch the doctor himself. Yes, he could see that they thought it funny that he was worrying about that now, when it was all months away, but he wanted it made plain from the start and let them just remember his commands when the time came.

'Yes, Squire,' said Mary, winking at Hannah. They all knew how embarrassed he was by this title.

He made an inarticulate noise and stamped out, leaving even serious-minded Hannah chuckling.

–

The villagers might be starting to accept Will's new status, but Edward Sewell naturally shared his father's hostility to the Bedhams. He was a weasel-faced young man of twenty-five or so, with narrow shoulders and scrawny legs. In spite of his father's mockery, he tried hard to figure as a gentleman of taste and refinement, but unfortunately, his tendency to overdress only emphasised his personal defects, and he could never understand why he did not get the respect he felt he deserved. In truth, he fitted neither into his father's business life, nor into the life of a country gentleman, and so spent most of his time with his mother, who doted on him, or his tailor, who loved his open-handedness and offered him unlimited flattery in exchange.

One day, Edward encountered Sarah and Will on foot as he was riding through the village and, on an impulse which he was later to regret, deliberately rode through a muddy puddle near the pump and splashed them from head to foot.

In the old days, Will would have dared do nothing to avenge this deliberate insult, but this treatment of his wife made him see red. He wasn't going to let a puke-stockings like Edward Sewell treat Sarah like that, especially in her condition! He ran forward and seized the horse's reins.

'Get down off that horse at once and apologise to my wife!'

'How dare you, fellow! Take your hands off my reins this minute!'

Will planted his feet firmly. 'You're going no further until you've apologised, and if you ever do such a thing as that again, you'll feel a taste of my whip about your shoulders!'

Edward, as lacking in courage as he was in inches, took fright at the expression on Will's face and slashed at him with his riding crop. Will tore it out of his hand and sent it whistling across the village green. 'Let's see how brave you are without a whip and a horse to use it from!' he roared.

Faces began to appear at the windows and peer round corners. Sarah, watching aghast, saw Will seize the blustering young man by his embroidered coat sleeve and drag him down from his horse.

'Apologise!'

Even greater than his present fear of Will Pursley was Edward's fear of what his father would do to him if he publicly apologised to a Bedham.

'No!' It was a squeak of despair, rather than a defiance.

The next moment Edward Sewell found himself being frog-marched across the village green, yelping and flailing ineffectually at his captor. His yelps grew shriller as he realised that their destination was the big stone trough of water outside the smithy, then they cut off abruptly as he was thrust into the greenish liquid that filled it and pushed right down.

Will didn't wait for Edward to surface, spluttering and yelping, but marched back across the village green to slap the horse on its fat rump and send it galloping home to its stables.

Those villagers who were fortunate enough to witness the incident laughed about it for years, and took great glee in telling and retelling the tale of this exquisitely humorous occurrence to those who had missed it. All were agreed that 'It served'n right' and that 'twere best not to get on the wrong side of that Will Bedham.'

'Proper Squire he's turnin' into,' they added with a grin. 'Us'll hev to watch what us do, eh, or us might end up in that old horse trough too.' And they'd roar with laughter again.

Matthew Sewell went off into a near apoplexy when his shivering, dripping son squelched up the drive and spilled out his tale of woe. His face turned such a dark red that his wife froze in her seat. She had seen her own father die of a seizure and wouldn't be unhappy if her husband followed suit. But she didn't dare hope for this. Men like Matthew always seemed to escape scot-free from the consequences of their wrongdoing.

She worried constantly about whether she, too, would roast in hell, for Matthew had forced her to use her artistic skill to forge signatures on false debts on several occasions, and guilt for that lay heavy on her conscience. As the tirade continued, she clasped her hands together tightly to prevent them trembling.

'You palsied maw-worm!' Sewell roared at his son. 'Can you do no better than splash the fellow with mud? And have you no more wit than to do it in front of witnesses? Next time, take a carriage and drive them down – but do it somewhere quiet, where there is no one to see!'

'But Father, I... Pursley put me in the horse trough. Absolutely *ruined* my new coat! Aren't you going to do anything about it?'

'What can I do, you snivelling turd? You started it... you finish it! I'm not going to enter into litigation I haven't a chance of winning. Think Tarnly would judge in favour of us, if we took Pursley to court for this? Eh? Do you?'

Several pokes with a bony forefinger emphasised this point and left livid bruises on Edward's thin chest.

'Well, I'll tell you the answer to that, since you haven't the wit you were born with,' Sewell sneered. 'Tarnly wouldn't. So leave the men's work to me and stay with your mother. She can wipe you wet arse for you! I have better things to do.'

Edward shuddered and looked across at her. She had her head bent over her embroidery as usual when his father was ranting on.

'And stay out of the village for a week or two!'

Hugh, who had just come in, eyed his master's son curiously.

Sewell ground his teeth, but they would find out one way or another. 'Pursley tossed him in the horse trough.'

Hugh, a man of few words and only one loyalty, threw his master a puzzled look.

'Don't worry! We'll make Pursley pay for that later. If we did anything now, they'd connect it to us, thanks to Master Piss-Breeches, here. So pay off those men you hired and tell them to come back in a week or two.'

'Yes, Squire.'

'And you, you jelly-brained fool, get out of my sight! How I sired a half-wit like you, I'll never know! Or a gawking lump like your sister who can't attract a decent husband! There must be bad blood on your mother's side.' The sight of his cowering son so angered him that he picked up an ornament and threw it at Edward, narrowly missing his head.

Edward ran out of the room like a startled rabbit and took refuge in his bedroom.

His mother stayed where she was, head bent, praying her husband wouldn't turn on her now. And this time, at least, her prayers were answered.

–

Lord Tarnly laughed so much at the tale of Edward Sewell's ducking that he burst a button off his waistcoat.

Passing Mr Sewell senior in the street in Sawbury one day, he chuckled quite audibly and the words, 'horse-trough, egad!' floated back to further stoke that gentleman's ire.

His lordship took great pleasure in repeating the tale on several further occasions during the next week or two to divers gentlemen friends over a glass of port. 'Dumped him in the horse trough, damme! They say he was as covered in green weed as a water meadow. And since Bedham had sent Sewell's horse galloping back to its stables, the fellow had to squelch all the way home! Damme, but I wish I'd been there to see it!'

So pleased was he with Will's hasty act that Lord Tarnly insisted his wife invite the young couple over to dine with them. 'Better show people we approve of the fellow. Not a gentleman, but a man after my own heart, damme, right after my own heart. And besides, her mother *was* my god-daughter. You won't forget to invite them, will you, my dear?'

'No, Henry, I won't forget.'

He suddenly guffawed. 'Perhaps we should buy another water trough for Sawbury. It might deter the Sewells from comin' into town, eh?' He nearly choked at the brilliance of this witticism, but his wife was growing rather tired of references to water troughs and did not so much as blink at it, so he eventually subsided.

—

When the summons came to dine at Tarnly Hall, Will was fetched in from the fields and a conference hastily held.

'We'll have to go,' said Sarah. 'We can't refuse.'

'Dine with Lord and Lady Tarnly! Me!' Will was horrorstruck. 'I wouldn't know what to say or do with grand folk like that!'

'You managed well enough when they came to our wedding.'

'But—'

'We'll *have* to go! It's an honour to be invited. We have no choice in the matter.'

Will advanced a great many arguments as to why he could not go. He had no clothes fine enough for such a visit and they'd no money to buy new ones. He wouldn't know what to talk about and would surely make a fool of himself, and that'd do no one any good, would it? He couldn't leave the stock. It was her they wanted to see, anyway. Why couldn't she go on her own?

Sarah was adamant, though she had hard work persuading him firstly that he'd have to go, and secondly, that he would definitely need to buy himself a good suit of gentleman's clothes for the occasion. In the end, after consulting parson, he agreed to submit himself to this dual ordeal, and they drove into Sawbury together. But he had his sticking point and nothing she or the tailor said could persuade him either to purchase a wig or to cover his hair in flour! Some things a man could stomach, declared Will, folding his arms, and others he couldn't. To walk around with flour all over your head was just plain silly, and he'd never do it. It was nearly as bad as shaving off your own hair and borrowing some from a horse!

In the event, the visit to Tarnly Hall went off better than anyone had expected. Her ladyship had very wisely invited only a few guests, and those carefully picked for their interest in agriculture. Will, primed by Mr Rogers not to try to appear anything he wasn't, let the others do most of the talking and listened attentively, which offended no one. However, he did contribute one or two shrewd remarks about stock-breeding, which won him the accolade of being a sensible man and a forward-thinking farmer.

He also displayed perfect table manners, thanks to Sarah's tuition, far better than those of his host, and since he was a rather good-looking fellow when properly dressed, if a trifle serious, that was enough to win the ladies' approval too. Moreover, he didn't drink to excess, a thing Lady Tarnly deplored in everyone but her husband.

'Fellow shows a deal of sense,' said his lordship afterwards. (Will had agreed with everything his host said about the political scene, being too unsure of the finer points to have any opinions of his own.) 'We'll invite 'em over from time to time from now on, eh?'

'Certainly, my dear. The experience will do Mr Bedham good. He lacks somewhat in style and polish, but he cannot do better than to model himself upon you.'

'And maybe I will buy that horse trough. What?' He choked with laughter again.

She rolled her eyes at the ceiling and discovered pressing business elsewhere.

After a week of seclusion, during which his mother's tender care narrowly averted a cold settling upon his chest, Edward Sewell left the district, ostensibly to deal with some business affairs in Bristol for his father.

Gone off to hide till the gossip died down, said the uncharitable.

A week after that, Sam Poulter passed on the information to Will that Izzy had got drunk the previous night in The Golden Fleece and let slip the information that his master had had a few bits of bad luck, businesswise, and would have to spend more time away from home himself in the near future, tending to the concerns which had gained him his fortune in the first place.

Good riddance, said Will, and the sentiment was echoed by most of the people in the village, who found life a lot easier without Sewell popping up to shout abuse at them if they so much as looked up from their work for a minute or two.

Smiling at his own cunning, Sewell made sure as many people as possible saw him driving off in his fine new carriage, but left his wife at home. She had dared refuse to forge a new bill of debt for him, and none of his threatening had persuaded her. She was even talking of confessing her sins to that doddering old fool of a Parson. Well, he'd soon put paid to that. She'd not dare tell the tale to her own shadow now, or it's be the last tale she ever told.

And he'd meant that. Better no wife at all than one who betrayed you.

The peace in Broadhurst didn't last beyond the autumn.

Every alternate Saturday saw Jessie setting off for Sawbury market in the cart, sometimes accompanied by her son, sometimes by one of the Haplin boys. One week, however, they were fired upon by an unknown assailant on their way back and the shot narrowly missed Will, who was driving.

Since he didn't wish Sarah to worry, he made light of the incident. It was probably someone out shooting in the woods, someone who hadn't taken care where he was aiming and who was afraid to admit his fault.

'Who would that be?' demanded Jessie. 'We know everyone round here. None of them'd be out shooting at people.'

'Well, perhaps it was a highwayman, then.'

'A likely tale! A highwayman would find such poor pickings round here, he'd starve to death, and well you know it, our Will. No, there's only one person in Broadhurst as hates you.'

'It couldn't be him. Sewell's been in Bristol for the last few weeks, and his two bullies with him. Now, don't you go worrying Sarah with this, mother. I'll keep a better watch out in future, I promise you.'

But Jessie couldn't help mentioning the incident and Sarah didn't take the matter lightly, either. 'Highwaymen don't haunt the roads round Sawbury,' she said, gazing in terror at Will. What would she do if anything happened to him? She didn't want to raise a child who didn't know its father. She'd hardly known her own and had felt the lack of that many a time, and not just because of their shortage of money.

'Then perhaps my first guess was right and it was an accident,' Will said.

'Accident! You don't believe that any more than I do. Sewell might be away from home, but he could have hired someone else to do it for him, couldn't he? In fact, he's more likely to have hired someone else, because he never does the worst things himself.' She clutched his arm with one hand, the other resting on her swelling belly. 'He hates us, Will. He'd stop at nothing to get our land. Please take care.'

But another week or two passed and nothing happened, so Sarah had to admit that perhaps her fears were groundless.

–

Robin Cox was a happy man again. He and his family were put into the home farm when the Pursleys moved out, though its management remained in Will's hands. Bessie Cox wept with joy the day they moved in and Robin wasn't far from tears either. Since being turned out of his cottage at Hay Nook Farm when his master was dispossessed, Robin had had to eke out a living in a series of casual day-labouring jobs. The other farm workers had got positions out of the district and moved away, but Robin had a stubborn streak and refused point-blank to leave Broadhurst. It was *his* village! He'd been born there and by dang, he'd die there, too!

He, his wife and his six children had gone to live in a one-room, tumble-down cottage belonging to the Old Squire, which was the only place available in the village. There, two of the children had died from one thing or another, and his Bessie had grown so thin and listless he'd thought to lose her too. All he'd clung to was the determination that Sewell wasn't going to drive him away from Broadhurst, not if he had to watch all his family die, no, and not even if he followed them into the churchyard and had to come back to haunt their tormentor.

Now, Robin had a regular job again and a house that was a palace, even compared to their old cottage. Mistress Pursley had left them a lot of fine furniture to help fill all those rooms and no king could have been happier than they were. Moreover, there was occasional work for Bessie in the dairy, like in the old days, or helping with the rough work in the big house, and there was regular employment for his eldest boy, Johnny, a sturdy lad of ten, quite big enough now to bring in a shilling or two.

'I'm grateful to you for all you've done for us, Squire,' he said gruffly one day, determined to voice his gratitude.

'What did you call me?' demanded Will, stiffening.

'Squire,' repeated Robin, a man of few words.

'I'm not the Squire!'

'That you are!' retorted Robin, who could be just as stubborn as Will. 'Bedhams hev allus been Squires in this village. You be a Bedham now, only male there is, an' you live at the Manor. So it stands to reason you be the Squire. Everyone says so. Well, them as dares.'

'Don't be stupid, man!'

'I ent stupid!' And nothing would stop Robin from addressing Will as Squire and talking about him in the same way. Because of this, he twice he got into fights with Sewell's employees, who also drank at The Golden Fleece, for lack of anywhere else, but kept their distance from Bedham employees.

Robin remained quite unrepentant about it, even to the point of boasting to his wife about the good thump he had given that Eb Mendle. Why, that blow alone was well worth a torn shirt and a black eye, and he wasn't going to change his ways for her or for anyone. He'd tell the truth and shame the devil.

'But Mr Sewell will find a way to get back at you, because Eb's one of his men,' she pleaded. 'Couldn't you just… be a bit quieter about it all, Robin lovie?'

'No, I couldn't.' Just let Sewell try anything, he thought. There were a few men ready to side openly with the Bedhams now, even if the womenfolk were a bit nervous about it all. In fact, it was a great pity Sewell had stayed in Bristol so long, it was that. Time he got his come-uppance. More than time.

Chapter 14

By November, the days had closed in and frost was beginning to glisten on the leaves of the evergreens, crackling underfoot on the edges of puddles in the mornings. Sarah had stopped feeling sickly, but this had been replaced by a tendency to drowsiness, of which she was secretly ashamed.

The other women in the house, who had all been through this, smiled sympathetically and reminisced about the vagaries of their own pregnancies. Even Mary learned to tiptoe into rooms instead of clattering in on a trail of words, for you never knew when you'd find the mistress taking a nap somewhere.

Although Sewell returned to take up residence again at the Hall, less was seen of him around the village than usual, and even his two bully-boys seemed quieter and less aggressive. The rumour spread, though no one quite knew whence it came, that Sewell had suffered financial reverses of considerable magnitude and needed to live quietly for a while.

'That'n could no more live quietly than a blackbird can stop calling in the spring,' Thad said to Will one day. 'Nor he won't have forgotten his quarrel with you.'

'I agree. Let me know if you hear of anything going on.'

'I will, Squire.'

'Not you too!'

Thad shrugged and grinned. 'Well, I ent callin' that'n Squire. An' you be a Bedham now.'

Will didn't waste his breath arguing, but changed the subject. 'I came here to discuss that seed drill you're making for me. I think…' And the two were lost for over an hour in their favourite pastime.

Then several disasters hit the village in quick succession, which quite took the heart out of the Christmas festivities. Sarah, wrapped in her drowsy cocoon of personal happiness, noticed them less than anyone else, but even she was beginning to realise that something was wrong, and badly wrong, in Broadhurst.

'Is it that man again?' she asked Hannah, for no one else would discuss it with her.

'So most folk believe.'

'I had hoped…' Sarah let the words trail away.

'Can the Ethiopian change his skin, or the leopard his spots?' quoted Hannah.

'What can we do?'

'You can do nothing, mistress.' Hannah nodded towards the swelling belly. 'Your business is to have a healthy child, so leave the worrying to the menfolk.'

But Sarah couldn't do that. Worries began to creep into her mind, and she couldn't forget that someone had shot at Will on the way to market. It hadn't happened again, so maybe it had been an accident – but maybe it hadn't.

The first disaster wasn't recognised as anything other than bad luck. One of the village hayricks caught fire and burned to the ground, causing a shortage of valuable feed. The men worked quickly to stop the fire spreading and managed to save the other stacks. No one thought it more than an unlucky chance.

Until the second incident.

One evening Mistress Bell heard a noise and went into the shop to find two men throwing flour across the floor, then adding her chunks of sugar and trampling them underfoot. They only laughed when she screeched at them to stop, then continued to destroy her goods and livelihood methodically.

Without thinking she rushed across the room to stop them. One of them grabbed her, pushing her to the other, who pushed her back again with a laugh. The first one then began to feel her breasts and though she tried to beat him off her, he was much bigger and stronger and she could do nothing.

'Been a long time,' he said to the other with a grin and lifted her skirts.

Her screaming brought her children running and the other man brandished a knife at them. 'Keep back, or I'll slit your throats. Stay there, you!'

The first man made short work of raping her, clouting her hard across the side of the head when she tried to scratch his face. He got up afterwards to button his breeches and grin at his friend. 'Want a turn?'

'I would but one of them children's just run off. Better get going before someone comes. We've done the job now, anyway.'

The neighbour was already at the door, but the man with the knife threatened him and he backed away. The two strangers then ran across the green and shortly afterwards came the sound of horses galloping away.

The neighbour's wife went in to see what was wrong and found Mistress Bell, huddled in a tight ball on the floor, her clothes in disarray, sobbing in a whimpering, desolate way that tore at your heart strings, 'deed it did.

Everyone was shocked to the core. Such a thing had never been heard of before in their little community.

The men were never caught or even seen in the district again, but people locked their doors carefully at night from then onwards.

The younger Bell children had nightmares for a long time, and the slightest sound after dark would make them freeze in their places and send the colour from their cheeks. Mistress Bell became a ghost of her old self, too, paler, thinner and jumping at sudden noises.

Even young Ned lost his cheerful grin and took on a grim look, his expression too old and wary for a lad of his age. He began to do some investigating on his own account. Thad had always considered Ned Bell a very smart lad. Now he proved himself to be much smarter than Sewell and his men realised, for they continued to discuss their plans and options without checking the stables for eavesdroppers.

Ned took his findings to Thad, who rewarded him by allowing him to join a small determined group, formed mostly of Waste dwellers, whose existence was unknown to most of the other villagers.

'We intend to keep an eye on Sewell and his henchmen,' Thad explained.

'I can help,' Ned said eagerly, 'find things out.'

Thad set his huge lumpy hands on the lad's narrow shoulders. 'You have to be careful about this – more careful than you've ever been in your life before. If they catch you spying, they might kill you – and what would your mother do then?'

Ned's mouth fell open.

'What's more,' Thad went on, driving his point home remorselessly, 'If they did catch you, they'd know we was after them. So that's another reason for you to be careful.' He shook the lad, gently and repeated, 'Don't… take… *any*… risks.'

'I won't, Thad.'

'In fact, don't do anything without asking me first.'

'No, Thad. But we are going to stop them, aren't we?'

'Oh, yes. And you can be part of it if you follow orders.'

Ned went home, saying nothing to his mother, but his heart swelled with pride that an important person like Thad Honeyfield should trust him like this.

When he grew up, he wanted to be just like Thad.

–

Sewell demonstrated great indignation after the attack on Nancy Bell. He stopped Sam Poulter one day on the green to harangue him about doing his duty as village constable, and he even approached Will publicly after church one Sunday.

'I know we've had our differences, Pursley, but we must unite against this lawlessness that has crept into the district.'

'We definitely need to drive it out again,' Will agreed in an expressionless tone.

'And if there's ever anything I can do to help in that, I'm ready to set aside my personal feelings for the common good.'

'Yes.' But Will ignored the outstretched hand and whisked his wife away before Sewell could summon his own wife to join them.

'What did he mean by that?' Sarah whispered as they walked away.

'He's trying to fool folk about who's behind it all. Ha! As if we don't know what he's trying to do, which is terrorise folk till they daren't say him nay.' Will sat and fumed all the way to the edge of their land, then got off the trap abruptly at the new gatehouse. 'I need to have a word with Ted. I won't be long. You can drive back, can't you?'

'Of course I can. The baby doesn't make me incapable of doing normal tasks.' But she was talking to herself. He had already moved away, a frown on his face.

His needing to talk to Ted so soon after the encounter with Sewell only added to her worries.

Since everyone in the village had overheard what Sewell said, it was discussed in every cottage and most of all at the inn for the next few days. Some said the man had shown a few proper feelings, for once. Others scoffed at them for being credulous. Foxes didn't turn into kittens overnight, did they? No more could Sewell turn into an honest citizen!

He hadn't offered any help to Nancy Bell, had he? Not like Squire had. Bought her some new stock, Squire had, and fitted strong new bolts to her doors with his own hands.

As for the small group of secret observers, they kept their thoughts to themselves, but not one of them doubted that Sewell was behind the troubles. It was just a question of how best they could catch him out.

Thad was the next to suffer, less than a week after he had refused point-blank to obey a command to address Sewell as Squire.

'You'll be glad to change your mind one day,' said Sewell, swishing his riding crop viciously through the air.

'That I won't! Bedhams are Squires round here, and allus will be.'

'Bedhams! There are no Bedhams any more.'

'Lawyers don't seem to think so, nor Lord Tarnly, neither. An' if that Hugh of yours takes one step inside my smithy, he'll find himself sitting in the horse trough.' Thad flexed his muscles and Hugh stepped back hastily.

'I ent afeared of him,' Thad went on, speaking in an over-amiable tone of voice, 'Nor of that other one as is tryin' to sneak round the side of me, neither.' He raised his voice to shout, 'Michael! Here, boy!'

His eldest son, a budding young giant of fourteen, came out of the smithy carrying a hammer. 'Yes, Dad?'

'Just see to it that Izzy don't come too close to the smithy, will 'ee, boy? Even when he brings horses to be shod, he's to stay outside.'

'Yes, Dad.' Michael hefted his hammer in his hand, his eyes sparkling with anticipation. 'Can I hit him if he comes too near, Dad? Can I?'

'Yes. But see you hit him hard, so he don't try to clout you back.'

Michael hefted the hammer again and looked hungrily at Izzy, who began to edge away.

Sewell signalled to his men to remount. 'That's the last of my business you'll see!' he growled.

But it was Thad who had the last word. 'Ent seen much of your business, anyway. You let that clumperton over in Sawbury do most of your smithing work. Thass why that mare of yours be limping – an' it'll only get worse. Too tight fitted, that back shoe is.'

–

Less than a week later the smithy caught fire one night. Fortunately, Thad's dog woke everyone by howling loudly. As soon as he smelled the smoke, Thad raced downstairs to find out what was going on and what he saw made him bellow, 'Fire! Fire!'

This brought the other villagers rushing to help.

A chain of them filled buckets at the duck pond, while Thad and his son raked away the burning thatch so that fire couldn't spread to the house. The flames were soon under control, but not before Thad had suffered some loss and damage, not only to the smithy but to the part of the cottage which abutted it.

When the fire was out, Thad stood looking at his half-ruined smithy. 'That were no accident,' he said to the friends who stood around him, his fists clenching and unclenching. 'I ent a careless man, an' I tell 'ee that it were *no* accident!'

'Makes you wonder about that there rick, don't it?' said his neighbour, wiping the sweat off his smutty forehead.

'Ah. It do indeed.'

Another of the cottagers had slouched over to join them. 'We'd all best be more careful from now on, I reckon.'

'Very careful,' agreed Thad. 'An' since the Lord helps those who help themselves, we'd best make shift to take action ourselves. We can't delay too long if this sort of thing is going to happen. Eh, that Sewell hev got me fair roiled up now, an' I don't roil up easy.'

'Thad!'

He turned to look at his wife, Meg, whose face was grimy with smoke, through which paler lines showed the tracks of her tears. 'What if she'd got hurt, or dealt with like poor Nancy?' he said softly to the man next to him. 'Or what if it'd been one of the childer hurt. It don't bear thinkin' of!'

Meg came up to him and put her hand in his. 'If the fire's all out, Thad love, we might as well get some sleep.'

'You get some sleep, my dear. I'll just stay up an' keep watch tonight, case there's any embers still alight.'

She swung round to face him. 'Thad, you won't do anything – well, silly, will you?'

'No. I won't do nothin' silly. I won't do nothin' tonight 'cept keep a watch on the house, I promise. You get yourself off to bed, now.'

Nate Pinkly, who worked for Sewell, came over to join them and Thad whispered 'Shhh!' to his wife as he turned to greet Nate.

'Thass a bad business, Thad,' Nate muttered.

'Ah. We'll all have to be more careful next time, won't we?'

Thad pushed his wife towards the house, and she went with a reluctant glance over her shoulder. Nate wasn't popular in the village, for he had been one of the first to work for Sewell and to call him 'Squire'.

'Thanks for your help,' Thad added, for Nate had at least formed one of the chain passing buckets from the duck pond. Well, there'd have been trouble for any villager who didn't play their part in trying to avert such disasters.

'Least I could do. But how'd it all start?'

Thad studied Nate's face. Either the man was a better liar than anyone had ever suspected, or he wasn't involved in this. 'Musta been a spark.' Thad's face was as guileless as a child's. 'Happens sometimes, don't it?'

'Ah. An' you hev to leave that fire o' yours banked up of a night, don't you? Can't be too careful wi' fires. Good thing the cottage roof didn't go up, eh? Thatch burns quick.' Nate yawned hugely. 'Well, I'd better get some sleep. Sewell d'keep a body on the hop all day long.'

Thad nodded and waited till Nate was out of earshot. 'I'll draw a jug of my new cider come evening and we'll hold a little meeting in my house,' Thad said, his voice a quiet rumble that carried only to his friends' ears. 'Don't let anyone see you comin' here. We don't want word gettin' back to Sewell that we're meetin' secretly, do we?'

They nodded and melted away into the darkness. Only when he was alone with the half-ruined smithy did Thad allow his emotions to show on his face. His eyes suspiciously bright, he stared at the charred tool handles and the collapsed wall.

'They won't stop me! Nor I won't never call him Squire,' he muttered. 'An' I'll make 'em regret this one day, or my name's not Thad Honeyfield.'

Unlike most of the villagers, he had some savings, though he bitterly resented having to dip into them. When Sewell rode through the village the next day, unable to resist the opportunity to gloat, Thad ignored his remarks completely, simply turning his back and continuing to work on rebuilding the wall.

Michael, labouring next to his father, didn't turn away. He stood and stared back at the trio of men on horseback. He knew who held a grudge against his father.

A few of the other men in the village drifted over to stand near the smithy, their hostility as plain as Michael's. In the end, Sewell rode off with his men, laughing loudly.

–

Within the month, everything in the smithy was fully operative again, and only a few scorch marks were left to bear witness to the fire. The two seed-drills on which Thad had been working for Will were completely ruined, but there was still time enough to build others before sowing came round. Will not only provided more wood for this, but also lent a hand himself to put the new ones together.

'You watch out for yourself, Thad,' he warned.

'Ah. There's a few of us keepin' our eyes open here now at nights, takin' it in turns, like. You'd better see you do the same up at the Manor, Squire. Need a bit o' proof, though, afore we can stop'n properly, don't we?'

'Yes. But I can't see him giving it us, can you?'

'Mebbe not. But we might persuade him to show his hand if we set about it right.'

'Don't leave me out of this.'

'Ah.'

'I mean it.'

'Well, we ent ready to act yet, so you tend to your business an' leave us to see what we can work out.'

–

After that, people eyed the few strangers who passed through the village warily. Men who had never even had locks on their doors bought themselves stout bolts or made wooden drop bars, and began to keep a careful watch on their homes. It were all dangy peculiar, and they misliked it. Their fathers hadn't had to have bolts on the doors, had they? And they shouldn't have to, neither! Their anger, slow to fuel, began to smoulder hotly beneath their stolid exteriors.

Will was particularly vigilant out at Broadhurst, even going so far as to patrol the grounds occasionally at night, and the Haplins certainly didn't skimp their new duties. But they found nothing at all suspicious at the Manor. The latest rash of incidents seemed to be confined to the village.

Then Sewell also suffered, to everyone's amazement. It seemed someone had tried to break into his stables one night, and had damaged the lock. Fortunately one of the grooms had disturbed the thief and he'd run off.

This incident made some of the less astute villagers wonder if their suspicions had been correct, but it left others unmoved.

Thad's lip curled scornfully when Nate eagerly poured out the tale of the supposed break-in one evening in The Golden Fleece.

'Much damage done, then?' Thad asked.

'Well, no.'

'Didn't think there would be.'

'Well, coachman sleeps over the stables an' he heard a noise. Him an' the groom chased 'em away,' Nate confided.

'Ah. So nothin' was touched?'

'Well, the lock was broke. Saw it myself, I did. Tore off the door frame, it was. Must've been horse thieves or gipsies, they reckon.'

'Must it?' Thad's expression was bland.

'Well, who else would break into the stables?'

'Who else, indeed?'

But there had been no sign of gipsies in the district, and if there were any horse thieves, they'd go after Lord Tarnly's prime stock, not the heavy-footed brutes Sewell favoured simply because they were showy.

As village constable, Sam Poulter got another haranguing from Sewell as a result of this, which made him very resentful, for what did they expect one man to do on his own? He couldn't patrol the village every night, could he, as well as do his own work by day?

'You find yourselves another constable,' he yelled at the village elders when they too complained. 'I've had enough of the job, for 'tis a hard one, that it is, bein' called out at night and who knows what besides! I've done my best and if it ent good enough, you elect someone else and be done with it. If you can find'n.'

It took quite a while and several pots of cider, before the elders were able soothe Sam down again. This they did very zealously, because being constable was a thankless task at the best of times and no one else wanted the job, thank you very much! However, it was decided that Bart Potter should be elected as assistant constable, in case there was more trouble than one man could handle.

Sam, secretly delighted to have an assistant to order round, for it was Prue who ran things at The Golden Fleece, condescended to give the job another try.

Thad watched these ineffectual preparations with a curl of his lips, but kept his own counsel. Bart Potter and Sam Poulter were no match for young Ned Bell in cunning, let alone Sewell.

Perhaps as a result of the increased vigilance, an attempt to break into The Golden Fleece one night, after its occupants were all in bed, was easily foiled by Prue Poulter, who was a light sleeper. Her shrieks were loud enough to wake everyone in the group of houses bordering the green, and two men were spotted and chased.

Unfortunately, the villains had horses tethered on the other side of the duck pond and they managed to reach these and make their escape. The villagers' dogs, who should have warned of the approach of strangers, were found to be drugged and one of them, noted for his hearty appetite, never woke from that sleep. But how could a stranger have got close enough to the animals to drug them in the first place? It had to be someone they were used to.

Nate went around looking uneasy and began to get some funny sideways looks from his neighbours.

Sewell made a great play of sending his daughter to stay with friends in Bristol for safety, and this caused nothing but scorn. Afeard of broken locks, was she? Well, that young madam wouldn't be missed. Too grand to walk into Broadhurst, she was, let alone stop and pass the time of day with anyone. No wonder she couldn't find herself a husband, for all her father's money! She had a face that'd sour milk in winter.

Without telling anyone, Mr Rogers took the unprecedented step of going into Sawbury and calling on Lord Tarnly to lay the matter before him.

Two days later, in his role as Justice of the Peace, Lord Tarnly came over to Broadhurst and asked a lot of questions which got him precisely nowhere. What could you say or do when you didn't even know who your adversary was? Or at least, when you had no proof. Thad and his friends kept their suspicions to themselves and played dumb.

'They gentry allus stick together,' said Bob Wraggins afterwards. 'No use expectin' one of them to go after another.'

'Besides,' added Thad, puffing slowly on his clay pipe, 'we got no proof. *Yet.*' He spat into the fire for emphasis. 'Best we wait our time, eh, lads?'

'Ah.'

Lord Tarnly called at the Manor while he was over that way, and was very gallant to Sarah, complimenting her on her coming addition to the family and promising to hurry over at once with his militia if there was any further trouble. They had only to send for him.

Hannah had the last word on that, as she took her anger out on the dough she was kneading. 'It takes an hour to get over to Sawbury, unless you have a horse, which most people ent got, and another hour to get them militia of his lordship's together, *plus* an hour again for them to march here! What help could they give us! You tell me that. I'll put my faith in the Lord with a little help from our dogs, thank you very much! Hetty's taught 'em not to eat from anything but their own bowls now, so no one's going to feed them any poison.'

After that, a proper watch was organised by the villagers. Sewell, still pretending to be a fellow victim, volunteered the services of his men, and the villagers dared not refuse them. But Hugh and Izzy were treated with extreme caution, and always set to guard Marsh Bottom, because no one liked being alone at night with such rascals.

There was not the slightest piece of evidence that they were involved, but apart from that one minor incident supposed to have happened at Marsh Bottom, it was noticeable that all of the victims had been people who'd crossed or offended Sewell.

'Don't have to poke me in the eye to make me take notice of who gets hurt and who doesn't,' Thad said. 'He thinks we're stupid, but we ent, and so he'll find out.'

Chapter 15

One day in early January, Will heard a rumour that there were to be some new-style farm implements for sale, the sort he had read of in Mr Tull's book, at the monthly stock market in Sawbury.

'I can't resist going over to see them,' he told Sarah.

'It's a dreadful day. Is it really worth it?' She had woken up with a feeling of dread and she didn't want him going anywhere, but knew he wouldn't listen to such vague worries and would put them down to her condition.

'It is if I can get a good look at them. Thad and I are thinking of making things like that and selling them to other folk. There might be money to be made from it.'

'Well, you'd better take him with you, then, hadn't you?'

'He's busy here.' He stared at her. 'It's not like you to fuss so, Sarah.'

Tears welled in her eyes. 'I can't forget that someone shot at you once.'

He smiled, indulgent with a pregnant woman's fancies. 'That was months ago. If they'd done it on purpose and were serious about it, they'd have had another go at me before now.'

'Well, take Robin with you, then.'

'He has his own work to do. Do you think me such a weakling as to need a nurse-maid for such a short journey?'

'No-o-o, but—'

'It'd be different if I was going into Poole or further afield. I'd take someone with me then. But this is just Sawbury, a few miles away. What do you think will happen to me on a busy road? There'll be other people coming and going the whole way.'

She brightened at that thought.

In fact, he had underestimated the effects of the cold weather. A week of sleet and rain had left only the hardiest buyers with any desire to attend the market. There were fewer folk around than Will had ever seen, and those who'd made the effort to come left as soon as their purchases were completed or their wares sold.

And the rumour proved to be false; no new implements were to be seen and no one from Sawbury had heard tell of any. They seemed to think this was something to be pleased about, but Will was bitterly disappointed. He made the few purchases his womenfolk had asked for, then met a kindred spirit, interested in new farming methods, so stayed for a drink of mulled cider in the inn. The conversation was so interesting that he stayed for longer than he had intended.

Now he would have to travel home in the dark, and Sarah would be fretting and worrying till he got back. This wasn't good for a woman in her condition and he was annoyed with himself for being so selfish.

–

The day passed very slowly for Sarah. By mid-afternoon, it had grown damp and misty. Long before Will was due back, she began peering out of the window and pacing up and down in her little parlour, where a high-banked fire of logs kept the chill at bay.

As it grew dark, with still no sign of him, she became more and more anxious, for it was unlike Will to be this late. Twice she thought she heard a noise and rushed to open the front door, only to be met by a blast of icy air, for frost was now threatening after the milder damp weather of the past few days. She stood staring out at a wall of impenetrable darkness, but strain her ears as she might, she could hear no sound of hoof beats, no sound of movement at all, except for the thin whining of the wind. The people at the Manor might have been alone in the world.

When Mary came in to check the fire and bring fresh candles, she saw her mistress looking out of the window. 'Squire's late, ent he?' she said, ever a Job's comforter. 'He did say as he'd be back afore dark.'

'Yes. I feel a little worried, I must admit.'

'Ah. Bad time of year to be out after dark. An' the weather's turned frosty, too. Catch a chill, he will, staying out in this.'

Another hour went by and Jessie came to join Sarah, for she too had grown uneasy about her son. 'It isn't like Will to be this late,' she said, adding more fuel to Sarah's worries.

'What do you think can have happened to him? Has he ever been so late before?'

'Not often.'

The two women sat on together in silence, stealing surreptitious glances at the clock, each trying not to add to the other's worries.

After a while, Jessie got up to put some more wood on the fire and the noise she made raking out the ashes to get it to burn more brightly must have masked the approach of footsteps. Suddenly, there was a hammering on the front door and a loud hallooing that brought everyone in the house running to see what was wrong.

Jessie Pursley got to the door first and when she wrenched it open, the Haplins stumbled in, carrying Will's unconscious and bloody body between them. 'Dear Lord! Don't tell me he's dead!' she cried as they laid her son's body on the floor.

Sarah rushed over to kneel by his side with an anguished, '*Will!*' The figure lay motionless and she couldn't even tell whether he was breathing.

'He ent dead,' said Ted, 'but he's bleedin' like a stuck pig.'

'Lord ha' mercy!' quavered Mary. 'What happened to'n?'

'Let me see to him, Sarah!' Jessie commanded, pushing her daughter-in-law to one side. Like every farmer's wife, she'd had experience of tending the inevitable accidents. 'Do as I tell you!' she said sharply when Sarah didn't move. The chalky whiteness of Sarah's face made her afraid for her unborn grandchild as well as for her son, especially when Sarah looked wildly around, as if she could not recognise anyone.

'I must tend Will's wound,' repeated Jessie, 'And 'twill do him no good if you make yourself ill and lose the baby!'

Hannah stepped forward. 'She's right, mistress. Do you come and sit down over here on the settle. We'll see to the master for you.'

'No, I must...'

Because Sarah suddenly felt breathless and dizzy, she let the two women lead her to the settle.

Once she was seated, Hannah pushed her head down towards her knees. 'Don't try to talk for a minute, mistress, just take deep breaths,' she ordered, in a firm voice. 'You've had a shock. You must think of the child! Mary, go and fetch some of that brandy for the mistress! Quickly, now!'

Mary clattered off, ignoring Petey, who was whimpering with fright in a corner of the hall.

At Jessie's command, Ted and Joe moved Will so that he lay on the rug in front of the hall fire, then she bent over him to examine the wound. When she called for more light, Hetty ran to get a candle from the parlour and hold it over her master's body. The two Haplins moved back and left explanations until the blood that was still trickling from Will's shoulder had been stanched.

'Hot water!' ordered Jessie and Hannah went running.

'Fetch me some clean cloths, Hetty. One of those sheets that Mary washed yesterday will do!'

'Ted Haplin, hold this candle for me.'

Mary came back with a jug of brandy and a battered pewter tankard. Hannah took them from her trembling hands and told her to go and help Mistress Pursley.

'More candles,' ordered Jessie, holding her rolled-up apron against the wound.

Joe, seeing that everyone else was occupied, poked his head into the nearest room, from whence he fetched and lit some more candles.

'Build up that fire!'

Again, it was Joe who hurried to obey.

'Bullet's passed clean through him, the Lord be thanked,' said Jessie, after a while. 'Be you all right, Sarah girl?'

'Yes.' But Sarah's voice was faint.

Jessie spared a moment to look at her. Dear Lord, not that too, she thought. 'Lie down, my lovie!' she commanded. 'That's always the best thing to do if you've had a shock. Won't do Will no good if you lose his son for him.'

'Is he...'

'He's all right. Not going to die, but he's lost a lot of blood. Best if we sent for Doctor Shadderby. I've seen him sew people up so they're as good as new. I do b'lieve that's what our Will needs now. Ted Haplin!' Her voice was so sharp that Ted jumped and spilt some wax on the floor.

'Watch what you're doing with that candle! Now, did you bring Will's horse back with you?'

'Ah. 'Twere the mare as found us in the first place. That's how we knowed somethin' were wrong. She come gallopin' along to the gatehouse with no rider, so me an' Joe caught her an' run back along the road to see what'd happened to Squire. Found'n fighting with two men. Another one were up on a horse, tryin' to get a shot at him. They rode off when they seen us, so we couldn't catch 'em, more's the pity. But one of 'em turned round and loosed off a shot, bad cess to him! When we saw

Squire was hit we reckoned we'd best leave off chasin' 'em and carry him home.'

'You did right, but you can talk your head off about it afterwards,' cut in Jessie. 'Just now we need someone to go and fetch the doctor from Sawbury. You take Will's horse, Ted Haplin, and get off as fast as you can.

He stood gaping at her.

'Well, go on! What are you waiting for?'

Joe lounged forward. 'I'll go, mistress. Ted don't deal so well with horses.' He pulled a mocking face at his brother and was out of the door before anyone had time to agree or disagree.

Soon after he had left, Will stirred and began to mutter. Sarah immediately tried to sit up.

'Lie down, Sarah!' ordered Jessie, and Hannah pressed her mistress back onto the settle, because her face was still white and her breathing ragged, as if she were holding back sobs. After a moment, she stopped trying to move, but lay watching her husband, her feelings for him showing in her face.

She do love him true, thought Jessie to herself. She's a nice woman and doesn't deserve all this trouble. Then her son claimed her attention again.

Will's eyes flickered open. 'What happened?' he muttered thickly. 'My shoulder... hurts.'

'Lie still, son,' said Jessie in a calm, reassuring voice. 'You been shot, but they only hit your shoulder. No real harm done, but if you move, you'll start it off a-bleedin' again.'

'Oh yes... I remember now.' He winced as he tried to move his arm. 'Three men. I thought... thought they wanted my money. Two of them attacked me, pulled me off my horse…' His voice trailed away, but he didn't lose consciousness. 'Sarah?' he asked, after a moment.

She slipped off the settle and went to kneel at his side. 'I'm here, Will.'

'You were right,' he murmured. 'Shouldn't have gone alone.'

He seemed to drift off into unconsciousness again, and after a while, she let Hannah help her back to the settle. Oh, God, she prayed silently over and over, don't let him die, don't let my Will die! She gave no thought to herself, but Hannah and Jessie were worried about the effect of the shock on a pregnant woman.

Petey was still whimpering in the corner. 'Mary, take that son of yours down to the kitchen,' ordered Jessie, without looking up, 'or he'll drive us all mad with that whining! Then you can go round and make sure that all the doors and windows are locked.'

Mary gasped and hesitated to go off alone.

'I'll go with her,' said Ted, 'if the little lass will hold this here candle. I got a sharp knife, Mary. If we find anyone we shouldn't, I'll stick it into him quick as a flash. We'll jest make sure the house is safe, eh? You got any cider in that kitchen o' yours? Gives a man a thirst, a bit of excitement does.'

'Get him some cider, Mary,' said Jessie. 'He's earned it.'

Sarah pulled herself together after a while and sent Hannah to brew the women a dish of tea. She went to sit on the floor by Will to allow Jessie to stand up and stretch her legs.

'Oh, my love, my dear love, what have they done to you?' she whispered, thinking no one could hear her.

But though his eyes were closed, Will caught what she said. He lay there without moving, savouring the thought that a Bedham could love a common farmer like him, for he had doubted that she could do more than grow fond of him. With a great effort he opened his eyes and whispered. 'I'll be all right, Sarah, lass. I'm just a bit tired now.'

She clasped his hand convulsively and there she stayed while they waited for the doctor.

It was two full hours after Joe had left before they heard the sound of horses galloping up the dark driveway. Footsteps crunched across the gravel towards the front door and Ted Haplin lounged in again from the kitchen, a loaded gun in his hand, which he had found and appropriated during his tour of the house.

'Best take no chances,' he said and motioned Hannah back from the door, before opening it himself, just a crack. Immediately he saw who was there, he lowered the gun and threw the door wide open. 'It's the doctor,' he said unnecessarily.

'Good evening, ladies,' said Dr Shadderby, his manners as polished as ever. His glance lingered for a moment on Sarah, struggling to her feet, then he left her to Hannah and turned his full attention on to Will.

'We didn't like to move him,' said Jessie. 'He keeps breaking out a-bleedin'. Bullet passed straight through, though.'

'Mmm.' The doctor examined the wound with gentle fingers. Seeing that Will had roused again, he said cheerfully, 'You're very lucky, sir, very lucky indeed. The bullet just missed a main blood vessel. But it may have glanced off the bone, in fact, yes,' he ignored the way Will winced beneath his probing, 'I think it probably did. We shall need to clean out the wound very carefully before I sew it up – we can't leave any fragments of bone in it or they will putrefy. And then afterwards, we'll just bleed you a little, to be on the safe side.'

Three voices spoke as one. 'No!'

The doctor blinked at them in surprise.

'You can clean the wound and sew it up, but his arm'll be empty if you take any more blood out of it,' declared Jessie, arms akimbo.

'My good woman…' the doctor began but was not allowed to continue.

'I'll take the responsibility for this,' intervened Sarah. 'I don't want him bled, either, doctor.'

'I can take my own responsibility!' declared Will, incensed at the way they were talking over his head. 'And no one's taking any more blood out of me!'

'The risk of fever requires me to…' began Dr Shadderby, but was not allowed to finish.

'I'd rather risk fever than lose any more blood!' said Will.

Had his patient not been a man of some importance and the bearer, albeit by marriage, of an ancient and honoured name, Dr Shadderby would have taken umbrage and walked out at this flouting of his expert advice. As it was, he swallowed his anger and concentrated on cleaning the wound and sewing up the torn flesh as neatly as he could. Will endured this ordeal without crying out, but he became very pale and at one stage groaned and fainted as a sliver of bone was removed.

When Dr Shadderby had finished, he tried again to make them see sense and allow him to bleed his patient. 'I still think…'

'No!' Will's voice was a mere thread of sound. 'I'll not… be bled.'

'Then on your own head be it! Remember, if anything goes wrong, that you flew in the face of my considered professional advice and that…'

'Ah,' said Jessie, cutting him short, 'we'll remember. Now do you stop goin' on about that and take a look at my daughter-in-law. I reckon she needs to be got to bed herself. Shocks aren't good for women in her condition.'

With which the doctor could not but agree. In fact, he thought Mistress Bedham was looking very pale.

'Has she been well lately?' he asked Jessie as if Sarah could not reply herself.

'Well… now I come to think of it, she has been looking a bit tired the past day or two.'

'Hmm. She must go to bed and rest, then.'

Ted and Joe were summoned from the kitchen to carry Will upstairs, which made him groan again, and Sarah was persuaded to go and sleep in Jessie's room.

'But I'm his wife. I want to watch over him.'

'Do as we say, Sarah,' said Jessie. 'You've the child to think of now.'

But she couldn't be persuaded to lie down until she had seen him safely to bed.

When the two invalids had been settled, Hannah was left to keep watch over Will, and Jessie took Dr Shadderby downstairs. 'Do you think you should stay till morning? It's very raw outside and I'm just a bit worried about Sarah. It isn't like her to go to pieces like this. I can't help worrying about the baby.'

'Yes, I will stay. And if Mr Bedham has taken a turn for the worse in the morning, I shall bleed him, whatever any of you say.' Besides, the doctor wasn't fond of riding alone along dark country lanes, with the frost gleaming black in the wheel ruts and an icy wind cutting through one's clothing and taking one's breath away.

'A glass of brandy, perhaps?' she offered. 'And a bowl of soup. I have some good broth in the kitchen.'

'I thank you, yes. Brandy is a sovereign preventive on chill nights. And a bowl of soup would be most welcome too. Nothing like hot soup for warming a man up without taxing his digestive processes.'

The doctor was always full of breakteeth words, she thought as she made her way to the kitchen, but she'd be glad to have him around, nonetheless.

–

At the hall, Sewell didn't know whether to be pleased or angry. The men had been paid off and Hugh, who had led them to the place of ambush, reported that he had certainly wounded Will Pursley. However, no one could be sure whether he was dead, thanks to those damned Haplins turning up just then.

'If he doesn't die this time, we shall have to try again,' said Sewell, who had been imbibing rather freely of rum, a low habit which his wife deplored, but which at least put him in a better mood. 'Have the men left?'

'Yes.'

'Hire some others next time. Those two weren't up to the work.'

'He's a good fighter, Pursley,' Hugh commented thoughtfully. 'You've got to give him that. I couldn't believe how he struggled, and I didn't dare intervene in case he recognised me.'

'Hire four of 'em next time and hang the expense. I want rid of the fellow.'

And there they left the matter till morning should bring them the latest gossip.

–

In the middle of the night, Jessie, lying fully clothed in the bed beside Sarah, woke up suddenly. By the light of a flickering candle, she saw that Sarah was doubled up and heard her gasping in pain. She rushed to rouse the doctor, but he could do nothing, and an hour later, Sarah lost the baby.

Afterwards, as Sarah lay sobbing on the bed, beyond comfort for the moment, Hannah tiptoed in to say that Will was awake and wanted to see his mother.

'What's happening?' he askcd, before she was even through the door.

Jessie hesitated.

'For God's sake, tell me? I'm not deaf – I can hear Sarah sobbing. Is it… is it…'

'I'm sorry, son. We did all we could, but she's lost the baby.'

He struggled to sit up. 'I must go to her.'

'You shall not! You'll start your shoulder bleeding again. And besides… there's nothing you can do now.'

'I can comfort her.'

'No one can do that now. It… it would have been a boy, too.'

'Then I can share her grief. I'll not be stopped, mother. Either you help me, or I'll damned well crawl there, but I'll not be kept from her.'

In the end, Ted was summoned from downstairs, where he was scaring away intruders by snoring loudly on the settle, and he helped Will in to see Sarah.

'Now go away and leave us be!' Will ordered everyone. 'Will...'

'Leave us, mother, please!'

An hour later, he allowed them to carry him back to his own bed and Sarah agreed to take some laudanum to put her to sleep, though it was more to set Will's mind at rest than because she wanted it.

When he had been settled comfortably again, Will feigned sleep so they would leave him in peace, but he lay awake for most of the night, his face grim and bitter. It was time to put an end to this trouble, by fair means or foul. They wouldn't wait for something else to happen, they would find a way to *force* Sewell to show his hand.

Sarah had made him promise that he wouldn't put his life in danger again, that he would take care of himself, for she couldn't bear to lose him as well as the child. Well, he would be careful, and he would stay inside the law if he could, but if he couldn't, he'd work outside it, as his enemy was doing. He'd find some way to put a stop to Sewell's depredations. They'd waited too long already, put up with too much bullying and villainy. You needed to fight fire with fire.

And now his infant son was dead because of Sewell.

Once he himself was recovered, he would plan a trap... If only his head didn't ache so, he'd start thinking it all out now. But that would have to wait... wait till he felt more...

–

Mrs Sewell knew better than to leave her bedchamber when the news was brought that Will Pursley had survived the attack. She couldn't help feeling glad about that, for she still had nightmares about her part in her husband's villainies, and no matter what he threatened her with, she wasn't going to forge any more documents for him. She'd kill herself first. Or maybe he'd kill her.

What she really wanted – and most desperately – was to talk to Parson about it all, to confess what she had done and ask how she could earn forgiveness. She read her Bible assiduously, but it didn't seem to show her what to do.

If she could only get her son and daughter away from her husband, maybe she could still do something about their characters, for their father hadn't given them any moral guidance and they were both more callous about others than she liked. But she could see no hope of that.

She begged Matthew to let the three of them go and stay in Bath for a while, to take the waters, and he refused point-blank, laughing at the mere idea.

'You'll stay here where I can keep an eye on you – all of you. We'll send for Dorothy to come back from Bristol. She's done no good there that I can see, and has attracted no men of substance. I'm going to have to buy her a husband – and for that we'll need a gentleman who is down on his luck. I'll buy Edward a wife, too, but it must be someone the gentry can't ignore.'

She didn't know where Matthew got this obsession about becoming part of the gentry. They'd had a comfortable house in Bristol and she'd been as happy as was possible married to a man like that, for he'd been out and about most of the day. Here in the country, she had him descending on her at any hour of the day or night, and could never sit easy, even in her own parlour.

Dear Lord, she prayed every night, deliver me from this man, even if death is the only way out for me.

–

After he recovered, Will made no more fuss when people called him Squire. He gave his commands in a new, sharper way. Some folk commented on his increasing resemblance to his father's cousin, the clever one of the family, who had left to go and seek his fortune in London. The man had never come back to Dorset again, though he'd sent his mother money regular till she died, so he must have been doing well. Will was still polite enough to everyone, but somehow, he was no longer one of the villagers; he really was the Squire now.

The only one with whom he was still on friendly terms was Thad Honeyfield, who was awed by no man. The two of them consulted regularly about the new equipment Thad was making for him.

Even Sewell noticed that Pursley was beginning to ape the gentleman. 'Pity you aren't a better shot, Hugh,' he snarled one day, 'then we'd be spared his damned posturings. You'd better practice before you try again.'

Nate, who had been mucking out the stables, gasped and cast a frightened glance out of the doorway, but to his enormous relief they hadn't noticed him. He kept still and quiet until they'd walked away. If they thought he'd overheard, who knew what they'd do to him?

It took him two days' wrestling with his conscience before he took his tale to Thad Blacksmith. And it was the fact that Will Pursley had helped him once when he'd been in trouble that tipped the scales. He crept over to the smithy just as Thad was locking up for the night and spilled his news, with many a look over his shoulder.

'Ah,' said Thad, patting him on the back. 'You've done very well coming to me, Nate, very well indeed.'

'I can't... can't help you in any other way, Thad, so please don't ask me. I still need to earn my family's bread, and Sewell is still my master.'

'You've done what you can, though, and we'll not forget that.'

Chapter 16

February was cold, even worse than usual. The freezing weather had everyone in the village shivering and sneezing, and beasts lowing miserably in their shelters. It wasn't until the end of the month that Will recovered his health and strength fully, and not only did the scar still burn red across his shoulder, but another scar burned on his soul – the loss of his son.

He thought often of Sarah's soft words of love, overheard when she thought him unconscious, and he treasured them in his heart, but would not, he felt, be worthy of her love, worthy to tell her how much he loved her in return, until he had avenged his son's death and made the world safe for his wife to bear another child.

He and Sarah couldn't discuss the loss of their son in words, but he showed her every tenderness he could think of, and treasured those he received from her. The way she nursed him with many small loving acts had, he was sure, made him recover more quickly. They would look at one another sometimes and smile slightly. They never said anything at those times, but it meant a great deal to him – and to her as well, he knew.

For her part, Sarah continued with her life because what else could you do when disaster struck? How much her life had changed! she often thought. Was it really only a year since her mother had died, and she'd had to bear her grief alone? Well, she wasn't alone in this grief, at least.

She felt better in the daytime, because she could keep herself busy, but at night in bed, she couldn't always hold the tide of sorrow back. Then Will would hold her in his arms, stroke her hair and wipe away her tears. Without this comfort, she didn't think she'd have been able to continue.

She did her best to immerse herself once again in the restoration of her home, but it was no longer enough and the chair seat cover she was embroidering in the evenings sometimes lay still in her lap for hours. She no longer tried to drive herself beyond her strength. Will had said they would have other children, but an icy fear lay within her that they might not be able to. At her age, you could never be sure you would even quicken again, let alone carry a baby to full term.

And all the time, Sewell strutted around the village as if he owned it, unpunished for the harm he had done to them, free still to harm others. He swept her a bow if they ever met, but she didn't deign to recognise his existence. His presence in the district, she often felt, was one of the things which prevented her from recovering her spirits totally. What if he attacked Will again? That fear lay like an icy stone in her heart every minute of her waking hours, yes and sometimes cast a shadow over her dreams.

–

The group of plotters was slowly gathering its ideas together. They were slow-thinking, these men, used to taking their time, waiting for wind and weather – but once set upon a path of action, they would follow it through, whatever it cost them. And they were set firmly as rocks in their purpose now.

Their lack of immediate action was deliberate, to fool Sewell into a false sense of security. And it succeeded. Clods and dolts, he called them, when he talked to his men, too stupid to look after themselves, just asking to be taken advantage of by someone who had his wits about him.

Nate overheard several such diatribes and duly reported them to Thad.

Thad nodded, told him he was a good lad, and sent him back with an encouragement to use his ears, but take no risks.

Sewell's family suffered his scorn and his iron hand as much as the villagers who worked for him.

'Can you not be kinder to the villagers?' his wife begged one day, having nerved herself up to make some gesture when he'd thrown a family out of its home.

'Fool of a woman. What do you know about anything? You haven't even the wit to do what you're best suited for to help me, so, since thinking is clearly beyond you, keep your ideas to yourself. I treat these clods as they deserve. This is *my* village and its folk shall run meekly at my heel, as suits their station in life – or move elsewhere.

Her trembling lips and tear-filled eyes suddenly annoyed him so much that he shoved her violently away from him, sending her tumbling to the ground like a marionette whose strings had been cut. And he laughed as he watched her scramble to her feet and back away from him, her eyes wide with terror.

Sewell's daughter was also warned to mind her manners and her tongue. She had become too pert in her ways.

No wonder he was having trouble finding her a suitable husband.

'I hope you'll not find me an old one, then,' she declared, 'for I'll not marry someone who revolts me.' Her best friend had just been forced into this and she shuddered to think what Frances whispered about the fumblings of an elderly husband.

He leaned across and pinched her ear hard, forcing her to stand on tiptoe. 'An I give you to a boss-eyed mule, miss, you'll marry him.' He threw her to the floor as well.

Dorothy crept up to her mother's room to nurse her bruises. 'What's got into Father lately?' she whispered. 'Has he run mad?'

'I think so,' Rosemary Sewell whispered back, one eye on the door. 'But don't speak so loudly. The servants tell him all they hear. And perhaps he'll find you a handsome young man – though kindness is more important than good looks, as I know to my cost.'

'Good looks?'

'Aye. Your father was handsome enough when I first met him. He quite won me over, but I have lived to rue the day I met him.' She touched her daughter's hair timidly, for they hadn't been close before. 'The marriage has given me you and your brother, at least. That's my only consolation or happiness in life.'

Dorothy gave her a sudden convulsive hug.

Edward also sought his mother's company and comfort. He, who loathed the country, had been set to learning how to run an estate, ready for the time when he should inherit. The satins and silks he delighted in were forbidden and sombre, hard-wearing country clothes commanded for him from the tailor in Sawbury. Day after day, throughout that bitter winter, he was sent out to accompany the harsh-tempered bailiff whose views on dealing with those who worked for him exactly coincided with his master's.

Edward was there to learn the duties, but he also learned to hate his tutor almost as much as his father, and to pity those who worked at Marsh Bottom. His skin became chapped, he developed a continuous sniffle and the miseries of his daily existence drove even his weak spirit near to rebellion – but not quite near enough to stand against the juggernaut will of his father.

Sewell embarked upon the further embellishment of his estate. It became his main obsession, that and how to get rid of the Bedhams. Trees were felled, vistas opened up, exotic shrubs ordered from London. And two families, whose cottages were an unsightly lump on the newly-cleared horizon, were evicted with only a day's notice.

Will, who could still remember the pain of losing his own home, allowed the families to stay in one of his barns until they could find something more permanent. He ignored Sewell's gibes after church about being too soft for his own good, though it took all his strength of will to walk past the arrogant figure, with its jutting belly, for Sewell had put on a lot of unhealthy flesh in the past year. But Will kept his mouth closed, because the time was drawing near for action.

–

One day at the beginning of April, Ted Haplin strolled into the village and had a quiet word with Thad Honeyfield. As a result, Thad slipped up the icy lane to the Manor after dark, when all sensible folk were in their beds, cursing the darkness and the mud that sent him measuring his length once or twice.

Will was waiting for him in the library, with Ted and Joe in attendance. That night he had had sharp words with Sarah for the first time since the shooting because he refused to tell her exactly what he was planning. Better she be angry with him than dead.

He let Thad in through the old estate office door at the back of the house. 'Come and warm yourself by the fire, lad. No one saw you?'

'No, Squire.'

'Make sure they don't see you going back, either!' He grinned. 'And try not to play in the mud.'

Thad grinned back and brushed at the muddy stains on his clothing, but it was a futile effort.

'I want nothing to go wrong with this,' Will said, the smile fading and grim determination taking its place. 'Well, sit down, man! We can't discuss this with you standing up like that.'

Thad sat down gingerly in one of the chairs, which looked to him as if it would scarce bear a man's weight. In a similar chair, Ted Haplin was sprawling at ease, a glass of the late Squire's port in his hand.

Will told Thad to help himself to cider or port and, then got down to business. 'Are you still willing to help me put paid to Sewell once and for all?'

'Aye.' Ted gathered moisture in his mouth to spit out his scorn of their enemy, then looked down at the clean polished floor and thought better of it. 'He's like a mad bull of late, that one is. Needs penning up and a ring putting through his nose.'

'Lord Tarnly is the only one who can pen him up, though, so we have two choices. Either we get proof that Sewell has been behind all the troubles and hand him over to the law – or we deal with him ourselves.'

''Tis easy enough for accidents to happen,' said Ted mildly. 'Dreadful easy, it is, for a man to get hisself shot in them woods – even if Sewell takes them two bullies with him every time he goes out. *They* can't see a bullet coming. No one can.'

'Well, you'd better make sure no such accident happens,' ordered Will, 'because I intend to stick within the law – more or less, anyway.'

They smiled at that.

'And if your way doesn't work?' Ted asked.

'We'll have to think again. I'm not giving up, that's for sure.' Will's sole concession to Sarah had been a promise to do nothing against the law, if he could help it.

Ted shot a wolfish look at Thad, but the blacksmith's eyes were fixed on the Squire.

'Tell us what needs doin',' he said simply, anger simmering in his chest, as it always did when he thought of the fire that had damaged his smithy. 'There's me an' our Michael just waitin' for a chance to sauce that one's goose for him, an' Nate's ready to carry back to his master any gossip we tell him to, because he's afeared of what his neighbours will do to him if he doesn't help us.'

He thought about that for a few seconds and added in all fairness, 'And because what Sewell does to folk sticks in his gullet. Nate's terrible feared of what Sewell will do to him if he finds out he's thrown in his lot with us, but his neighbours live closer than Sewell does, an' his wife's a cousin of my wife.'

'Ah, see, even a fool like Nate can't stomach it,' agreed Joe.

Ted nodded. 'He's not a bad fellow, just puny and nervous of trouble.'

Will cleared his throat to regain their attention. 'It seems to me we need to do two things. Firstly, we need to catch Sewell's men in some unlawful act, and secondly, we must connect what they're doing with him.'

''Tisn't Hugh and Izzy as do things lately, though,' objected Ted. 'Thass why we couldn't set them other attacks straight to Sewell's door. Them two bully-boys is allus somewhere else when things happen, some place where folk can see 'em and swear they couldn't ha' done it. They fetch others in from Poole and beyond to do their mischief. They must be a lot of dangy scoundrels up that way.'

'When we catch the hirelings, we'll *make* them tell us who's paying them,' declared Will.

'Ah, we might persuade 'em to do that, but Sewell will still deny it afterwards, won't he? He'll say as we forced 'em to bear false witness. An' his lordship won't hang him just on our say-so. They don't hang the gentry all that easy, even when they deserve it. It's the poor folks as gets hanged. Besides, Sewell's got that lawyer in Sawbury eatin' out of his hand, tame as a pigeon in a loft. That fellow has all sorts of tricks up his sleeve to trap honest folk.'

'Suppose… just suppose Sewell heard that some of you had captured the men hired to make mischief and were making them speak, but that you hadn't yet sent for Lord Tarnly,' said Will, thinking aloud. 'Suppose he thought he could rescue them and save himself a deal of trouble.'

Ted scratched his head, Joe frowned and Thad looked deep into the flames, mouth pursed in thought. There was silence for a while. Will sat and waited for them to think things through. He wanted no mistakes.

'Might turn the trick,' allowed Ted at last, smacking his lips over the dregs of the port. 'Yes, well, just a smidgen more, Squire. It d'warm you nicely on a cold night, port wine do.'

'We'd need a bit of help to do it,' warned Thad. 'There'd hev to be enough of us to make sure none of 'em escaped.' He waved aside the port bottle and reached for the jug of cider.

'That's your job, Thad. You know who in the village can be trusted to keep his mouth shut and who can't. Will you find me some men?'

'Ah. Dare say I can. I'll ask around.'

'Good. Then this is what we'll do.'

–

In April, it became known that Will had purchased some new cows, and was to drive them home himself, with Robin Cox's help. He would use the main roads and keep a sharp eye out for attackers, he told those who worried about his safety.

His foolhardiness in risking his life was loudly debated in The Golden Fleece, and though the men always stopped their discussions when anyone connected with Sewell came in. Hugh nonetheless managed to glean from Nate all the information his master needed.

Sewell's smile became so smug and gloating that his wife took to her bed again, praying and weeping. Dorothy stayed upstairs, too, declaring it to be her duty to nurse her mama.

Poor Edward couldn't escape his father. As Sewell's temper became more unpredictable, his grown son even suffered the occasional thump or kick, for Sewell had decided he'd brought Edward up too soft and was determined to harden him.

Hugh and Izzy got their share of abuse, too, but unlike Edward, they thought nothing of a blow here and there.

The next Sunday, after church, Sewell made a point of stopping Will in the porch and warning him not to risk his life fetching the cows.

'I reckon I'll be safe enough now,' Will said slowly, at his most phlegmatic. 'His lordship reckons it was a band of thieves wintering in the district who attacked me last time. Nothing's happened for three months or more, so I reckon they'll have moved on by now. Besides, I'll not forget to take my pistol this time.'

'Better still, send one of your servants to fetch the cows.'

'Nay, I can't do that. Paid a precious lot for those beasts, I have, and I'll not trust 'em to anyone else.' He always spoke more broadly to Sewell than he did to others, because he could see that it irritated him.

Sarah came up to join him.

'Your servant, Mistress Bedham,' Sewell flourished a mocking bow.

Keeping her hands in her muff, she stared through him as if he were invisible, though she nodded briefly to his wife and daughter, hovering in the background. Of the son there was no sign that day.

As they drove home, Sarah said fiercely to Will, 'I know you're planning something to do with this trip!'

'Nothing you wouldn't approve of, my lass.'

'Tell me!'

'No. Best you know nothing. This is men's work.'

And that was all she could get from him. He knew his Sarah now and didn't want her joining in, for there would inevitably be some risk involved.

—

The weather was kind to the plotters. It rained on the day they went to bring the cows home from market, a steady downpour that made everyone who attended muffle themselves in their cloaks, pull their hats down over their noses and hurry back to their homes as soon as they could.

Robin Cox plodded stolidly out of town behind the new cows, ignoring the rain, and Will followed him in the cart, so muffled against the sleeting rain that you wouldn't have recognised him. The horse was used to the route and he'd fastened the reins to the rim of the cart, the better to shelter himself from the weather. Behind him, in the back of the cart, lay a pile of bundles covered in sacking.

To the four men lying in wait in the woods, it was all ridiculously easy. They let Robin pass with the cows, then fired at the figure driving the cart. And as they were all professional thieves or highwaymen and had kept their powder dry, their guns didn't misfire. They had the satisfaction of seeing two of their bullets strike home, then heard the figure grunt as it toppled slowly sideways on the seat.

The only thing that didn't go as expected was the way Robin Cox behaved. Instead of running to his master's help and setting himself up nicely as a second target, he fled into the woods.

'Easy as pickin' off crows,' said one of the killers. 'Don't know why they were so worried about this fellow.'

'Better check that Pursley's dead, though.'

'And what about the other one? Shouldn't we go after him?'

'No, he'll be half way home by now. It's not him as we're being paid to kill and he'll never recognise us.'

One rode across to hold the horse's head, sitting easily on his own mount; another stayed by the side of the road; and the other two dismounted and clambered on to the cart to lean over the still figure lying hunched across the driver's bench. As one of them stretched out a hand to roll the body over, the sacking behind the seat was tossed aside and Will stood up, holding a cocked pistol in each hand, pointed at them. The savage expression on his face made them freeze in shock, and before either of them could make a move, there was a warning shout from the man at the horse's head.

Other figures had run out of the woods and were already snatching at his reins.

Heedless now of the pistols trained on them, the two unmounted men fought viciously to escape, for capture would result in certain death for them at the hands of the law. But they were greatly outnumbered and were soon pulled to the ground.

The fourth man saw his chance and managed to knock his two assailants aside and spur his frightened horse into rearing up and clearing a path for him to escape. His spine was itching as he pounded along the track, in case they shot at him, but although one bullet came whistling past his ears, no others followed it.

The men he'd left behind went down under a rain of blows and kicks from men who had so far had no chance to get back at those terrorising their village. The strangers were battered and bleeding by the time they were trussed up and stowed in the cart.

'Dearie me, Squire,' said Ted, 'one of them got away.' He winked at the other villagers. 'Careless of you, lads, very careless!'

'Keep your comments till later, Ted Haplin!' said Will curtly. 'We haven't finished yet.' He drove the trap along a circuitous route, ending at Joe's cottage, and the others wiped out its tracks. When they stopped, the men were unceremoniously dragged out and locked in a sturdy shed, still bound hand and foot.

'Don't let them escape!' warned Will.

'Don't you worry, Squire, me an' Joe'll make sure o' that. They might get a bit hungry, though. I ent goin' to waste good food on bastards like them!'

'Are your wife and children well away, Joe?' whispered Will, unable to take things as lightly as Ted.

'Ah,' replied Joe. 'They'm over stayin' with Poll. And young Ned Bell is all afire to keep watch for us. A real smart lad, that one.'

'Then we'll wait and see what happens, as we agreed. I want Hugh and Izzy involved – those devils aren't going to get away scot-free if I have any say in the matter – and I need them to lay a clear trail back to Sewell. I'll be back later. If they haven't found our men by then, we'll have to drop them a clue or two.'

Will walked away, feeling all his senses twice as alert as usual. He welcomed the icy wind in his face, the cold drops of rain on his skin, because they helped cool down his anger. He had been filled with rage against Sewell ever since Sarah had lost their child. Now, as the possibility of bringing his enemy to justice seemed within his grasp, he felt it like a great dam, ready to overflow.

It would take very little to make him lose control, whatever his promises to Sarah. Pursleys were slow to anger, but when their fury rose, nothing short of death could stop them giving vent to it.

–

That evening, when Mr Sewell's man Izzy slouched into The Golden Fleece and bought himself a pot of cider, he found a noisy group congregated by the fire, giving all the appearance of men celebrating something.

'On your own tonight, are you?' asked Prue, who was dying to find out what was going on and why Thad, who had drunk only one small pot of cider, was feigning drunkenness.

'Aye.' Izzy swivelled round as a roar of laughter erupted from the group by the fire. 'Not like Thad to go on the tipple.'

'Oh, he's celebrating something. Went into Sawbury today and came back fair set up with himself. But you're right. He don't often get himself tipsy. His Meg'll have something to say to him when he goes home, that she will!'

'I heard tell Pursley were gettin' some new cows today.'

'If you mean Mr Bedham, yes he was. Nice beasts, too. Robin brought 'em through earlier.'

'Thought Pursley were goin' with him to get 'em.'

'I wouldn't know, I'm sure! Excuse me, I have a few things to do.'

Izzy sat down on one of the corner benches and looked casually round the room. So Pursley hadn't come back yet. But the fellow couldn't be seriously injured or those clods wouldn't be celebrating. The man who'd escaped after the ambush said that at least a dozen men had come out of the woods. Sewell had been furious, but had refused to take any action till Hugh and Izzy had spied out the land.

The first thing was to find out where they captives were being held. So Izzy went and sat in the corner with his brows knitted in thought, sipping at his ale and listening intently to what was going on around him. What had happened today? He had misliked this plan from the start, feeling they'd tempted providence too often, but his master had a bee in his bonnet and was absolutely set on killing Pursley. And it wasn't wise to question Sewell's orders, not when your master knew so much about your own past. Besides he paid well for the sort of services Izzy provided.

Another roar of laughter was followed by the black-smith declaring loudly that he'd settle those gallow-cheats good an' proper this time. His friends hastily shushed him, and one cast an anxious glance towards Izzy, who was looking in the other direction, as if he hadn't a care in the world.

'…won't try to burn down my smithy again…' said that loud drunken voice and once more, Thad's friends shushed him hastily and started speaking at the tops of their voices to cover any more indiscretions.

After sitting there for a while longer, Izzy decided there was nothing more to be found out here and drained his pot.

'Good, that were, Mistress Poulter,' he said, giving her a gap-toothed smile. 'Squire Sewell don't keep any half as good in his cellar.'

She nodded with professional politeness, but allowed her features to relax into a scowl once his back was turned.

As he walked towards the door, Izzy caught the words, 'gone to fetch his lordship' from another of the group and heard pots clink together merrily. He stiffened, but kept on walking. They could only mean Lord Tarnly and that didn't bode well for his master – or for himself. And where in hell's name were the other three men they'd hired to do the deed? He and Hugh had checked everywhere they could think of. They had to be found and got out of the way as the one who'd escaped the ambush had been – and quickly, too.

Just outside the village, Hugh was waiting for him, sheltering under a tree. 'Took your bleedin' time, didn't you? I thought you was just nipping in for a quick pot to see if they'd heard anythin'?'

'Worth stayin' a while, Hugh my lad, well worth it. Thad Honeyfield is as drunk as a lord back there.'

'Is he, now? And what's that got to do with us? It's Pursley as master wants settled. And as soon as may be. Honeyfield can wait till later.'

'That blacksmith's celebrating something. In fact, there's a whole group of 'em roaring with laughter an' drinkin' themselves under the table. I doubt you'd get any sense out of them, even if you could ask 'em straight out.

But I did hear that someone had gone off to fetch Lord Tarnly.'

'Ah.' Hugh scowled at him. 'That could be a mite nasty for us, that could, if anyone talks.'

'Just what I thought.'

'Better find out where our dear friends hev got to, then, eh, Izzy? Can't have them tellin' tales about us to his lordship, can we? And if we can't rescue 'em, then we shall just have to make sure that they're in no condition to talk.'

'Aye, I suppose so. But I don't like killin' friends. I don't think it's safe to kill anyone in such a small village, come to that. Fair gives me the creeps at times, this bloody place, the way everyone knows everyone else. Give me a city like Bristol any day.'

'Too late to worry about that now, not if you want to keep away from the hangman's noose.'

'Ah. I reckon Sewell were a bit hasty with Saul tonight. Who'd have thought a man's neck could break so easily? And we've still to get rid of the body. That's not as easy as master seems to think.' Izzy shook his head.

'Ah, he just got a bit angry, that's all. A man's entitled to get angry when he pays out good money to get a job done, and then it's bungled twice. Hey, where are you goin' now?'

'To tell Mr Sewell what I heard.'

'No time for that. I saw two men creeping off down East Lane while you were sitting guzzling that cider. I followed 'em a little way and they turned off into the woods. It's plain as anything they were up to no good. I reckon they've got our men down there.'

'But...'

'Look, you fool, you know Sewell will want it all settled, an' he won't want to come with us to help do the job, so we might as well get on with it. He doesn't like to get his hands dirty these days, our precious master. When I think o' what he done in the old days…'

'Mum's the word on that, if you don't want to go on breathin'.'

'Aye, I suppose you're right. But if we go an' tell him what's happening first, we could be too late to do anything before Lord Tarnly gets here. I've no mind to swing for it, even if you have!'

'But…'

'But nothing! We've got to find out where they're keeping the lads and make sure they don't talk about us.'

A small figure hidden in the bushes watched them go, then slipped back to The Golden Fleece, where Thad and his friends had miraculously sobered up. When they heard what he had to tell them, they all left in a hurry.

Those remaining in the tap room looked at one another. 'Somethin' up,' said Richard Bennifer, with the smug interest of an old man who is past the stage of getting personally involved in trouble.

'Ah,' agreed one of his cronies. 'Thass for sure.'

'We'd better get ready for trouble, then,' said a third, who was still young enough to resent being left out of the conspiracy. 'They might need a bit of help.'

'Now, don't you go a-starting anything!' warned Sam, torn between his duty as constable and his own desire to join in.

He was ignored.

'I'll go an' get my fowling piece. She's old, but she still works all right. Been oilin' her up lately.'

'I sharpened my pitchfork,' said another man. 'Do a mort o' harm, a nice sharp pitchfork can. Hev to be careful I don't poke it into someone, shan't I?'

Within minutes, the atmosphere inside the inn had changed completely. Men slipped out to their homes and returned with their chosen weapons, then settled to wait with a heavy patience few town-dwellers could match. If there was any chance of striking back at Sewell, they would be ready.

Even Will had underestimated the depth of their anger.

Nate took one look at their faces and thanked God he'd changed allegiance. He shrank back into a corner and buried his nose in his ale. No one had included him in their earnest discussions, but at least they'd left him alone. He wasn't going home, though. He wanted them to see plain that he wasn't warning anyone.

Deep in the woods, Izzy and Hugh dismounted and led their horses, the better to see the tracks they were following, footprints clearly visible in the mud. Dusk deepened around them as they made their way along a little-used path, stopping at regular intervals to listen carefully and make sure they were not being followed. Any poacher would have laughed at the amount of noise they were making in between their pauses, but they had been bred in the stews of Bristol and their few years in the country had not taught them how to blend in with the woodland noises as they moved – which their pursuers were doing with their usual skill.

When at last the cottage came in sight, the two men paused and Izzy let out a soft 'Aaah!' of satisfaction. Two voices could be heard from inside, raised in raucous song. Were all the villagers drunk that night?

'They've run mad,' marvelled Izzy. 'Think they've won already, they do! Stupid dolts!'

'Shhh!' A punch in the arm emphasised this command and Izzy scowled as he rubbed the bruised flesh.

As they moved further down the track, they could make out the words:

> Oh, we'll hang him with a rope, rope, rope,
> Yes, we'll hang him with a long, long rope!
> And he will not have a hope, hope, hope,
> When we hang him with our long, long rope!

Every now and then the music stopped as pots were clinked together and toasts drunk.

'To Sewell!'

'To Sewell!'

'Hope he don't catch jail fever!'

'Not afore they hang him, anyhow.'

Another burst of laughter followed this exquisite piece of wit, then, 'To Izzy! To Hugh! Long may they swing on the gibbet!'

'Try to get us hanged, will they?' muttered Hugh. 'We'll see about that!'

'*Will* you shut up, you fool!'

Outside the cottage, hidden in the eaves, young Zacky Haplin was keeping watch. He'd heard the sound of the approaching horses a while ago, but not till he caught sight of two shadowy figures approaching the cottage did he pull hard on a piece of string attached at the other end to his father's wrist. Two sharp tugs a moment later showed him that Ted had got his message, and the tune the two Haplins were singing changed abruptly.

Zacky sank back into the shadows. His part was played now, unless something untoward happened, and his Dad had threatened to flay him alive if he tried to join in the fighting, or even stirred from his perch under the eaves till he was given permission. And Ted Haplin's children all knew when to do as they were told. But Zacky wasn't complaining, because he was in a prime position to see everything, unlike his brothers and sisters.

When the song changed, something stirred briefly in the shadows behind the new shed, and Zacky noted the movements with satisfaction.

The two conspirators stopped to confer.

'We'll try the outhouses first,' whispered Hugh. 'If they've got 'em locked up there, it'll be easy enough to deal with 'em. You got your pistol and knife ready?'

'Course I have!' An' he'd use them on some of them bastards afore this night was through, Izzy added mentally, angry now — and afraid as well. Hang him with a rope, would they? Sing an' laugh about it, would they?

Slowly they crept forward. Izzy waited outside while Hugh slipped into the first shed, checked that it held no prisoners and returned to pass on that information. It seemed to the hidden watchers that the two were in disagreement about something.

'I'm checking that new shed next, I tell you!' Hugh moved forward again. The door opened, then reopened and he hissed at his companion, 'They're here! I told you they would be.'

The men inside strained against their bonds and made gurgling noises into their gags as their rescuers took out their knives.

One of the hidden observers turned his ankle in a rut, and the slight noise made Izzy and Hugh freeze where they were for a moment.

'No time to get'm away! They're on to us!' hissed Hugh, and raised his knife.

'Stay where you are!' Will roared, unable to stand by and see men killed in cold blood, even murderers like these.

His command was ignored. Knives flashed and the night erupted into noise and confusion as shots were fired and an attempt was made to catch the intruders. A villager yelled in sudden pain, and one of the prisoners writhed against his bonds and then jerked slowly into eternal stillness.

Then, as suddenly as they had begun, the noises subsided. Will roared for lights to be brought. Ted's lantern revealed one dead prisoner, a second badly wounded and the third safe but hysterical with terror at his narrow escape. There was also a wounded villager, but he'd mend.

Sewell's man, Hugh, had been caught and was struggling vainly against those who held him, cursing them all. Of Izzy there was no sign.

'Damnation!' said Will. 'I didn't want any of them to escape until we were ready. He'll warn Sewell before we can get Lord Tarnly here! We'd better follow him as quickly as we can.'

Ted Haplin, on the edge of the group, judged it time to call in reinforcements, whatever the Squire had said about keeping this business to themselves. He beckoned to his son. 'Run to the village, Zacky. Tell 'em what's been happening. Say we're going over to Marsh Bottom an' we need a bit of help. Look sharp, now, boy!' He hadn't the slightest doubt that the other villagers would come. Enough of them, anyway.

'We'll have to capture Sewell before he has time to get away,' Will was saying, as Ted turned back to listen to his leader's instructions. Ted's mouth curved into a slight smile. Will Pursley had become Squire and turned gentry, so he'd be bound to try to take Sewell alive, but he, Ted, knew when it was time to rid the country of vermin. If Sewell were taken alive, he'd find some way to wriggle out of this. Ted wasn't having any more trouble around his village, not now he was set fair for a life of luxury in the gatehouse, with a wife as sweet-tempered as she'd been sharp before. And no one, *no one in the world*, was ever going to threaten the safety of his family again!

When Will had finished talking, the group of men set off towards Marsh Bottom, dragging Hugh and the other prisoner along with them, making sure they bounced off a few trees on the way, and leaving the badly wounded man behind, tied to Joe's bed. Time enough to deal with him later.

Chapter 17

Zacky Haplin arrived in the village out of breath and wild with excitement. He erupted into the Golden Fleece, panting so hard that he could scarcely get the words out.

'They... got 'em,' he managed to gasp at last.

'Who?'

'Sewell's new bully boys. First my Dad an' Squire got one lot as tried to kill Squire this afternoon, then they shut 'em up in our new pigshed.' He stopped to gulp for more breath. 'Hugh an' Izzy come to rescue 'em, an' when my Dad tried to catch 'em, they fired their guns and stabbed folk with knives an' it were a right old turn-up. One of the bully boys is dead, an' good riddance to him, an' Squire's caught Hugh, but that Izzy got away. He's run back to warn Mr Sewell, so Dad says you're all to come down to Marsh Bottom an' help us catch them afore they get away again. An' he says not to come empty-handed.'

While the precise details of what had happened might not be totally clear, the main message was. Sewell's hour of judgement had come and they were needed.

For a few minutes, the inn was filled with noise, as each man turned to his neighbour and claimed to have expected this all along. It was Sam who called for silence and got their reluctant attention.

'Thass agin' the law, goin' after Sewell is! We hafta send for His Lordship, like I been tellin' you all along. Us don't want to be took up for rioting.'

'Well, you go off to find his lordship, if you like, but we're goin' to get Sewell,' said Nancy Bell's brother Ralph. 'I been waitin' for this ever since they attacked our Nance.'

They poured out of the inn at his words, unwilling to wait a moment longer to get their weapons and leave.

Inevitably Mr Rogers was awoken by the tramping of heavy feet, the hushed voices and the clinking of spades, picks or other improvised weapons. He appeared suddenly among them in his nightshirt and cloak, his breath steaming in the cold air, his sparse white hair standing out like a halo.

'What are you doing?' he demanded. 'What is this?'

They stared at him unblinkingly, earth-coloured men in homespun garments, broad, callused hands clasping a strange mixture of weapons, their unity of purpose holding them together in a way that was almost visible.

'What are you doing?' repeated the parson.

Ralph took it upon himself to act as spokesman, 'Them sods hev been shootin' at Squire again. It were Sewell behind all them troubles, like we allus thought. Now we're goin' to settle with him once and for all.'

'Will!' gasped the parson, clutching his thin chest. 'Will's been shot again?'

'No. Just shot *at*. They missed him this time.'

'He's all right? You're sure he's all right?'

'Ah, right as rain. But now we hev to get Sewell, afore he escapes. Ted Haplin sent to let us know. Thass right, ent it, Zacky lad?'

'Yes. My Dad sent me to fetch help. He said people were to come to Marsh Bottom.'

Someone stepped forward to support the frail old figure, for the parson had suddenly started shaking like a leaf.

'You can't take the law into your own hands,' he quavered. 'You must not!'

'If *we* don't do somethin', who will?'

'First our hayrick,' said a voice at the back.

'Then my sister Nancy,' said Ralph.

'Then the smithy,' growled a friend of Thad's.

'And they nearly got my inn, too,' said Sam Poulter, his features flickering in a demoniacal way in the light of a lantern he held aloft. 'But I still say us should do it right an' call out Lord Tarnly an' that there militia of his. Us shouldn't try to do it on our own.'

'Where was Lord Tarnly an' his precious militia when Squire was shot after Christmas? What did he do to help then?'

'Nothin'!'

'Now them sods are startin' at it again, an' we're not havin' it!'

A deep growl approved this statement.

'It's time us did somethin' about it ourselves. Long gone time!'

'But you can't go after Sewell!' cried the parson, afraid for his flock. 'The law will deal harshly with you, if you try to take matters into your own hands!'

'If us don't, who'll they attack next?' demanded Ralph. 'He laughs at us, Sewell do. Calls us bumpkins an' clods. Laughs when he turns folk out o' their homes, too. Won't laugh after tonight, though. Nor will them two bullies of his. If I had my way, they'd never laugh again.'

Another rumble of approval greeted this statement.

'No, no!' begged Mr Rogers, but the men were already melting away into the darkness, and soon he was left standing alone in the flickering light of a lantern which hung on the wall outside the smithy. Its flame, blowing first this way, then that, lit up the still-blackened outer wall, then the old man's white face, with the thin plume of breath trailing from his lips, then swung back to show the wall. So long did the parson stand there that Prue eventually came out of the inn and begged him to get indoors before he caught his death.

'I must fetch help,' he stammered. 'I must fetch help!' But what help was there to be found in a little village like this?

'Nothin' to be done, Parson,' said Prue grimly. 'They'll not be stopped. An' my Sam's goin' for help, isn't he? Goin' into Sawbury.'

'But His Lordship won't be able to get here in time!'

At that moment Sam came round the side of the inn, leading a horse. He nodded to the two figures standing in the small pool of light and heaved himself up into the saddle.

'Ride as fast as you can, Sam,' begged the parson. 'Tell his lordship to come at once, with as many men as he can raise. Tell him to come straight to Marsh Bottom, and I'll meet him there.'

'Sam, take care!' wailed Prue, suddenly afraid that her husband would be hurt.

He galloped off into the night without even a glance over his shoulder.

Mistress Jenks stepped out of the shadows, making Prue squeak in fright. 'Come and get dressed, Parson!' she said quietly. 'You can't go to Marsh Bottom in your nightshirt!'

'You'll not stop me going!' warned Mr Rogers.

'No. No, I'll not even try to stop you. Some things have to be done, whatever the cost, and if you're there, maybe you can speak up for those misguided fools to his lordship. But I'll not let you catch your death of cold to do it.'

Prue whirled and ran back into the inn, terrified now for Sam's safety. If Lord Tarnly came out to Broadhurst with the Sawbury militia, then there were sure to be arrests. Men would fight viciously to avoid the harsh penalties of a law that could hang a man for something as small as the theft of a handkerchief. No use going after the village men to try to stop them; they'd not listen to her!

She stood frozen for a minute, then said slowly, 'But they might listen to Squire's wife. She's Mistress Elizabeth's daughter, after all. They might just listen to her.' Moreover, if Prue was there with them, she might be able to keep her Sam safe when he returned. She knew him. He was already torn between doing his duty as constable, and joining in with his friends.

Throwing on a dark dress over her nightgown, she crammed her bare feet into her shoes and went to harness the other horse to their trap, sobbing aloud as her chilled fingers fumbled with the stiff leather straps.

As the parson began to make his way on foot towards Marsh Bottom, accompanied by Mistress Jenks, Prue drove as fast as the fitful moonlight would allow towards the Manor, and Sam rode towards Sawbury, lashing one of the most placid horses in the district till it galloped hell for leather through the dark countryside.

–

Will and his men arrived at Marsh Bottom first and made their way in silence round to the stables. There they found a horse that bore signs of having recently been ridden furiously, its chest heaving and splashes of mud on its withers, not to mention spur marks showing clearly on its flanks.

'That's how Izzy got away from us,' said Thad. 'He must have had a horse waiting. In a mighty hurry, he were, ridin' the poor creature like that.' He stroked the still-nervous animal's sweaty nose, but it blew through its nostrils and tried to jerk away from him, its eyes still wild with fear.

'Let's go to the house,' Will said. 'It's time to confront Sewell.'

Sombre-faced, the group of men slipped outside again and surrounded the house, then, at a nod from Will, Ted went up and banged on the front door.

–

At almost the same time, Prue was hammering on the door of the Manor, sobbing under her breath, sure this night would see her losing her husband if she didn't do something about it.

Sarah, still fully dressed, woke from an uneasy doze in the parlour, thinking at first that Will had been hurt again. She rushed out to fling the door open, heedless of her own safety and gaped to see Prue Poulter standing there, her hair in wild disarray on her shoulders.

Once she realised that Will was all right, Sarah's brain started to function clearly again and she wasn't slow to grasp the dangers of the situation.

'I'll come!' she said quietly. 'We must stop them killing each other!'

The same inflexible unity of purpose that had drawn the men of the village together to redress their wrongs was now making other women follow them to the Manor to protect their husbands, it was hard to bear the waiting. They began creeping through the night to find out what was happening.

—

At Marsh Bottom, Sewell refused to open his door and when some of the men tried to break in, he loosed off a shot through an upstairs window that grazed Thad in the upper arm.

Will and his men withdrew to places of safety and held a conference that resulted in several of them, who knew the house and grounds, approaching it from the rear, while the others continued to create a diversion at the front. Stones were thrown at windows, smashing some of them with satisfying crashes and tinkles of falling glass, and threats were yelled at Sewell.

'You'll not escape this time.'

'We know what you've been doing.'

'You'll not be alive tomorrow.'

The rest of the men from the village arrived in the middle of all this and joined in with a will, howling insults and shaking their pitchforks at the house.

Inside, Mistress Sewell and her two grown children cowered together underneath her bed. 'You'll not join in, Edward,' she kept saying over and over. 'Promise me you'll not join in!'

'I promise, mother, I promise.'

Other shots were fired sporadically from the house, but no one else was hit. None of the besiegers quite knew what to do next to break the impasse, so they settled down to wait.

Mr Rogers arrived but could make no impression upon the attackers. They would not leave till they'd dealt with Sewell, whatever he urged.

Will was as polite as ever to the parson, but implacable in his resolve to capture Sewell and hand him over to the law. And he wasn't going to waste any more valuable time in arguing about it. The men at the rear hadn't yet got into the house and were waiting for further distractions from the front to draw the defenders' attention away from the rear. It was to Will that everyone turned for orders.

Setting the old cleric gently aside, he followed his men round the house.

Then the party from the Manor arrived.

Thad slipped over to the trap when it came to a halt at a safe distance from the fracas. He listened impassively to Sarah's pleas to stop the attack and wait for Lord Tarnly and his men to arrive. When she found out that Will had gone round the back to confer with the men there, they had to restrain her from following him.

While she was speaking to Thad, the other men at the front kept up a desultory assault with stones, breaking several more windows, and causing Sewell to yell at them that he'd have the lot of them locked up for trespass, and the ringleaders hanged for the damage to his property they were causing.

'Thad, can't you do something to stop them?' begged Sarah. 'Sewell's right. They could hang you all for this.'

'Can't stop now, mistress,' said Thad. 'We hev to put an end to this wickedness once and for all – or die trying.'

Will came back and ran to join them when he saw his wife. 'What the devil are you doing here, Sarah? I told you to stay out of this.'

'Prue came to find me. I couldn't refuse to help her. I was too worried about you. We're all worried about what you're doing! Will, you've got to stop this now and wait for Lord Tarnly.'

'We'll stop it when we've captured Sewell and not before. Then we'll hand him over to his lordship.'

Thad joined in. 'If Sewell gets away from us now, Mistress, he'll wriggle out of it, and then he'll get up to more mischief. We must capture him.' His great deep voice rang out above the yells and crashes of stones against window panes, making the three women shiver, for Mrs Jenks had come out of the shadows to join them.

A few men standing nearby nodded in agreement.

'Since my sister was attacked, her little 'uns cry of a night,' said Ralph. 'An' so does she. Must I wait till they come after my wife, too? Must I let them frighten my children senseless as well?'

'I lost my cottage because of him.' Robin Cox appeared out of the shadows, 'An' my old master was murdered. I never did believe he killed hisself. Two of my children died after that and my wife near broke her heart. I ent forgot that. I've waited a long time for this day.'

'Robin, not you too! Have you all run mad tonight?' exclaimed Sarah.

'No,' Robin answered quietly. 'We hev all come to our senses, mistress.'

Mr Rogers stepped forward. '*Vengeance is mine; I will repay, saith the Lord,*' he cried in his quavery old voice. 'I charge you in the name of the Lord to stop this foolishness while there is yet time!'

There was a sudden silence, for they were used to heeding his words, but a yell of triumph from the back of the house, followed by a shot, then a sudden cessation of noise, broke the spell. Silently they all turned to watch.

A face appeared at a brooken window. 'We've got him!' it yelled and disappeared again.

A rumble in the throats of the men who had remained outside showed how near to the surface their savage instincts had risen. They turned as one towards the house, cheering when the front door was flung open and a group of men appeared, dragging a struggling Sewell. Behind them, Joe Haplin shoved Edward Sewell along and two others dragged a cursing Hugh. Mrs Sewell and Dorothy hung around at the rear, for since everyone knew that the poor lady was helpless against her fierce husband, she and her daughter had been treated with respect.

Sewell's face was bloody, but he was still spitting defiance at his captors.

'Hang him!' shouted a voice half-choked with fury, and the cry was taken up by a dozen hoarse throats.

'Where are the others?' demanded Thad? 'He's got other men as work here. Hev you let 'em get away?'

'They be takin' a little nap in the stables,' someone replied. 'We'll fetch them out in a minute an' tell 'em to leave their jobs or suffer the consequences.'

Sarah stood there, terrified by this tide of savagery. Anger swirled around them, as visible as the mist from their breaths. Faces had turned into animal masks and hands trembled on weapons. At any moment, it might erupt into a blood bath. And her Will was at the centre of it all, would be seen as the ringleader. She was terrified for his safety, felt helpless to know what to do.

Beside her, Mr Rogers was leaning against the back of the cart, weeping aloud for his congregation, with Mrs Jenks trying vainly to comfort him.

Some of the men began to drag their most important captive away from the house, looking for a strong tree and calling for a rope. Sarah stepped forward. 'Will, no!' she pleaded. 'You said you'd take him to Lord Tarnly. You *promised* me you'd keep within the law!'

He nodded and put his arm briefly round her shoulders. 'It won't do any harm for them to frighten Sewell a little first, though. He well deserves it.'

After watching the confusion for a few minutes, he stepped forward. 'That's enough, lads! We'll hand him over to the law now.'

Ted barred his path. 'I don't think you could stop us now if you tried, Squire, so why not leave us be and take Mistress Bedham home? That rascal lost you your son, didn't he? Tried to kill you as well. It don't pay to treat such as him soft. Once let him loose an' he'll be up to his villainies again. You leave it to us. We know what to do and we ent afraid to do it. You hev to kill a mad bull.'

Will hesitated. At heart, he agreed with this, but he had promised Sarah to stay within the law and anyway, he owed it to his new position as Squire.

Before he could move, they all heard the sound of hoof beats in the distance.

Mr Rogers raised his tear-wet face. 'Oh, Lord, Thou hast answered my prayers,' he whispered. 'I pray You now to continue Your mercy and save these poor souls from hanging!'

The space in front of the house was suddenly surrounded by men on horseback. The militia were afire for some real action. Some had drawn their swords and were looking for permission to use them.

Lord Tarnly dismounted and strode towards the group of men still holding Sewell. 'Let him go!' Years of command rang in his voice.

Sullenly, they released their captive and moved back. Rumbles of discontent eddied to and fro, but they moved away. They had no quarrel with his lordship who was known to be a fair landlord and employer, as well as being more lenient than most in his judgements from the bench.

Sewell stumbled towards Lord Tarnly, quick to take advantage of the situation. 'These men have broken into my house, attacked my servants and threatened my life!' he cried. 'I demand that you arrest them! They must be made an example of, or a gentleman will not be safe in his own home! And Pursley here led them!'

A zealous captain of militia stepped forward and stationed himself next to Will, gesturing to one of his men to stand on the other side of him.

Sarah rushed forward and clutched His Lordship's arm. 'That's not true! They were only protecting themselves!'

she cried. 'And my husband was trying to *stop* them from hanging Sewell!'

'My dear Sarah!' Lord Tarnly bowed, gallant as ever. Nonetheless, he gave no orders for his men to release Will.

'Someone shot at my husband again today when he was coming home from the market,' she said urgently. 'He followed the man here.'

A nod from his lordship and Will was brought to stand before him.

'What happened, Bedham?'

'We laid a trap for them, your lordship. We caught the men who attacked me and then we let Sewell and his men know about it. His men tried to rescue our captives, but we fought them off and followed them here.'

Mr Rogers stepped forward to range himself at their side. 'We sent for you, sir, and are glad to see you here.'

'Ah,' said Ted, his anger cooling quickly in the face of authority. 'We caught them rascals for you. We didn't mean to break no laws, just protect ourselves. Ain't that right, lads? But we got no militia here, your lordship, and when they shot at Squire again, we did fear to wait for you to arrive, else the rogues would hev escaped. But here they be, all took up like rabbits in a trap!'

Mr Sewell spluttered with rage. 'Lies! All lies! They threatened to hang me!' He pointed down at the rope with its rough noose at one end, still lying on the ground. 'Don't let them get away with it!'

'That rope was just to frighten him a bit,' someone shouted from the back of the crowd. 'Like he frightened our wives and children.'

'Haven't you done enough harm?' Sarah asked Sewell bitterly.

He turned a look on her that was frightening in its malevolence. 'I haven't yet begun,' he said softly, keeping an eye on Lord Tarnly, who was giving orders to his men. 'You lost your child last time.' He actually smiled as he spoke those words. 'Beware for your husband this time! I *always* get what I want.'

As she fell back, pale with horror, Will launched himself at Sewell. This threatening of his wife, this casual reference to the dead child, was the final straw. It took four men to drag him off Sewell and even then, they had difficulty holding him back.

'What in God's name made him attack Sewell like that?' demanded Lord Tarnly.

'He were saying how happy he were that Mistress Bedham lost her baby a while back,' said Ted, 'An' that he'd see she lost her husband too this time. Proper villain, he be, your lordship. See as you keep a careful eye on him.'

Lord Tarnly drew himself up to his full height. He wasn't used to the lower classes telling him how to do his job. 'You can be sure the due processes of the law will be followed, my good fellow.'

'And you can be sure, too, that the King's laws will protect *me*,' declared Sewell. 'My lawyer will know how to act. I am a gentleman, sir, and demand to be treated as such!'

Will struggled again and Sewell laughed in his face. 'I shall sue you for this attack upon my person and property, Pursley. And I shall win. I shall get the Manor and its land through that, make no doubt about that. I am very well acquainted with the law.'

Sarah took a step backwards, shivering with cold and feeling suddenly defeated. She almost wished that the villagers had managed to extract their vengeance. How could Sewell be so confident, even now? Why did his lordship not do anything? What hope was there for anyone if a villain like Sewell could get off scot-free and his victims suffer the harsh penalties of the law?

She turned away, sick at heart, then swung round again, as a low murmur and hiss of surprise warned her that something else was happening.

Sewell was clutching his throat and clawing at the air, his face suddenly congested and dark with blood. The parson uttered the word, 'Seizure!' and would have run to his side, but Ted caught hold of his coat and yanked him back. 'Beggin' your pardon, Parson, but we wouldn't want you to get hurt when he falls.'

Watched in silence by the people he had wronged and by the newly-arrived militia, and helped by none of them, not even his own son, Sewell sank to his knees, still clawing at the air and uttering incomprehensible gurgling sounds.

He writhed on the ground, but still no one moved to help him. They didn't even stir. It was as if they were all held in some invisible grip.

The expressions on the villagers' faces made Sarah shudder, for they showed a savage, gloating satisfaction, eyes gleaming in the fitful light of the flares from the torches, earth-stained hands stilled on their makeshift weapons.

Even Lord Tarnly made no move to help the man, for the general paralysis seemed to have affected him and his militia as much as the villagers.

Finally, after struggling half to his feet again, Sewell toppled over, twitched once or twice and was still.

Only them did Ted allow Mr Rogers to move forward. No one else moved as the parson bent over the body and closed the staring, bulging eyes, then bowed his head in prayer. He had seen death too often not to recognise it now.

A long sigh of primeval satisfaction rippled through the crowd and Prue buried her face in Sam's shoulder, sobbing aloud in utter relief.

Will took Sarah in his arms. His voice was hoarse with emotion. 'I couldn't bear it when he said that to you. I'd have killed him for it if I could!'

Lord Tarnly jerked back into control of himself, coughed to hide his emotion and moved over to join the parson. It seemed to his lordship that justice had been done tonight by a power greater than his own.

Behind him, Sarah put her arms round her husband. 'Will, Will, I couldn't live without you. I love you so!'

'And I love you, my dearest lass!'

Mrs Jenks sighed quietly at the devotion on their faces.

Edward Sewell remained near the front door, shivering and shuddering. His mother stood beside him. Neither made any attempt to approach the body.

Lord Tarnly looked down at the corpse, bent his head for a moment, in respect for the parson's prayers rather than for the dead man, then took charge. 'Taking the law into your own hands is not to be encouraged,' he said loudly, 'but as you people were going to hand the villains over to me, I will not take you in charge this time.'

There was an audible sigh of relief from the villagers, some of whom had already slipped away to the shelter of the woods.

'Now, get back to your homes and go about your business *peacefully* from now on! Some of you will be called upon to bear witness at the inquest.'

He went over to Edward Sewell. 'I shall leave your father's body with you, sir. And the inquiry will show whether you have anything to answer for. Do not attempt to leave the district.'

'I had nothing to do with it,' said Edward hastily. 'Nothing! He was a wicked man. We were all terrified of him! Ask my mother! Ask my sister!'

'Quite,' said Lord Tarnly, failing to hide his disdain.

'You don't have to worry about that one, Your Lordship,' called out a hoarse voice. 'He's a proper mammy's boy, that one is! Only good for splashin' folk with mud an' swimmin' in horse troughs, he is!' Derisive laughter followed the words, dispersing the last of the anger.

Lord Tarnly coughed to hide a chuckle, then turned to his men. 'Take the prisoners away. You two, stay here with me. The rest of you, return to Sawbury with your officers.'

'You'll want to take this one with you, though,' Joe Haplin said, shoving Hugh forward. 'We caught him trying to sneak off. He killed a man today at my shed. We all saw him do it.'

Lord Tarnly gestured and two of the militia stepped forward smartly.

'Pretty, ain't they, in them fancy uniforms?' said Ted Haplin. 'Almost makes you want to join that there militia, your lordship.'

Lord Tarnly grinned at the expression of horror on his elegant Captain's face.

Slowly the tension evaporated and the people dispersed, leaving Edward Sewell looking in vain for someone to help him carry his father's body inside.

Only then did Mrs Sewell approach Lord Tarnly, plucking at his sleeve to gain his attention. 'He made me do it,' she sobbed. 'Forced me.'

'Do what, madam?' he asked gently, beckoning to Mr Rogers to come and help him with the distraught woman.

Quickly she explained about the forgeries and Will, standing listening nearby, felt his heart twist within him as he learned that his father had indeed been murdered.

'I'll pay back all the money. I don't care if you hang me,' Mrs Sewell wept, clinging now to the parson. 'As long as you'll let me make my peace with God.'

Since Mr Rogers was now shivering with reaction to his exertions, Lord Tarnly detached her hand from the parson's sleeve and jerked his head to beckon her daughter over. 'Take your mother inside and put her to bed. Parson will come over tomorrow to offer her his counsel.'

They two women turned and made their way slowly towards the house, the mother still sobbing as she stumbled along.

'I don't intend to bring the law down upon her, unless you insist, Bedham,' he murmured. 'She was coerced into helping, I'm sure, and she's no danger to anyone now. You will, of course, get the money they falsely claimed from your father back, if that's at all possible.'

Will bowed his head for a moment. 'Let her go. But I hope she leaves the district, for I doubt I could ever be civil to her.' The sight of her would always remind him of his father's murder.

From behind him someone cleared his throat and he turned to see Edward Sewell.

'I'll be selling the Hall as soon as I can.'

'Not,' said Lord Tarnly, looking Sewell straight in the eye, 'until you have agreed to make restitution to the people your father cheated out of money. Otherwise,' he let the word hang in the air for a moment, 'I shall be forced to resort to the law.'

'Oh, yes. Of course, of course. Whatever you say, your lordship.'

Will watched Sewell step back. The man didn't look happy at that, and Will wasn't happy, either. Money wouldn't make up for his father's death. And yet... there was still the Manor to restore. His spirits lifted as he suddenly realised he'd now be able to make a proper contribution.

He put an arm round his wife and gave her a quick hug, as Mrs Jenks came forward and helped Parson on to the trap, wrapping him in a thick blanket.

'You must come home with us, Mr Rogers,' Sarah said. 'It's much nearer and you're chilled to the bone. You, too, Mrs Jenks.'

They nodded agreement. It was not a night for being alone.

Sarah waited to mount the trap herself, her eyes on Will, who had gone over to give instructions to some of the villagers. Even the Haplins were listening intently and nodding.

She smiled, something she'd not have believed possible earlier. Tonight Will had said he loved her in front of everyone, and she would treasure that memory for the rest of her life. She knew he wouldn't often be able to express his feelings for her in words, for he was a man of action, and she knew just as clearly that his affections, once given, wouldn't change.

Tomorrow she would share with him the other news which would, she was sure, gladden his soul. There would be no Mr Sewell to blight this coming child's life and she was suddenly gloriously certain sure that she would bear it safely.

As Will turned and walked back towards her, she couldn't wait, but ran into his arms, laughing and crying at once, and raising her face for his kiss.

Mr Rogers allowed Mistress Jenks to tuck the blanket more securely around him and watched them in delight, settling back with a sigh of relief. Strange, he thought, dear Sarah looks quite beautiful tonight. A trick of the light, perhaps.

He watched benignly as Will helped his wife up into the vehicle. Suddenly the world seemed full of moonlight and peace. He bent his head for a moment. *Thank you, dear Lord, for saving my flock and for bringing Will the happiness he deserves.*

On the front seat of the trap, Sarah nestled against her husband as he told the tired horse to walk forward. She was going home, where she would be able to sleep in safety. And after today, they would begin a new and more peaceful life together.

At that moment she wouldn't have swapped places with Queen Caroline herself.